THE
TICKLER'S JAM
MURDERS

PETER TICKLER

I dedicate this book to my wife Fiona,
and all Ticklers near and far

AUTHOR'S NOTE

THIS IS A work of fiction.

The Crowthorpe Jam Company never existed.

Tickler's Jam (or, more correctly, Tickler's Fruit Growers and Preservers) did exist. It was active through much of the first half of the twentieth century, but became best known after winning a contract with the Ministry of Defence to supply jam to the British army during the First World War. (They had also done so to the troops in the Boer War.)

As boys, my twin brother and I were sent away to a preparatory school (Winchester House in Brackley) where we encountered Mr Bates, a teacher with a formidable reputation. When he read out the register in the first lesson and got to us – 'Tickler H, Tickler P' – he burst out with delight: 'Plum and Apple'. The jam meant so much to him. I think that as a consequence we received a much easier ride than the rest of the class!

That was the first hint to me of the emotional connection that Tickler's Jam had for those many, many men who served on the Western Front and elsewhere. It was a connection to their homeland and homes which they clung onto through dreadful circumstances.

Later, I was to discover that:

- The British troops sang songs about Tickler's Jam

- They made home-made bombs/grenades out of the empty jam tins

- The poet Robert Graves, who was nearly killed in 1917, wrote a poem 'Escape' in which he attributed his survival to Tickler's jam

- Tickler's jam even appears in a George Formby song

Finally, T G Tickler ran the company during its most successful period, but any reference to him made in this story is entirely derived from my imagination.

A DEATH

SIR WILFRED WALKER was not a man easily taken by surprise. He had throughout his life been a man who anticipated things and took whatever action was necessary to ward off any perceived threat. At prep school, when his friend Briggs had had his tuck box filled with broken eggs by 'Slasher' Seligman, he had taken precautionary measures of his own, cunningly inserting three of his father's razor blades inside the lip of his own tuck box and then provoking Seligman in public. Three days later Seligman had to be taken to hospital for surgery on the fingers of his right hand. As a consequence, the first XI's opening bowler and captain was forced to sit out the rest of the season on the boundary. When Walker was summoned to the headmaster's study, he half expected that he was going to be expelled or, at the very least thrashed with the cane, but all he received was a verbal dressing down. 'Slasher got what he deserved' was the unspoken message, and from that day on, Walker's reputation as a boy to be respected and secretly admired was established amongst both pupils and staff.

This was one of his favourite memories because it had taught him a lesson which had stood him in good stead throughout his life. Tricky situations required clear-sighted thinking, careful planning and decisive action. He had that very evening reached the decisive action phase to resolve another very tricky situation, and already he felt better for it. Light hearted even. His mood had been enhanced by the glass of brandy in his hand and the very fine Cuban cigar that he was smoking as he sat in the driving seat of his much beloved Rolls-Royce Silver Ghost – 50-horsepower of wonderful engineering and craftsmanship.

When he heard the door of the garage creak open, he didn't bother to look to see who it was. Why should he? If they wanted to speak to him, to beg and grovel, then he would know soon enough. Besides, turning round to see who it was would be an act of weakness. But whoever it was didn't come into his eye-line, didn't even move. They were silent and still, summoning up the courage, he imagined, to plead their case.

Still not a word or sound. He drained his brandy and tossed the glass onto the floor where it exploded into multiple fragments.

'Well, who the devil is it? I'm not in the mood. I just want to finish my cigar in peace and then I'll go to bed. You can save it for the morning.'

But the person behind him wasn't saving anything for the morning. There was a clatter behind him and Sir Wilfred, suddenly annoyed, turned round as far as his over-padded body would allow. He saw momentarily who his visitor was and then felt an excruciating pain as the Rolls-Royce's starting handle crashed into his skull.

That was not the final conscious moment of his life. He was not that fortunate. Later – moments or minutes later, he didn't know – he returned to some sort of consciousness and became aware of a strong and distinctive smell. Petrol! He felt a groundswell of panic. He tried to move, but his wrists were bound tight together with rope. His mouth was gagged and, in the dim light afforded by the garage's lamp, he saw more clearly who his assailant was. But they had no interest in looking at him as they silently rammed a very familiar object into his hands and then with great deftness twisted another piece of rope round that object and his hands. He tried to shout, to call for help, to shake himself free of his bonds, but he couldn't.

Now fear kicked in as he realised the vicious intent in the face of his assailant and the reality of what was going to happen to him. He shook his head vigorously, in a vain attempt to communicate and negotiate with his murderer. But nothing was going to save him. There was another sudden sprinkling of petrol, over what was left of his hair. It ran in terrifying rivulets over his forehead and down his cheeks. After that came the sudden flash of a match, followed by a noise like a blast of wind, and then all around him was the searing heat of flames. Terror gripped him and moments later so did an agony such as he had never experienced in his life before. And soon after that, mercifully, he lost all consciousness.

WHEN SIR WILFRED WALKER DIED…

- His wife Lady Beatrice was asleep in bed, dreaming of the day she met Queen Victoria
  – or so she said.

- His son Captain Alec Walker was lying still dressed, in an inebriated stupor, on his bed
  – or so he said.

- His daughter-in-law Elizabeth Walker was dozing in her newly purchased nursing chair in her bedroom, intermittently cursing the fact that her unborn child had such powerful and active feet
  – or so she said.

- His daughter Maud Walker was sitting at the desk in her father's study writing a pamphlet entitled 'Votes for Women: the Unanswerable Case'
  – or so she said.

- His trusted factotum and chauffeur Frank Tomkin was asleep in his attic room dreaming of rats in the trenches
  – or so he said.

- Rose Bates, maidservant to Lady Beatrice, was lying awake in her attic room, studying the personal columns of a copy of *The Lady* magazine which Lady Beatrice had given her
  – or so she said.

- David Graves, his loyal Production Manager at the Crowthorpe Jam Company, was sitting in his bed reading the newspaper with a nightcap of brandy *– or so he said.*

- His devoted secretary, Miss Mary Graves, had fallen asleep in her bed while reading a crime novel about a murdered businessman *– or so she said.*

- The Reverend Justin Ransom was writing and rewriting his latest sermon on the sins of the fathers *– or so he said.*

- Mrs Jane Ransom was asleep on her bed after imbibing too much wine, the consequence of a certain marital disharmony *– or so she said.*

ARRIVAL

DETECTIVE SERGEANT THOMAS Kite felt as if he had been banished to the ends of the earth. Lincolnshire in the winter is a county where the wind whips relentlessly in from over an inhospitable North Sea, chilling the bone and numbing the spirit. He was already missing London more than he could have imagined – the familiarity of the streets, the cosiness of the lodgings he shared with his sister and her family, even the dank smell of the Thames and the choking smoke of innumerable coal fires, not to mention the sound of humanity from before dawn to long after sunset.

'Not far now, sir,' shouted Constable Sparrow.

Sparrow was an incorrigibly cheerful young man. He had served three years in the trenches, seen several 'good friends' die, had witnessed one of his officers blow his own brains out rather than lead his men over the top, and yet he had emerged from the hell of what they were already calling the Great War with his sparky spirit and zest for life apparently undiminished. *Apparently*. Kite was suspicious of men like Sparrow, and already in their very short acquaintance he had found himself resenting him. He knew he wasn't being reasonable. Maybe living life to the full was the only sane reaction to surviving what Sparrow had been through over the last few years, but Kite couldn't help his feelings. In these times, sailing through life without a care in the world seemed to him to be somehow morally reprehensible.

'Ahh!' Kite bit back his cry of pain as the bike bounced into and out of a deep rut. He was stuck on the back of Sparrow's pride and joy – a Lincoln Elk 6 hp Twin Model A. Not that it belonged to Sparrow. It belonged to the Lincoln police force, who had purchased two of them only a few weeks previously. And Sparrow, who knew how to blow his own trumpet, had been quick to put himself forward as an experienced rider based on his time as a despatch rider for the British Expeditionary Force on the Western Front. So when there was suddenly a murder to be investigated, and it was some thirty miles from Lincoln, Sparrow and his motorbike had been assigned to Kite.

'He'll get you there,' Chief Constable Bostock had insisted. 'He had a very good war, and he grew up in the area, so he should be a great help to you.' The bike lurched again, wheels spinning in the mud, and Kite hung on even more grimly.

'This is my first murder.' It was Sparrow again, bellowing his way into Kite's musings. 'It'll be a feather in both our caps if we can catch the bastard who did it.'

'It will,' Kite shouted back. *If we get there in one piece*, he might have added. Because Sparrow, apart from being a very chirpy man, was also a man who drove his motorcycle as if he was being pursued by a squadron of demons from hell. In the pub the night before, he had regaled Kite with stories of his time on the Western Front. 'There were even nurses riding around on bikes. I met two of them, Elsie Knocker and Mairi Chisholm. Helped them repair their carburettor.

Elsie drove and Mairi whooped and hollered from the sidecar.' At that point in the conversation Sparrow had raised his glass as if toasting them and then knocked back the remainder of his pint in a single gulping gurgle. Then he belched and laughed. 'What a madcap pair they were!'

Madcap summed up Sparrow too at this precise moment, skidding around and through the mud and puddles, squealing like a kid on ice-skates. But if Sparrow had survived the blasted landscape of France, surely (Kite reassured himself) he wouldn't come to grief here on the agricultural outback of Lincolnshire. Kite huddled down a bit further behind his constable and wished he believed in the power of prayer.

'Not too far now, sir.'

The welcome words broke Kite out of his reverie. He sat up a bit and looked around.

'Over there, that's Crowthorpe village, sir, where the jam factory is, and where I grew up. Crowthorpe Manor is another two or three miles, but Sir Wilfred owns all the land in between and more.' Sparrow waved his right arm carelessly to indicate the extent of the man's domain.

A man of considerable wealth then, Kite surmised, and a man on whom a lot of locals must rely for their livelihoods.

'Hell's teeth!' The bike skidded viciously, and Sparrow hurled himself to the left to try and stop them crashing over. Somehow, he managed it and seconds later they were on firmer ground – bumpier but safer – and Sparrow bellowed out his delight. 'That was a close one, sir. The road is worse that I remember it. They need to bloody well repair it.'

'I'd like to get there in one piece, Constable!' he yelled back.

'Don't you worry, sir,' was the reply. 'I ain't ever lost a sergeant.'

'Here we are, sir,' Sparrow announced proudly as he skidded to a halt on the gravel drive.

'Thank you, Constable.' Kite groaned in relief.

Sparrow swung his leg over and was off the bike in a moment, but for several seconds Kite couldn't move.

'You all right, sir? Need a hand?'

Kite shook his head. His back was rigid with pain, and he couldn't feel his right leg. Both sensations were familiar to him, the legacy of a struggle two floors up on a scaffolded house and the subsequent fall. He had been lucky, much more so that the thug who had tried to clobber him with an axe and had ended up breaking his own spine instead. With a determined effort, he eased himself off the bike, conscious of Sparrow's gaze and hoping against hope that the back pain would recede and some sensation return to his leg. His shoulder, which under his layers of clothing sported an impressive scar where the thug's axe had dug into him, by contrast betrayed only a slight stiffness.

He limped forwards a few steps, trying to straighten himself up fully while eyeing up the stone edifice which was Crowthorpe Manor. It was an unevenly structured house. The central block was symmetrical:

a main entrance – two dark red doors framed by a pair of plain classical columns – was flanked on either side by two pairs of bay windows, and these were matched on the floor above by slightly smaller windows. And above them two small windows indicated the presence of further bedrooms under the roof. To the right of this was tacked on a single-storeyed room with two smaller windows. A later addition Kite surmised. A billiard room perhaps. Didn't every knight of the realm aspire to a billiard room in his house?

By contrast on the left-hand side of the manor, there stood a much more impressive three-storeyed structure topped by a square turret which exceeded the height of the main house by three or four feet. It also sported a clock. Five minutes to two. Kite pulled his own watch out of his jacket pocket and checked it for the time. They had taken nearly three hours to cover the thirty miles from Lincoln to Crowthorpe Manor. Given the state of the roads, this was impressive, and a tribute to Sparrow's skill. Kite slowly turned around, scanning the area and trying to familiarise himself with where they were.

The village of Crowthorpe, which they had driven past without pausing, was some three miles away, and yet would have been invisible were it not for the tip of a church spire. That was where they were due to stay that night, in the Red Lion pub. Otherwise the land all around was grey and almost featureless under the heavy clouds. God, he hated the place. He had only been stationed in Lincolnshire a month, but it felt like half a lifetime. 'Put out to grass,' his sister had said, and she had been right. All because he had said the wrong thing, ruffled feathers and made one mistake which they could fasten upon.

'Good morning.'

The greeting came from behind him, clipped and upper class. Kite turned to see who it was. A man had emerged from the house and was striding across the gravel. 'I am Sir Wilfred's son, Captain Alec Walker. I have met the constable before, so I presume you must be Inspector Kite?'

Kite took the proffered hand. 'Sergeant, sir. Detective Sergeant Kite, sir. And I am only sorry that I have had to meet you in such sad circumstances.'

'Quite.' Walker released Kite's hand. His eyes went from Kite to Sparrow and back to Kite. 'It has been, it is... awful. Bloody awful.'

'I'm sure it is. But let me assure you that Constable Sparrow and I will make every effort to spare you further distress. It is, of course, our duty to investigate the killing of your father and bring the killer to justice, so we will need to ask questions of the family.'

'Not too many, I hope. I don't believe any of us witnessed anything,' Walker said again, 'so I cannot see that we can be a lot of help. It must have been a burglar or someone with a grudge against my father, jealous of his success and his lovely car. In my opinion, you would be better off starting your investigations in the village.'

'I understand your distress, Captain, but I have my methods, and I would like to start with everyone living in the house and also of course I would like to examine the scene of the crime.'

Walker frowned. 'If you must ask questions, you

must. But let me warn you that the ladies are very distressed, in particular my mother of course. In addition her health is somewhat delicate.

'I fully understand,' Kite said.

'I do hope so.' Captain Walker turned away and stalked back towards the house. Kite followed.

'Before you do anything, you will need to meet my mother,' he said over his shoulder as he entered the manor. He turned sharply to his right, swivelling on his heels, and with boots clacking on the stained oak floorboards he marched into a sombre sitting room. Despite the large windows, Kite didn't immediately see the figure who was submerged in the deep armchair until Captain Walker came to a halt right next it.

'Mother, this is Inspector Kite. Inspector, this is Lady Beatrice Walker.'

'Detective Sergeant Kite,' he said, suppressing his irritation. Was the captain deliberately making a point? That a family of their standing should be dealing with someone of a higher rank.

Kite hovered in front of the tiny figure, uncertain if he should say anything more. Maybe it was better to wait for her to respond. Despite his own ambivalent feelings about the upper classes, he knew the importance of gaining Lady Beatrice's co-operation and thereby the co-operation of her household. He might have been exiled to Lincolnshire, but this was an opportunity, not just to solve a case, but also to win back some favour, which he badly needed.

'You are far too tall,' she said with a wave of her hand. 'I shall get a terrible crick in the neck if I have to stare up at you.'

Kite looked around and located a matching armchair several feet away and immediately opposite her. He sat down heavily into its comforting shape, sensing the tell-tale sweat on his forehead and a feeling of light-headedness. God knew, it had been a long time since he had eaten. The family would no doubt have eaten a hearty breakfast, whereas he had eaten nothing since his rushed and meagre meal in his digs. He tried to focus his attention on Lady Beatrice. She was clothed in black, a full-length dress, a shawl round her shoulders and a lace veil over her face. He could sense rather than see her eyes, peering birdlike at him through the fine material.

'As I have already informed Captain Walker, I would first like to express my sincere commiserations for your very sad loss.'

'Pah! I do not want your commiserations. It is not as if my husband or I have ever met you before. I merely want you to do your job and arrest the thug who murdered him.'

'Of course. I understand.'

'And how do you intend to achieve this?' Behind the veil was a sharp and commanding tongue. She was a woman used to issuing orders and expecting them to be carried out.

'I would like to start by interviewing everyone who was in the house at the time of Sir Wilfred's death.'

'He was killed outside, sitting in his car, which he kept in the old stable block. Perhaps you should concentrate your efforts on outsiders. A house like this is bound to attract the attention of ne'er-do-wells, envious of our good fortune. The last thing they would have expected was to find my husband sitting in his car…'

'I can assure you, Lady Beatrice, that my constable and I will leave no stone unturned outside or inside.'

She raised her hand suddenly. 'I really need to go and lie down. I have delayed my afternoon rest sufficiently. If you have any questions for me, I suggest you ask them at four o'clock, before I have my cup of tea.'

Kite nodded. He had been dismissed like a servant, but saw no point in resisting. As he stood up a wave of light-headedness swept through him, more intense this time. He tried to steady himself, stretching his right arm out towards the arm of the chair, but his left leg buckled beneath him and he felt himself falling. Somewhere in the far distance he heard the sound of Sparrow's alarm: 'Sir, sir!'

'I think he's stirring.'

It was a woman's voice, earthy and firm. 'You alright, my dear?'

Kite opened his eyes and found a round face framed by dark curly hair staring down at him.

'I'm Rose. I think you've had a bit of a turn.'

'Lady Beatrice has offered to send for her doctor, sir.' It was Sparrow, also looking down with concern on his face.

'No.' Kite forced himself to sit up. 'I just need to eat something. This happens sometimes. A cup of sweet tea and something to eat and I will be fine.'

'Don't you worry. The constable has just told me

that neither of you have eaten since breakfast. We can soon put that right.'

Sparrow helped him to his feet and escorted him along the corridor until they reached the kitchen. They sat him at the end of the long table which was oak, old and worn smooth from many years of service. Kite let his hands caress its surface and shut his eyes. When he opened them again, there was a platter of food in front of him. Sparrow ate alongside him, meat pie and potato, washed down with deep mugs of strong sweet tea. Gradually he began to feel more like his normal self, although what had just happened to him – not eating for a long time and then collapsing – was for him not entirely abnormal.

'What now, sir?' Sparrow was full of energy.

'I think we should go and view the scene of the crime.'

'Let me show you, sir.' Rose gave the impression of someone who was rather enjoying having a role in the drama which had enveloped the house. 'This way.' And she led the two men down a corridor, then left and right until they emerged outside in the gloomy December light.

'There,' she said with a flourish of her hand, pointing rather unnecessarily to the blackened remains of what had once been a building. Grouped round them were four men.

Kite advanced towards them, barely able to control his anger. 'What on earth is going on?'

Four pairs of eyes turned to towards him.

'Are you recovered, Sergeant?' It was Captain Walker, as calm as Kite was not.

'I am fully so. But what are you doing?'

'Isn't it obvious? We are having the remains of my father gathered up. I couldn't bear to leave them there in all the fire debris. They need to be gathered up respectfully, so that we can lay them to rest as is only right and proper.'

'Don't you worry, sir.' A short man in dark clothing and a bowler hat on his head stepped forward. 'Mr John Lamyman of Lamyman and Son, undertakers. We are very used to dealing with dead persons, in all sorts of conditions. Let me assure you that we will take great care to collect only the bones and other body parts. We will leave everything else in position for you to inspect at your leisure. However the afternoon is already well under way and I would like to complete the task before night falls.' He bowed his head in what was no doubt a well-rehearsed routine. 'Lamyman and Son are most expert in such matters.'

Kite nodded agreement, though in truth he would rather the undertakers had never been summoned by Captain Walker. He looked around. Any tracks which the killer might have made the previous evening had already been well and truly obliterated by the boots of these three men and of Captain Walker himself and presumably also by the various inhabitants of Crowthorpe Manor who had tumbled out of the house when the alarm had been raised.

'I have some tarpaulins,' Mr Lamyman said. 'I like to be prepared for all situations. We could lay them over the ash and fire-debris when we have finished if you so wished?'

'No. Just let me know when you have finished,'

Kite said, wishing he had got a better control of the situation, as well as his own temper. 'But perhaps you would leave your tarpaulins for my constable and myself, to make use of when we have completed an initial examination of the site.'

'Thank you, sir. That seems a very sensible plan.' He gave another bow and issued another obsequious smile as he backed away. 'In that case, we will continue.'

'And might I suggest,' Captain Walker said in a tone he probably used with his junior officers, 'that you come inside and start your interviews, until such time as Mr Lamyman has finished.'

'Thank you, but my constable and I will be making a full survey of the grounds while there is still daylight.' Kite looked up at the sky, conscious of the lowering clouds approaching ominously from the east. 'And before it starts to rain.'

'Very well,' he said, though his tone suggested he didn't think it was very well at all. He turned towards Lamyman, who was holding his hands together like a priest about to offer a prayer. 'Carry on then, man.' And he marched off back to the house, invisible steam pouring out of his ears.

Sparrow chuckled as he and Kite headed off towards the main gateway. 'Plenty of officers like him in the trenches. He'd have had you on fatigues, sir.'

But Kite's mind was elsewhere. 'Did you notice what the captain said? Told me to concentrate my efforts on the village, that I should be looking for a burglar. And Lady Beatrice called the killer a thug, a ne'er-do-well.'

'She has a point, doesn't she?'

'It could be one of the family.'

'What makes you think that?'

'Because it often is.'

'Is it?'

Sparrow's doubt was obvious, but Kite wasn't interested in continuing the conversation. When they reached the main entrance, there were plenty of signs of people and horses who had come in and out of it, and the fresh tracks of Sparrow's motorbike. But none of that proved or disproved anything as far as Kite was concerned.

'So, let's suppose you're a burglar, Constable. What would you be hoping to steal, and would you come on foot or by horse?'

'Whatever you could find, I guess. Food, drink. I expect they shoot game here in the winter. Maybe there's pheasants hanging in one of the outbuildings. Or stuff you can sell. Saddles and bridles for example from the stable area. Cans of petrol for the car. I expect there's a black market for that if you know the right people.'

'So heavy stuff to carry. You'd want something like a horse and cart to take it away, and to get away quickly if you were discovered. And you wouldn't come charging in by the main gate if you could avoid it because anyone looking out their bedroom window might spot you. So let's walk round the outskirts of the grounds and see what we can see.'

Walking the outskirts initially meant walking along the top of a ha-ha, designed to keep any animals in the grass field at the front from entering the garden.

Currently there was only one horse, a big hunter wearing a thick rug. There were no signs of attempted entry there or of a horse and cart being left out of sight in the dip to await stolen goods. Kite pressed on, alongside the outside of a tall garden wall which looped round to the back of the house before it gave way to a series of buildings – a large wooden barn, various brick structures, stables and sheds – before they found themselves back at the main entrance.

'So what do you make of that, Constable?' Kite stopped and leaned against the gate post, glad of a rest.

'Well no evidence of an intruder, though I guess someone on their own who knew the property wouldn't leave many traces. Sneak in by the front gate, keep to the shadows.'

'By intruder you mean a thief? Or someone intent on killing Sir Wilfred?'

Sparrow scratched the side of his face while he considered this. 'I suppose I'm thinking of a thief. He comes in hoping to steal something he can eat – a couple of pheasants maybe – or something he could sell. He sees the garage door open and slips inside not realising that Sir Wilfred is sitting in his car. He is startled, panics and hits him with something, sploshes petrol around and sets fire to the car before escaping.'

'But why do that when it was bound to alert the household?'

Sparrow frowned and scratched his cheek again. 'To make sure he was dead, I guess.'

'Hmm.' Kite took another sweep of the area. As theories go, it was pretty good. And if that was the case, then identifying that intruder would be difficult. And yet there was something that was bothering him. He nodded. He didn't want to discourage Sparrow by sharing his doubts. It was too soon for that. He glanced up at the darkening sky. 'Well, the truth is we need evidence. You go and check the inside of the gardens for traces before those rain clouds let rip. I'll go and see how Mr Lamyman and his men are getting on.'

But they weren't rain clouds. By the time he had limped his way to the remains of the burnt out car, large flakes of snow were drifting down through the fading winter light.

'We've just finished.' Lamyman was watching his two men strap down a coffin which, Kite assumed, contained the remains of Sir Wilfred Walker. Lamyman looked up pointedly at the sky. 'I reckon we're in for a fair old blanket of the white stuff. What shall I do with the tarpaulins?'

'Please, it would be very helpful if you could just lay them out across the site. And weigh them down.'

'Of course. As you say, sir.' By which he meant, *as I originally suggested*. There was a self-satisfied edge to his voice. A man of the country putting a big city policeman right. Kite tried not to care, but the fact was that there was already a thin white covering forming on top of the ashes and the snow in the air was intensifying.

'One more thing,' Kite said firmly, 'I'd like to look inside the coffin.'

Lamyman started. 'Why on earth…?'

'Just do it.'

'But we've just sealed it.'

'So unseal it. It's evidence.'

The tension was palpable. Lamyman's two men had stopped strapping the coffin onto the cart and were watching this stand-off with undisguised fascination. Kite turned towards them. 'Now, gentlemen, if you don't mind. The sooner I take a look, the sooner you all get home.'

Lamyman made a grunting sound and the two men undid the strapping and levered the lid up and removed it. Kite stood on the spokes of one of the wheels, using it as a step to clamber up. The bones were laid out in no real of order, though the skull – still attached to part of the spinal column – was positioned at the front end of the coffin. He levered himself up onto the cart and stretched out his arm to pick it up.

'I don't think the captain would like that.' It was obvious where Lamyman's loyalties lay. Kite glanced across at him and smiled.

'In that case, make sure you don't tell him. Then you won't upset him.'

'It's about showing respect.'

'It's about investigating a brutal murder in a methodical manner in order to find the truth.' Kite's gaze was fixed on the skull as he examined it. There was a crack in the back of it; a fine one admittedly, but distinct enough. He rubbed at it, clearing some of the ash away from it. In the midst of the crack was a slight indentation where a small piece of bone had been dislodged. He had studied skeletons during his time in London. He had talked to a sawbones or two as well. He had never seen a dead man reduced so spectacularly to a pile of bones and sinew, but he reckoned he knew how this had begun, with a blow to the back of the head. The killer must have set him alight after killing or knocking him out with that blow. That much was clear.

'Well, have you investigated enough?' Lamyman was growing more impatient by the second. 'I want to get home, not end up stuck in a snow drift.'

'All done, Mr Lamyman. Thank you. That's all I need to see for now.'

There was nothing to be done until the morning – at best. Kite trudged off, walking anticlockwise until he met up with Sparrow coming the other way.

'Nothing, sir. I thought maybe that gate in the wall, but it's securely bolted from the inside and there's no sign of it having been forced, or even used recently.'

'I didn't think so.' Kite liked it that his own theory had been – if not proved – then at least half proved. In his own mind it was almost certainly an inside family job. But it seemed tactful to keep that thought to himself – for the time being at least.

They had barely entered the house before they were intercepted by Captain Walker. Kite had already taken a dislike to him, so he was surprised by what he had to say. 'Inspector, I mean Sergeant, my mother says that you would both be most welcome to stay the night. Looking at the weather, getting to the village might be a bit tricky, and by the morning who knows how thick the snow will lie. There are two small rooms at the top of the west wing for guests. Mary and David Graves inhabit the lower floors, but I am

sure they will not object. In the meantime my mother
will happily receive you in the study.'

THE FIRST INTERVIEWS

LADY BEATRICE WAS sitting at a large desk. There was a pile of papers in front of her and for several seconds she didn't look up. Kite waited silently. He knew what she was doing, establishing her aristocratic superiority. There was a time when it would have annoyed him immensely, but now he was older and, he hoped, wiser. Instead he took the opportunity to survey the room. Behind Lady Beatrice the wall was lined with shelves. These contained on the lower levels numerous files which, Kite presumed, held the paperwork of the Crowthorpe Jam Company. On the higher shelves by contrast were a series of trophies and two-handled silver trophies with coloured ribbons hanging from them. On the wall to Kite's left – and indeed on the wall behind him – were a selection of framed posters, each an advertisement for Crowthorpe's produce – strawberry, raspberry, blackberry and apple jams, marmalade, as well as various chutneys. He had eaten their chutney more than once. It went very well with cheese and bread.

'So I suppose you want to ask me some questions?' Lady Beatrice snapped.

Kite had briefly been elsewhere. When he turned towards her, she was skewering him with her eyes. 'If you don't mind,' he said.

'What if I do mind?'

'Just a few questions. I will keep them as brief as possible.'

'Am I a suspect then? Do you think that I killed my

husband?'

'No I do not.' He tried to sound as emphatic as possible. 'I am trying to solve your husband's tragic murder, and to do that I really need to find out what happened yesterday evening. So all I am asking is that you answer a few questions.'

'If you must.' Lady Beatrice pursed her lips and then coughed. She removed a handkerchief from her sleeve and held it to her mouth, then picked up the glass of water on her table and took two sips.

'I would also be most grateful if you would allow me to question everyone else in the house.' *Allow?* Had he really said that? *Allow!* Kite hated himself for letting the word pass his lips, for giving her the power to say 'Yes' or 'No'. Of course, if she refused to give her blessing, then he would have to insist, but that would create tensions and problems. If he had to doff his hat and touch his forelock to get her co-operation, then that is what he would do.

'Well, I think you are being extremely impertinent. In fact I find this whole thing quite distasteful. When it is all over, I shall ring your superior and tell him exactly what I think.'

'You are fully entitled to contact the chief constable. But I hope you will not find it necessary to do so.' *Grovel.*

Lady Beatrice merely stared at him, silent.

'Your son tells me that, in view of the snow, you have invited Constable Sparrow and myself to sleep here overnight. That is most kind of you and we gladly accept the invitation.' More *grovel, grovel.*

'Oh, do get on with your questions! I would like to

have my cup of tea.' She waved her hand. 'And sit down. You make the room look untidy.'

Kite sat down, and motioned Sparrow to do the same. He wanted him to focus his attention on taking good notes.

'Perhaps you could tell me when you last saw your husband?'

'Well that's an easy one. At dinner, last night. We had a lamb casserole. It was rather tough to be honest. You would have thought that at the age of thirty-eight Mary Graves would have learned how to cook.'

'Mary is your cook?'

She laughed. 'Thank goodness, no. She is – she was – my husband's secretary. She calls herself his personal assistant, though general dogsbody would be closer to the truth. Since the beginning of the war, she's had to help out generally, not just with regard to the company, but around the house too. In return she shares a set of rooms with her brother David and gets all her meals free as well as a small salary, so she has no reason to complain. Rose is a much better cook, but she has to look after me too, so she cannot be expected to carry the full weight of the kitchen. But in difficult times, one cannot just go out and hire a new cook.'

'So,' Kite said, trying to steer the interview back on course, 'what happened after dinner?'

'What nearly always happens. The men went through to the library to drink their port and tell war stories to each other. But I had had enough. Quite enough. I went upstairs and got ready for bed. I read for a while, and then I dropped off to sleep and the next thing I knew was there was a most dreadful noise. I went out onto the landing, and everyone was wailing or shouting.'

'I see… May I ask, did Sir Wilfred come up to say good night before you fell asleep?'

She laughed again, as if this was the funniest suggestion he could possibly have come up with. 'Look, Sergeant, we sleep in separate rooms. He snores. And at my age, he doesn't come visiting any more. Not like when he was younger.'

'So, after you went upstairs, you didn't see anyone else?'

'That isn't what I said.' Her tongue was getting sharper with every passing moment. 'I didn't see my husband, but I did see Rose. She came up and helped me get ready for bed. She also brought me a cup of tea which I drank while I was reading.'

'What time was it when she brought the tea?'

She frowned. 'I am not sure. Maybe half-past nine or a little later.'

'And you read for how long?'

'Is that really of any importance? Twenty or twenty-five minutes I suppose.'

'I am merely trying to establish at what time you went to sleep.'

'Well why didn't you say so? It was shortly after ten o'clock. I have a little carriage clock which strikes on the hour. I wait for it to do so before I switch my light out.'

'That's very helpful.'

'And is that all?'

'One more question.' Kite paused. 'What was the

book?'

'What on earth has that got to do with my husband's death?'

'I'm curious, that's all. I like a good read.'

'It was *Bleak House*. By Charles Dickens. I have a complete set of his books in the library.'

Lady Beatrice eased herself up onto her feet. The interview was over as far as she was concerned. 'I think that is quite enough of your wretched questions! I need my cup of tea and my piece of cake.'

Kite nodded and stood up. 'Personally, I prefer *Oliver Twist*.'

'Yes, of course. Being a Londoner and policeman, you would.'

Kite followed Lady Beatrice out of the study only to find Captain Alec blocking his exit.

'Perhaps we could get your questioning of me over.'

'Of course.' Kite withdrew back into the study. He waved Sparrow back down into his chair, while wondering how long the captain had been hovering nearby. Had he been trying to overhear what his mother was saying? The doors in the house were thick and heavy, but there was a distinct draught from under this one.

The captain sat down in the chair beyond the desk, crossing one leg over the knee, as if disinterested and casual. 'Fire away.'

Kite opened with an easy question. 'You served in the trenches?'

'I was proud to do so.' *Proud to do so*. A sly dig at Kite who had not been there.

'And you were injured.'

'Some people would say I was lucky. I caught a piece of shrapnel in the shoulder. They brought me back to Blighty for a spell of recuperation, and then it was off to the front again for the last few months of the war.'

'And following your father's death, I presume you are now in charge of the Crowthorpe Jam Company.'

The captain stiffened, unfolding his legs, sitting upright in his chair, gripping the wooden arms of his chair. 'Are you insinuating something?'

'Not at all. But an important part of my job is to ask questions.'

'You didn't ask a question. You implied that I benefited from my father's death.'

'If a father dies, then someone always benefits.'

'Don't get clever with me, Mr Detective. My father was brutally murdered, and I take very great exception to your implication that I did it.'

Kite glanced to his right, where Sparrow was watching him intently, fascinated by what he was witnessing. Perhaps he was pressing too hard. 'I really do apologise. That was not my intention at all. But I am merely trying to establish the facts.' He paused, trying to find the right words, before continuing. 'I merely assumed that since you have been back here you've been helping your father run the company?'

'He wanted me to learn the ropes, yes, and I was happy to support him in whatever way he wanted. But he was still very hands-on in the running of the company.'

'Never easy that. Father and son working together. My father wanted me to help him with his business.

But he didn't want me interfering with the way he did it. Didn't want me to suggest how things could be done better. Which is why I decided to go and join the police.'

'My father and I understood each other very well. He wanted his company to live on after him. So did I. And I had no interest in telling him how to run his own business.'

'Perhaps you can just tell me what happened on the night of your father's death. I understand you had dinner together. When would that have been?'

'Half past seven. Regular as clockwork. Any later and my mother would have problems with her indigestion.'

'And who was there?'

'All of us. Not Frank and Rose of course. They served the food and drink and then they withdrew. I expect they ate afterwards in the kitchen. So my father and mother. Myself and my wife Elizabeth. My sister Maud. And David Graves and his sister Mary Graves.'

'So you finished when?'

'I suppose a little before nine o'clock.'

'And then what did you do?'

'My mother went upstairs as she normally did. Us men went into the library and had a glass or two of port.'

'And after that?'

'David challenged me to a game of billiards. In the end we played best of three.'

'And who won?'

'What?' His tone of voice was suddenly sharp.

'What possible relevance can that have to your investigations.'

'I was just curious.'

'He did. Two games to one. And only by the skin of his teeth.'

'And then you did what?'

'Went to bed.'

'What time was this?'

'God knows. I didn't check the time. The fact is that I had drunk more than I usually do, so I just lay down on the bed in my clothes and the next thing I know there was a God awful noise in the corridor. And then Elizabeth came in and told me the garage was on fire. Of course I rushed downstairs and outside, but it was too late to do anything.'

'Can you remember who else was there when you arrived?'

He shook his head. 'David Graves, Frank Tomkin, my sister Maud, I'm not sure. But soon enough we were all there, though we tried to get the women to go back inside. We tried to put the fire out with buckets of water from the stables, but really it was futile.'

'It must have been traumatic.'

'Yes, indeed. Just talking about it now, it's…'

'I am most grateful for your assistance. Perhaps I could ask if you saw your father after you had been drinking port with him?'

'No. He said he had things to do in his study.'

'But at some point he must have gone out to his car.'

'I am glad you have worked that out, Detective.' His voice was laced with a sneer.

'Was this normal, for him to sit in his car late at

night.'

'In the summer often. In the winter less so. But if he had a problem he would sometimes go out and sit in his car and smoke a cigar while he thought it through.'

'Even on a cold winter's night.'

'Yes.'

'Have you any idea what this problem might have been?'

'If I had, Sergeant, then I would have told you.'

Kite nodded. He wondered if he could squeeze in another question or two, but before he could, the captain leant forward.

'What about you then, Detective? You have asked me a lot of intrusive questions, so I think it is my turn to ask some of you.' The captain stroked his moustache as he prepared to counter-attack. 'Who exactly are you? Unless my hearing has been severely disordered by my time in the trenches, I am fairly sure you're not a Lincolnshire man.'

'No.'

'Some sort of Londoner, I would hazard.'

'I was born in Bishopsgate.'

'Oh, Bishopsgate.' His tone of voice was knowing and disapproving at the same time. 'And I suppose you joined the City of London police?'

'Yes.'

'And did you sign up for the army at the beginning of the war?'

'I lost an eye in 1910, trying to stop a robbery.'

'Ah. Did you catch him?'

'No.'

'So it's not true that every cloud has a silver lining.' He smiled thinly and flexed his hands together. The knuckles cracked and he looked up at Kite. 'And just out of curiosity, did you join in the police strike last year?'

Kite swallowed hard. The captain seemed well informed. Suspiciously well informed. As if he already knew about Kite's history. As if someone had tipped him off. No surprise there. People like him knew people who mattered – like Chief Constable Bostock in Lincoln.

'Our wages were very low. Married men couldn't support their families.'

'You're a married man, are you, Detective?'

Kite realised he had underestimated the captain. He was much more than just a stiff shirt.

'No.'

'No? But you had the effrontery to say you would not do your vital job unless you were paid more.'

'It wasn't like that.'

'It was exactly like that. You and plenty more like you, who weaselled your way out of fighting for your King and Country, instead tried to hold the government to ransom when we were still engaged in a war to the death. Have you any idea how many people died in the trenches, Detective? Millions. But instead you stayed at home, in the safety of London, and demanded more money.'

'I wanted to support my colleagues.'

The captain gave a hoarse laugh and stood up. 'Is that all then? Because I do have a lot of things on my plate.'

Kite nodded. He was being dismissed. He knew that and he didn't feel able to resist. The fact was he had been shaken by the course the interview had taken. And in any case, there seemed to be no point in trying to question the captain any further. He would have to wait for another opportunity. Come up with a plan. Catch him off his guard.

'Just one thing,' Kite said quickly. 'I wonder if I might ask your wife a few questions?'

'Is that really necessary?'

'She was in the house that terrible night. She might have seen something relevant.'

'I am quite sure she would have told me if she had.'

'Sometimes people don't realise the importance of what they have seen. Besides, whereas you were sleeping off the effects of alcohol when your father was killed, you said yourself that your wife woke you up.'

The captain clenched his jaw. 'My wife is carrying our first child. Not too long to go either. That is why I am very unhappy about the prospect of you asking her a series of unnecessary and distressing questions.'

'I do understand your concern, sir. And if I may say so, congratulations to both yourself and your wife.'

'Thank you.' The words were uttered grudgingly.

Kite smiled. 'My understanding of women in her delicate state is that they often sleep rather badly, so it may be your wife will for that reason turn out to be a very important witness.'

The captain twisted his hands in frustration. 'Even so, Sergeant, I am concerned that in her state she should not be unduly upset.'

'Of course. I will endeavour not to ask her any distressing questions, I can assure you.'

'I should hope not.

'Thank you.'

'Ah, good afternoon,' Kite said. He stood up. 'I think you must be Mrs Elizabeth Walker, the captain's wife.'

She nodded. She was tall, in a flowing black dress and her right hand was resting on the bulge of her stomach.

'Please sit down,' he continued. 'They have kindly provided us with some tea. Perhaps Constable Sparrow can pour you some.'

In the ten minutes while Kite had been waiting, Sparrow had disappeared to the kitchen and returned with a laden tray. He now proceeded to pour the tea and hand out pieces of carraway cake. Kite could hardly wait, sinking his teeth into it.

'Very good this is too. Did you make it by any chance, Mrs Walker?'

'No.' She smiled as if flattered by this suggestion. 'I am perfectly capable of making cakes, but given my condition I am afraid they treat me like a porcelain doll. "Sit down. Don't do that." To be honest, it all gets a bit tedious.'

'Perhaps I might offer you my congratulations, Mrs Walker. A first child. That will be quite something.'

'Please, call me Elizabeth. I do not stand on as much ceremony as my dear husband.'

'Thank you.' Kite took a sip of tea, and glanced across at Sparrow to check he was ready.

'Well, Elizabeth, I just want to ask you a few straightforward questions about the night your father-in-law died. And I have asked Constable Sparrow to take notes in accordance with our normal procedures.'

'I have never been interviewed by a policeman.'

'And I hope you never will be again.' He smiled at her and to his surprise she smiled back. Almost as if she was flirting with him.

Kite swallowed. He wasn't so naive as to think she was flirting with him. Was she trying to distract him? To put him off? If so, why?

Kite opened his mouth to say something, but she jumped in first: 'No!'

'No?' Kite was startled. He had thought she would be straightforward and yet…

'No, I did not kill my father-in-law.'

Kite felt himself blush. 'I… I really wasn't going to suggest that you had. I merely wanted you to tell me about last night. When, for example, did you retire to your bedroom?'

'Well, that's an easy one. Straight after supper. About nine o'clock I suppose.'

'Like your mother-in-law?'

'Yes, we staggered up the stairs together.'

'And after that?'

She gave another mischievous smile. 'I had a bath. Mary came up with a cocoa for each of us and we sat together and talked for a while. And then, I suppose it was about a quarter to ten, she took our dirty cups and saucers downstairs to the kitchen and I went to sleep.'

'Did you sleep well?'

'Not particularly. I don't do at the moment. In fact I

didn't actually go to bed. Instead I sat in the nursing chair which my mother-in-law kindly gave me. I put my feet up on a stool and dozed. Rather fitfully, but the baby seems to prefer me in that position.'

'When did your husband come up?'

'Much later I suspect. Until the baby is born, he is sleeping in the small room across the corridor. It suits the both of us.'

'And I suppose you didn't see your father-in-law at all after dinner?'

'No.'

'Well thank you, Elizabeth. You have been very tolerant of my questions.'

'Have I?' She looked down at her lap and then up at him again, as bashful as a teenage girl on the edge of puberty. Kite couldn't help but feel that she was playing with him, that she was a lot more knowing than she liked to pretend, but he couldn't help enjoying the moment.

'I hope you don't mind me asking, but I was just wondering when your baby might be due.'

'In six weeks' time, God willing – and if the doctors have got their timings right. I myself was born two weeks early, although my mother-in-law is of the opinion that first babies are nearly always late. We will see.'

'The tea and cake was very welcome, Constable. Thank you for arranging it.'

A smile burst across Sparrow's face. Kite wasn't quite sure what to make of him. He was part live-wire (especially when driving a motorcycle) and part model constable. Kite had checked his notepad earlier when Sparrow had gone to the kitchen and had been impressed both by the tidiness of his writing and the accuracy of his notes. But it was Sparrow's initiative in thinking of the tea and cake which had most surprised him – a constable who could see further than the obvious was someone to be encouraged.

'I was hungry,' he grinned. 'I always look after number one – don't you worry.'

Kite drained the last of his tea and picked up the few crumbs of cake left on his plate. 'I understand there is one more family member to talk to. A Miss Maud Walker.'

'A bit of a rebel from what I've heard.'

'Have you met her before?'

Another grin. 'Only from a distance. When I was a lad. Saw her riding her pony a couple of times. Never spoke to her. If I had, I'd have got a clip round the ear and that's for sure.'

'So where is she now?'

'I'll go and find out, sir.'

'Well, you take the tray back to the kitchen and ask there. I think I'll go and get a bit of fresh air.'

Getting a bit of fresh air wasn't entirely his intention. He retrieved his coat, slipped out of the front door, lit a cigarette and stood huddled in the porch looking out. The snow was still falling in huge flakes, silent and soft. There wasn't a breath of wind. If it continued like this until the morning, it was likely to be impassable. He scanned the yard. He could just about make out where the remains of the car and garage lay. The snow and the moonlight revealed too the shape of the various buildings. Far to the left, only just in sight, was a lamp flickering in the dark. Was that where the horses were stabled? Was Maud out there? If so, it would be worth a trudge through the snow to find her on her own and maybe catch her unawares. And he was curious to know why she had a reputation as a rebel. Was it her father who she had rebelled against?

Deep and crisp and even. The words from the Christmas carol blossomed inside his head as he made his way through the snow, now several inches deep, soft rather than crisp, but even and almost unspoilt except for a single trail of tracks which led him inexorably towards that beckoning light. When he got to the door, he paused, taking a final draw from his cigarette before tossing it away into the snow. Then he went in, calling out 'Hello' as he did so.

A figure turned towards him and for a moment he was uncertain if it was a man or a woman. Slim build, almost as tall as himself, scruffy country clothes, scarf wrapped tight about the neck and a woollen hat pulled down over the head, partly covering the ears.

'Ah,' said a voice. A clearly female voice. 'You must be the detective.'

'I am indeed. Detective Sergeant Kite, at your service. And I detect that you must be Miss Maud Walker, daughter of Sir Wilfred and Lady Beatrice.'

'I've just been cleaning out and feeding the horses. God only knows how long this weather will last.'

'You ride then?'

'Oh yes. When I can. But not in this sort of weather.'

'No?'

'When I was fifteen, we had snow, almost as bad as this. I decided it was so wonderful that I would go for a ride. But in these conditions, it is not the snow, but what is underneath the snow which is the danger: ice, frozen ruts, unseen obstacles.' She paused, staring into the dark. Her eyes were moist. 'I had a lovely horse called Lonesome. Fifteen hands tall, a beautiful bay, easily spooked. Anyway he was spooked that day, tried to take off across the snow, caught his foot in a rut and *Crack!* Broke his ankle. He had to be shot. My father made me watch. A lesson for life, he called it. It was my fault, he said. I should never have taken the horse out in those conditions.'

'I'm so sorry. That must have been hard for you.'

'Harder for the horse.' She stood stock still for several seconds before giving a sudden shake of the head, as if discarding the memory. Then she looked straight at him. 'Anyway, I expect you want to ask me some questions.'

'If you don't mind.'

'And if I do mind, what then?' Her face was smooth and emotionless, and her eyes unblinking. She gestured towards the door. 'You're letting the cold in and the heat out.' She was, Kite decided, very much her mother's daughter.

'Sorry.' Kite moved back to shut the door. The catch was stiff and it took a few moments to click it into place. When he turned round, Maud Walker had sat down on a bale of straw. She had taken off the woollen hat and was scratching vigorously at her short red hair.

'I've already been warned that you would want to know my name, rank and number – as it were. So let me save you some breath. I am thirty-one years old and unmarried. I helped my father run the company – the Crowthorpe Jam Company – through the war. Not that he was that keen on me doing it. He expects – expected – women to sit at home giving birth to children, above all male children. Then to look after those children, as well as the house and the husband, to wear pretty dresses, and to keep their mouths shut. That's not me. I am proud to call myself a suffragette. I believe women should have the same rights as men when it comes to voting. I also believe women are smarter than men, and that if we had the opportunity, we would make a much better fist of running the country than men.'

'That explains it then.'

'Explains what?'

'Constable Sparrow said you had a bit of a reputation for being a rebel.'

'Did he now?'

'When he was a child, he used to live in the village of Crowthorpe. Said he saw you riding a pony from time to time.'

'I did ride a lot. And not always where I was meant to.' She laughed. 'But, of course, we were not allowed to fraternise with the locals. Not the done thing!'

'Well, my constable may be wondering where I have got to, so perhaps I can just ask a few questions and then you can finish tending to your horses.'

'Carry on.'

'What time did you go to bed last night?'

'Ah, they said you would ask that. How predictable you men are. Unlike my mother and my sister-in-law, I did not retire upstairs straight after dinner. What I did do was help Mary clear up and put the leftover food away. She made Elizabeth and herself cocoa and took it off upstairs. But I went and joined the men.'

'Nobody mentioned that.'

'Perhaps you didn't ask the right question.'

Kite scratched his chin. It was itchy. Perhaps it was the straw, or perhaps he was unconsciously influenced by Maud, who was still scratching intermittently at her own hair.

'Miss Walker—'

'Maud will do.'

'Maud… what did you and the men talk about?'

'When I joined them, they were talking racing. But we soon moved on to politics. They disapprove of me and my views, but I like to challenge their outdated thinking.'

'Did you not discuss business at all? After all, things must have been difficult these last few years.'

'I find it best to avoid business when people have been drinking.'

'And how did your father seem?'

She looked up at Kite, her face tight and disdainful. 'As patriarchal and male as he always seemed.'

'So he didn't seem unduly concerned about anything?'

'Only about his horses. He owns three steeplechasers and was concerned as to how the weather might impede their training. He had his eye on entering them at a couple of big race meetings this spring.'

'And they are here are they?'

'God no. He pays…' She paused, suddenly stumbling over her words. 'He paid for them to be looked after and trained. He just went along on race day in the hope of picking up a trophy and some prize money.'

'I see.'

'Anything else? Only it is quite late and I'm keen to get finished here.'

'So after drinking with the men, you went straight to bed?'

'No. Alec and David wanted a game of billiards, so I took the opportunity to go to the library and do some work on a pamphlet.'

'What sort of pamphlet?'

'I have given it the title "Votes for Women: the Unanswerable Case". I hope that is self-explanatory?'

'And how long were you there in the library?'

'Until… until… until the noise and the shouting woke me up. You see I fell asleep. I fear crème de menthe often has that effect on me.'

'But did you see or hear anything before you fell asleep?'

'No. If I had, I would have told you already.'

'Just one more question.' Kite hesitated. He couldn't be sure how anyone might react to what he had in mind, but having met Maud he felt confident he could put it to her.

'Well?' Her impatience for this to be finished was obvious.

'I was wondering if you might have any idea why someone would want to kill your father?'

'Oh, that's an easy one. Because he made enemies. That's why.'

'And do you have anyone in particular in mind?'

'Really, Sergeant, do I look particularly stupid? I understand from my brother that that you are convinced that the killer was one of us. Not an intruder who chanced upon him while trying to steal something, but someone who was in the house last night. You can hardly expect me to point the finger of suspicion at any of them.'

'Perhaps not.' He wasn't surprised, but he didn't regret asking the question. Nor did it put him off slipping in one more riposte. 'Maud, this isn't a question as such, I don't expect you to answer, but I do wonder this. If you knew who killed your father, would you tell me who the killer was?'

To Kite's surprise, she laughed. Then she stood up, signifying as she brushed straw off her clothing that she had given up enough of her time. 'Look, Sergeant, what you have to remember is that my father was a most unlikeable man. When I looked around the breakfast table this morning, I realised that any of us could have killed him.'

'Any of you?'

'Oh yes,' she said, without a glimmer of humour in her voice. 'Even me.'

Kite's and Sparrow's bedrooms were on the second floor at the top of the west wing of the house. The third room on that level contained a toilet which they were to share. Kite opted for the slightly larger bedroom – and why not? – which gave a view across the front lawn (now white in the darkness). Sparrow's looked out across the walled kitchen garden at the back.

Kite lay on his bed to rest and stretch his back. It had been his intention to lie there awake for just a few minutes, but he fell asleep almost immediately and woke only when Sparrow tapped insistently on the door and told him that supper was ready. They were to eat in the kitchen, with Rose and with Frank Tomkin, a tall, broad-shouldered dark-haired man who introduced himself and offered them a beer.

'Been a long day for you, I reckon.' He grinned, revealing a gap where two or three teeth were missing. 'I bet it was a bouncy old ride on that motorbike.'

The food was a stew with a surprisingly generous amount of meat in it, plus baked potatoes and boiled cabbage. The conversation was mostly between Frank and Sparrow, exchanging stories about the war which became more and more improbable as each tried to outdo the other. To Kite's surprise Rose was largely silent. Perhaps she had heard Frank's stories too many times already, or perhaps like Kite she was fighting fatigue. It was she who seemed to have the greatest workload in the house, both acting as Lady Beatrice's maid and running the kitchen and much else of the domestic side of the house. Frank had apparently helped with taking the food through to the dining room and making up fires in two of the downstairs rooms, but he showed no sign of helping any further in the kitchen.

There was a temporary lull when Rose produced a portion each of queen of puddings, and that was when Kite decided to take his opportunity.

'Frank, tell me about Sir Wilfred's car.'

'A Rolls-Royce Silver Ghost. A beautiful piece

of precious engineering. Leather seats, mahogany dashboard. Lovely to drive.'

'Did Sir Wilfred drive it himself?'

'No, he liked me to drive him. Didn't trust any of the others.'

'And you maintained it?'

'I did. Kept it immaculate. Inside and out. Checked the fuel, oil, everything.'

'And it was in good working order?'

Frank looked up sharply from his pudding. 'Course it was.'

'No leaks or anything?'

'What are you getting at?'

'He liked to smoke a cigar in the evening, I gather. And he had had quite a lot to drink. So I was wondering if he could have dropped his lighted cigar into some petrol which then caught fire and...'

'Hey!' Frank lifted his hand and jabbed his finger in Kite's direction. 'What are you talking about? You're saying it was my fault. That I left petrol spilt all over the floor and that was the reason the place went up in flames?' He rose to his feet, towering over Kite and red in the face. 'I always left that garage in immaculate condition, everything tidy. The spare cans of petrol were stored up on a shelf on the far wall, at a distance, secured with wire. So don't you try and pin it on me.'

Rose, who was sitting at the end of the table, banged the flat of her hand down on the surface and now it was her turn to rise to her feet. 'Frank Tomkin, sit down!' She spoke slowly, her words like a hiss. 'I will not have shouting or drunken behaviour in my kitchen.'

'But you heard what he said? He was accusing me…'

'Sit down!'

Frank opened his mouth to argue, but something in her was stronger than his anger, and he slumped back down onto the bench.

'Frank,' she said, still standing and speaking with exaggerated calm, 'the sergeant was trying to establish whether Sir Wilfred's death might have been accidental. That was all. I will merely say that in my experience you always kept the car and garage very tidy. And so if Sir Wilfred's death was an accident, then I do not see that you could possibly be held responsible for it.' Rose looked around, waiting for a response, and when there wasn't one she sat down. 'I suggest we all finish our pudding, stop drinking beer and try to find something more cheerful to talk about.'

'It was my fault,' Kite said. 'It's hard to switch off being a policeman when you're involved in a case. No more questions until tomorrow. But I hope you understand that Constable Sparrow and I will have to interview you both tomorrow. After breakfast perhaps?'

'Of course.' Rose was quick to speak for both of them. She also refused any help with the clearing up. It was as clear as a frog on a log – an expression Kite had regularly heard from the lips of his mother – that she wanted the two policemen out of the kitchen. So they headed up the back stairs towards their sleeping quarters, each armed with a mug of water.

They had barely reached the first floor when a woman appeared. She was wearing a plain black dress. Her light brown hair was tied back tight behind her head, and her cheeks were flushed. 'Oh! Oh, gosh!' She was flustered. 'You must be the police.'

Kite nodded and introduced himself and Sparrow.

'I am… I am Mary Graves. Miss Mary Graves. Sir Wilfred's secretary. Well, not just his secretary, more his personal assistant.'

Kite nodded, remembering as he did so the less than flattering comments about her that Lady Beatrice had expressed. 'We will be sleeping on the next floor above you. I do hope we won't disturb you.' Kite spoke calmly and carefully. She gave the impression of being a highly strung, skittish horse. 'I am afraid,' he added, 'that I rarely have a night's sleep without having to get up to answer a call of nature.'

'I sleep very well,' she said defiantly.

'And your brother…'

'My brother David is in the study at the moment, I think, dealing with some company business. He is production manager of the business. Very important too in these times.'

'Of course.'

'I expect you would you like to ask me questions.'

'Well, yes but…'

'I know how these things work. I am an avid reader of mystery novels. Sherlock Holmes, of course, and the Father Brown stories. Have you read them, Sergeant?'

'Yes, a number of the short stories, though I fear they don't always show us police detectives in the best light.'

'No.' She frowned as if she had just realised that she had made a faux pas. 'I suppose not. But that is, I think, deliberate, to make the private investigators seem cleverer. I don't suppose it is like that in real life.'

'I hope not.'

Kite moved to carry on up the stairs, but she stepped across, effectively blocking him. 'Why don't you come and ask me your questions now?'

'Are you sure?' Kite wasn't at all sure himself that this was what he wanted now. It had been a long day, and he would have liked time to prepare some questions.

'Of course I am sure. I don't go to bed this early, and I do so want to help you solve the dreadful mystery. Sir Wilfred was such a benefactor to everyone who lived around here. I mean, you won't believe how many of them are dependent on the Crowthorpe Jam Company. Growing, picking, making the wonderful jams and chutneys, and of course transporting them to Lincoln and beyond for the people of Britain to enjoy. But clearly someone out there held a grudge against him.'

'Not necessarily someone out there, Miss Graves,' Sparrow said suddenly. He had been notably quiet since Frank Tomkin's outburst in the kitchen.

She frowned. 'What do you mean, Constable? Surely it must have been someone from Crowthorpe or possibly from further afield? A vagabond trying to steal something very likely.'

'The sergeant has not ruled out the possibility of it

being someone who lives in this house.'

Mary stared, first at Sparrow and then at Kite. Her cheerful red face seemed to collapse upon itself. For a moment she looked as though she might faint. She thrust a hand out to steady herself against the door frame, but missed. Kite lunged forwards and grabbed her arm. Sparrow grabbed the other.

Mary blinked at Kite. 'Oh!' she said. 'Oh dear! You think one of us killed Sir Wilfred?'

He ignored the question. 'I suggest we go and sit down, Miss Graves.'

Her room was large and much more than just a bedroom. Spanning the whole of the floor, it had a brass framed bed near the front window, plus a chest of drawers and a modest wardrobe. A round table was positioned near the rear window, with two upright chairs tucked in either side. In the centre of the room were two armchairs, carefully arranged opposite a fireplace, in which a fire was burning merrily.

'This is very cosy. Especially the fire on a night like this.'

'Oh yes. I am very fortunate. Sir Wilfred and Lady Beatrice have been very kind. I used to have rooms in Crowthorpe village, but once the war took a grip, they invited me to stay here and since then well…' Her words tailed away. She slipped a handkerchief out of her sleeve and dabbed at her eyes.

'Are you alright, Miss Graves? Would you like a glass of water, or perhaps Constable Sparrow can go and organise a cup of tea?'

She shivered. 'Thank you, a cup of tea would be most welcome.'

Kite nodded to Sparrow. Kite and Mary sat silently on either side of the table, as Sparrow trudged heavily down the stairs. 'Oh dear, Sergeant,' she said, suddenly looking up. 'You must think me very silly, nearly falling over like that.'

'Not at all. It must have all been a terrible shock to you, especially when you worked so closely with him.' He gave her an encouraging smile. 'But it would be helpful if you could tell me about last night. I gather you ate dinner with the family.'

She gave a final dab at her eyes, and straightened herself up. 'Yes, David and I joined them. We didn't always eat with them. After all, they are family and we are not. They are kind to us, but we are employees after all. To be honest, now that the war is over and with Elizabeth soon to give birth, I have been half expecting that they might ask us to move back to Crowthorpe village. But this is a big house, and it hasn't happened yet. So I count my blessings.'

'So there wasn't a specific reason why you and David joined them last night except as an act of kindness. Sir Wilfred didn't have any pronouncements to make about anything?' Kite stopped and waited for a reply.

'Pronouncements? I'm not sure I know what you mean?'

'I was wondering if the war had affected the company business at all. I mean, I imagine it must have. Either for the good or the bad?'

Mary did not reply for several seconds. Kite let the question hang in the air, wondering if she was nervous about what she should or should not say.

'The war was hard at times, not least because so

many of the men were away fighting, but Sir Wilfred was a shrewd businessman and never gave me any reason to doubt that things were going in the right direction.'

Kite shrugged internally. Mary gave the impression of being the archetype of the loyal secretary, unwilling to say anything detrimental about her boss. Maybe another time he would press her, but he didn't want her to clam up. So he leaned forward with a smile. 'Mary, you were going to tell me about last night?'

'Yes, of course. I'm afraid I am not quite myself. It has all been so much of a shock.' She sat up straighter, folded her hands in her lap, and took a deep breath. 'We all had dinner at seven thirty last night. That is to say, Sir Wilfred and Lady Beatrice, Alec and Elizabeth, Maud, David and myself. Actually, I was in charge of the stew. Mutton from a Lincoln Longwool. A good filling meal for this time of year. Frank and Rose brought it in and served it, and then they went back to the kitchen to eat their own portions there.'

'And what did you talk about?'

She frowned. 'Let me think. The weather, of course. Racing. Sir Wilfred is… was… very keen on his racing. Maud tried to talk about women's rights and them getting the vote. But the men shouted her down. Sir Wilfred, Alec and my brother David are all very opposed to such ideas.'

'And what about you?'

'Oh goodness me, I stay out of conversations like that. Besides, the men had been drinking and I knew nothing good would come of it.'

'I expect there was some talk about the business.'

'You mean Crowthorpe Jam?' Mary seemed puzzled by this. 'I am sure there was not. Whatever makes you think there was, Sergeant?'

'Just a hunch,' he said, feeling slightly ashamed of himself for trying to catch her out. 'And what happened after supper?'

'Well, the men went off to smoke and drink while I helped clear things away. Then I made a cup of cocoa for Elizabeth and myself and I went up to her bedroom. Alec wasn't there, of course, so I sat and chatted with Elizabeth for a while, and then I took our dirty cups back down to the kitchen, and after that I made my way up to my bedroom.'

'Was there anyone else in the kitchen?'

'No.' She said this very firmly. 'No-one.'

'What time was this?'

'Gosh, I'm not sure. I suppose it must have been some time before ten o'clock, but... oh dear, is it important? I do want to help you, but I—'

'Please, don't worry. It is not important.' Kite smiled, trying to put her at ease. She was a bundle of nerves. 'And did you go straight to sleep?'

'Well I got ready for bed, washed my face and brushed my teeth, but then I sat in bed and started reading *Trent's Last Case*, by E C Bentley. Elizabeth has let me borrow her copy. She says it is terribly good. We are going to discuss it when I've finished it.'

'Are you enjoying it?'

She glanced around nervously, as if someone invisible might be listening. 'It's about a businessman who is murdered in the grounds of his English country house.' The words came out like a whisper. 'Oh gosh. Don't you see? Like Sir Wilfred!'

Kite nodded. He wasn't sure how she was expecting him to react.

'Mind you, the man in the book is American, so it's not the same, and he was shot in the head, not burnt to death in his car, but it makes you think, doesn't it!'

Not really, Kite might have replied if he was being honest, but he wanted to steer her back to what had happened at Crowthorpe Manor, not in her book. 'So what time did you actually go to sleep?'

'I only read a few pages.' She simpered as she said this, and Kite suddenly felt uncomfortable, sitting here alone with her, in her room. 'To be honest I felt rather tired, so I think I must have turned my light off about half-past ten. But I couldn't get to sleep and…' She fell silent, frowning, as if lost in thought. Kite waited, massaging his hands together. The third and fourth fingers had been stamped on by a heavily built man wearing reinforced boots, and in cold weather they invariably ached. It was a harsh reminder of what a moment's hesitation might lead to. The thug had escaped and Kite had never seen him again.

He was woken from his reverie by the steady tread of feet on the stairs. He looked round to see Sparrow appear carrying a tray. 'Here we are,' he said merrily. 'Shall I be mother and pour?'

Kite waited for them each to get settled with their tea, though Sparrow remained standing, as if expecting that at any moment he might have to jump into action. Kite watched Mary take a dainty sip from her cup – it was rather fancy with gilt round the rim –

and then set it carefully down on her saucer.

'Maybe I did drop off,' she said, picking up on what she had said. 'I'm not sure. It's so hard to be sure about anything.' She looked up at Kite, then at Sparrow, and then down again, staring at her dress as if that might offer her clarity. 'Anyway, the next thing was there was a terrible noise. It sounded like a bang and I heard David shouting downstairs, and so I pulled my dressing gown and slippers on as quickly as I could, and I hurried down the stairs to see what was happening, and I followed the others outside and saw the fire and…'

Mary stopped, her throat gulping as if she was struggling to breathe.

'Please, don't rush,' Kite said. 'I appreciate that this must be upsetting for you, but anything you can tell us would most helpful.'

She sat up straighter, took in a deep breath and nodded. 'You are going to think this is a bit… silly.'

'I'm sure I won't,' Kite said, though he wasn't at all sure. She reminded him of a woman he had once come across who suffered from hysteria. As witnesses went, she did seem a bit silly, but did that make her unreliable?

'You see, I didn't follow the others to the fire. I waited in the porch. It was so cold and I was terrified of what I might see.'

Kite nodded encouragingly. 'Yes?'

She took deep breath. The fingers of her hands locked themselves together and then began to writhe as if half of them were desperate to escape. 'I saw someone,' she said firmly and paused. 'What I mean is: I thought I saw someone.' Then the words suddenly came tumbling helter-skelter out of her mouth, as if a blockage had been finally removed. 'Or something. I mean, there was definitely a movement in the darkness. Just for a moment or two. A shape. Hunched. Slipping through the darkness. And then it was gone.'

'Where was this?'

'Over by the main gate. Maybe I just imagined it. Maybe it was the stress of situation playing tricks with my mind.'

'Was this figure, whoever or whatever it was, coming in through the gate or going out of it?'

Mary didn't answer. She frowned, as if this was an impossibly difficult question. She lifted her right hand to her mouth, then began to rock forwards and backwards, her eyes wide open but focused on nothing.

'Mary?' Kite spoke softly.

'Out,' she said suddenly and quickly. 'Or maybe… maybe it was all in my head. But it seemed real!' She leaned forward intently. 'Or maybe…' She stopped. There was another long pause, as she looked from Kite to Sparrow, then back to Kite, then to Sparrow again before finally her eyes settled on Kite. 'Sergeant,' she whispered. 'You'll think me silly when I say this, but maybe it was just a ghost.' And after that she began to wail.

The next thing was the sound of heavy footsteps pounding up the stairs and David Graves bursting in with the words, 'What the devil is going on?' and Kite cursing silently and knowing he had lost his opportunity to find out more and very quickly beating a hasty retreat upstairs.

'Blimey, she's a right one!' Sparrow said, almost before they had reached the sanctuary of the second floor. Kite didn't respond. He pushed his way into his room and sat down heavily on the bed. Sparrow followed him in. He hadn't finished. 'I mean seeing ghosts! At first I thought she had seen the killer, but then…'

'Maybe she did.'

'What? See a ghost?'

'No. What I mean is, she can't quite credit the figure was real, so she imagines she saw a ghost.'

'You mean she actually saw the killer leave. But…'

Sparrow, unusually for him, fell silent, the sentence uncompleted. But Kite was pretty sure he knew what Sparrow had been about to say. That if Mary had seen the killer leaving by the front gate, then that would suggest that the killer wasn't someone living in the house, yet he had been insisting that the killer was someone living in the house.

They both fell silent. From downstairs they could hear the voices of Mary and her brother David who, after storming up the stairs from his ground-floor rooms, had driven them out. Kite felt shattered. The rigours of the trip and the situation were taking their toll. He just wanted to lie down and go to bed, but Sparrow was still hovering. From down below the sound of voices had dropped. That was a relief for Kite, but not for long. Thump, thump, thump! The sound of heavy steps on the creaking stairs heralded the approach of someone. David Graves, Kite assumed, and he was right.

'What in God's name were you playing at, distressing Mary like that? Lady Beatrice foolishly allows you to stay in her house and you repay her hospitality by reducing poor Mary to hysteria.'

'She wanted to talk to us,' Kite said, aware of the feebleness of his defence.

'Couldn't you have waited until the morning? What she needs is a damned good night's sleep.'

'But she insisted that we do it immediately. Constable Sparrow will confirm that. Sometimes people in distress just need to talk. And, in any case, as a member of the Lincoln Constabulary I can't avoid asking awkward and potentially painful questions. I can't pretend Sir Wilfred did not die – and very unpleasantly. It is my job to find out who did it and bring them to justice.'

'Mary was a gibbering wreck, and that is entirely thanks to you. She's calmed down now, so hopefully she will fall deeply asleep. But I must insist that if you must ask more questions tomorrow, then you should only do so if I myself am present.'

Kite gave the briefest of nods. 'Very well.' He couldn't afford to fall out any more with the man. But he also sensed an opportunity.

'Perhaps I can just ask you one question now, while it is fresh in my head.'

'If you must.'

'I do think now would be a good time. Because your sister told me that she thought she may have seen someone outside shortly after the explosion.'

'Someone? What are you talking about?' His face was red and aggressive. 'Are you suggesting she saw the killer leaving the scene? Or what? She never said any such thing to me. I certainly didn't see anyone. I sleep downstairs, as you know, and when I heard the explosion, I rushed outside to see what on earth had happened. Of course I did. We all did. But as for seeing someone else.'

'Mary believes she may have done.'

'May have done? Well did she recognise him? Was it someone from the village? Someone from the workforce? She goes into Crowthorpe every Friday with either myself or Maud to help pay the men and women. Anyway, wouldn't I or one of the others have seen this person?'

'She stayed in the porch when you went out to the fire. She thought she saw someone – or something. It was, I think, a very fleeting glimpse.'

David Graves stared at Kite for three or four seconds, and then suddenly the serious look on his face was displaced by a smirk. 'You mean it was there one moment and gone the next? An insubstantial figure?' The smirk expanded into a broad grin. 'You mean, a ghost?'

Kite shuddered, but said nothing.

Graves exploded into laughter. 'Is that what she said? That she saw a ghost.' He held his sides as if they would burst. 'It wouldn't be the first time. My sister is – how shall I put it – susceptible to seeing ghosts. Where we used to live, near Oxford, she claimed she used to see monks walking through walls en route to the site of what used to be the old abbey.

But of course all that was poppycock!'

'I saw a ghost once,' Kite said suddenly. Quite why he said it, he had no idea. Except that Graves had annoyed him intensely with his 'I know best' and 'silly little Mary' attitudes. And also because he felt that Graves' demeaning words were an assault not just on Mary, but on he himself. 'It was on the first anniversary of my wife's death.' The memory was as vivid as the snow outside was white. 'I looked out of the window and saw her walking down the street in her favourite dress and hat. She stopped at one point, looked up at the window and… and…' Kite couldn't finish. His throat was twisted into a knot.

For a few seconds, even Graves was silenced. Then he pulled himself up to his full height and straightened his coat. 'In that case, all I can say is that I am amazed that you were ever admitted to the police force.' With that he turned on his heel and headed for the door.

'Wait!' Kite snapped. And Sparrow, quick as a flash, stepped across and blocked Graves.

'Out of my way,' he snarled. But Sparrow didn't budge.

'While I'm about it, I'd like to ask you a few more questions,' Kite said firmly. 'Now!'

Graves spun round. 'You said that would be in the morning. I'm tired, for God's sake.'

'We are all tired, but neither I nor my constable have the luxury of retiring to bed as soon as we feel tired.' Kite pressed on, denying Graves the opportunity to argue. 'Tell me, Mr Graves, what is the financial state of Crowthorpe Jam?'

'I'm not the one to ask.'

'You're the production manager, so you must have a sense of how many tins of jam and chutneys you sell?'

'We sell whatever we produce.'

'And were your production levels up or down during the war?'

'I am not going to answer that. It is commercially sensitive information.'

Kite shrugged. The man's unwillingness to respond was surely significant, but there was, as his mother used to say, more than one way to skin a cat. 'I understand that Tickler's Jams had a very successful war supplying His Majesty's soldiers on the front line.'

'Yes indeed. I'm not sure about the quality of the product they provided.' Graves' tone of voice was dismissive.

'My impression is that it was very popular with the troops.'

'Popular? Maybe. But that doesn't mean their jam was good quality. Not like ours. Anyway, I'm not sure what point you are trying to make, Sergeant.'

'I am merely supposing that if Tickler's did very well through the war, then Crowthorpe's might have done rather less well.'

'You're wrong on that score, Sergeant. We had plenty of business. The people at home still needed to eat.'

Kite sighed. Like Graves, he was tired, but somehow the man's replies seemed evasive. He would have to wait for the morning and try and catch Mary on her own again. He was fairly sure that if he questioned her carefully, he ought to be able to extract information from her. After all, much of the day to day paperwork must pass through her hands. All he had to do was win her confidence. But how?

He got no further in his wondering because Graves started to speak again, though this time his tone was very different. 'Look, Sergeant, I fear I have been rather rude, and for that I apologise; what you have to understand is I am not family. I am well paid, I am allowed to live here, Mary and I are sometimes invited to join them for dinner, as we were last night. But I am not included in the decision making, even though I am damned good at my job. Now if you don't mind, I would like to retire to my rooms. It has been a very difficult last twenty-four hours.'

Kite shrugged. 'I do have just one more quick question. What sort of mood was Sir Wilfred in at dinner, and indeed after dinner?'

Graves looked puzzled by the question, and only answered it after a few seconds had passed. 'Actually, I would say he was in a very good mood, if you must know. He was, in point of fact, rather cheerful.'

Kite nodded. 'Good night then, Mr Graves. Thank you for your co-operation.'

Sparrow moved to the side and allowed Graves to leave. Kite himself slumped down on the side of his bed and closed his eyes. Working out who killed Sir Wilfred was not going to be easy. Not that he had expected it, but so far no-one had shown any genuine desire to help. Stall, feign ignorance, and occasionally counter-attack – it was as if none of them were interested in finding the killer.

Sparrow cleared his throat. Kite looked up and immediately sensed the intensity of his stare. He was waiting for him to say something. And he knew instinctively what it was that his constable wanted to know. *Did you really see your wife's ghost? Are you sure it wasn't a figment of your imagination? Were you just trying to annoy Graves?* Maybe even: *are you a bit deranged?*

But he didn't want to be interrogated about it. What he saw or didn't see was his own business, and the memory of it, a glimpse of his dead wife, was very important to him. But right now he just wanted to go to bed. 'Good night, Constable. We need to be up at first light. There's plenty we've got to do.'

Sparrow nodded and withdrew to his own room, clearly disappointed.

Kite went to the toilet before rinsing his face and lying down on his bed, fully dressed except for his jacket. Someone had laid out nightclothes for him, but he placed them on the chest of drawers. He preferred to be ready for action in case of… he wasn't sure of what. He pulled two blankets up over him. Despite his exhaustion, sleep didn't come quickly because there were too many thoughts spinning round inside his head. And he also felt annoyed with himself that during his questioning of Mary, when he had the opportunity, he hadn't even touched on what she did for Sir Wilfred, his state of mind in recent weeks, or anything much else. He cursed himself for his stupidity and waited for sleep to come.

THE NEXT MORNING

WHEN KITE WOKE, a thin strip of light through the curtains announced the coming of the new day. He heaved himself out of bed and methodically laced on his boots as he considered what he needed to do next. Five minutes later he rapped on Sparrow's door before heading down towards the kitchen.

His steps on the stairs were heavy, so much so that they must have alerted Mary Graves, for she opened her door and poked her head out.

'Sergeant,' she whispered, 'I need to tell you something.' She beckoned him inside and shut the door behind him.

'What is it?' Kite whispered back.

She was wearing her dressing gown, and clearly on edge. 'Don't clump around on the floor or David might come up to see what is going on.'

'You're not dressed. I really cannot stay here to—'

'Some money has been stolen. About a week ago. I told Sir Wilfred about it, and he told me he would deal with it, but since he's dead and you're a policeman, I thought I should tell you. We keep enough money in the safe to make sure we can pay the staff wages every Friday.'

'Who has the safe key?'

'Not me. It couldn't have been me.'

'But who? Sir Wilfred presumably? Maud, Alec, Lady Beatrice?'

'I expect so. As far as I know there is one key, and it is kept hidden somewhere. I am never allowed to open the safe, so I just don't know.'

'And how much was stolen?'

'One hundred and fifty pounds.'

Kite was stunned. Over half a year's pay for the likes of him.

'Sir Wilfred said not to worry,' Mary said. 'Told me not to say anything.'

'I must go,' Kite said quickly. He could hear Sparrow moving around upstairs. 'Try not to worry.' And with that he was out of the door and heading down to the kitchen.

He had half expected to find it unoccupied, but Rose was already there, stirring something on the cooking range.

'Morning, Sergeant. The porridge isn't ready yet, but there's tea in the pot there on the hot plate.'

Kite helped himself and sipped it as he stared out of the window. The snow was still falling steadily. There was no sign of a wind, nothing to herald a change of weather. Snow covered the ground like an expansive eiderdown. The likelihood of finding any trace of the intruder that Mary Graves might have seen had dropped from improbable to impossible. It would take a miracle and Kite didn't believe in them. He believed in diligent investigation, organised questioning and careful listening. If and when the snow let up, he wanted to take a proper look at what remained under Mr Lamyman's tarpaulin, but until then he would have to settle for questions and answers.

'Did you sleep well?' It was Rose interrupting his thoughts.

'Very well, thank you.' Which was true. He had

only woken once, peeing in the pot left under his bed because his need had been extremely urgent.

'So did I.' It was Sparrow, popping up in the doorway like a jack-in-the-box. He went over to the range and peered at the porridge. 'I'm starving!'

'You're also in the way. Now pour yourself some tea and then sit down, and I'll dish us each a bowl.'

Kite sat down too.

'Here you are.' Rose plonked two bowls of steaming porridge in front of them. She pushed a pottery jar towards Kite. 'And there's some of Crowthorpe's best three fruit jam to sweeten it. A very limited supply what with the war disrupting things, so consider yourself lucky.'

Kite took some and then pushed it across the table to Sparrow. Rose sat down at the end, presiding over the kitchen, her domain.

'This is very tasty jam,' Kite said after a couple of mouthfuls of porridge.

'This is the proper stuff, real fruit, but a premium price too – for those that can afford it.'

'So what goes into the cheap jam that I used to buy in London?'

'Best not to ask, or you might not want to eat it again!' She laughed. 'They were all at it, I reckon, not just Crowthorpe's, but Tickler's and the rest of them. Whatever fruit you can find, then throw in beet pulp or whatever to bulk it out. People say Tickler's raspberry jam had wood chips put in it. Maybe or maybe not. But what I do know is I wouldn't have it in my kitchen. Not that Sir Wilfred would ever have allowed it, of course. That suits me. I like to know what's in the food I serve, and in the case of Crowthorpe's I can find out from the horse's mouth.' She laughed. 'In a manner of speaking. No disrespect to Sir Wilfred and Lady Beatrice.'

Rose fell silent. She played with her porridge, making patterns with her spoon, as if she had no real appetite for it. By contrast Sparrow was attacking his like a child who didn't know where his next meal was coming from – a hangover from the war or an impoverished childhood. Whichever was the case, Sparrow was soon asking Rose if he could have some more. Rose paused before answering. 'Help yourself, but one spoonful only.'

The long spoon was in fact a ladle, and Sparrow returned to the table with a substantial second helping and a grin. 'Very nice porridge, indeed,' he said. Rose nodded acknowledgement. It was obvious she knew he was ingratiating himself with her, and Kite was pretty sure that she wasn't for a moment taken in by it. But who doesn't like a bit of praise?

When Kite had finished eating, he turned towards Rose. She was watching him, still and serious. 'You'll be wanting to ask me questions.'

'Yes.'

'Well, we might as well get it over and done with before I have to take her ladyship's tea up to her.' She glanced at the clock hanging on the wall. 'I can give you ten minutes.'

'Tell me about that night.'

'They had supper as they usually did at seven thirty. Lady Beatrice can't eat any later or she wakes up with indigestion in the night. Mary was in charge of the main course, to give me a break. She and David had been invited to eat with the family – that didn't always happen. Often they eat together in David's parlour. Frank and I served the food and drink, then we snatched a bit of food in the kitchen until we got summoned to clear up.'

'Summoned?'

'Bells.' She pointed towards the wall over Kite's shoulder. He turned to see a boxed-in panel, comprising a series of little windows each with its own label: *Dining Room, Billiard Room, Library, Sir Wilfred's Bedroom* as well as several bedrooms differentiated only by a Roman numeral. 'There's a bell pull in most of the rooms – except for mine and Frank's bedrooms up in the attic of course.' She laughed. 'Even if there was, who would come if I rang the bell?'

'So after supper?'

'We cleared the table. Mary helped, and so did Maud. Then I made a cup of tea and took it up for Lady Beatrice. I helped her get ready for bed and she said I could go as she wanted to read a bit.'

'And what time was this?'

She thought about this for several seconds before answering. 'I suppose it must have been about half past nine.' She paused and frowned. 'Maybe. Or a bit later.'

'Then what?'

'I went back down to the kitchen. It was all tidied up, I'm glad to say, except that Frank was lounging in my chair drinking beer. I shooed him out of it, but he pleaded with me for a game of dominoes. I beat him three times, and then I told him to clear off to bed.'

She paused. Kite glanced at Sparrow and was pleased to see that he had produced his notebook and was scribbling away in it.

'What else then, after Frank went upstairs?'

'Well I checked the front door was locked and soon after that I went upstairs to bed.'

'Is it your job to check the front door?'

'No. But I always like to do so last thing. Force of habit, I suppose.'

'What about the back door?'

'That one too,' she said quickly. Too quickly, maybe. Kite scratched his cheek, and realised he hadn't shaved.

'I understand Sir Wilfred made a habit of sitting in his car smoking a cigar after supper.'

'That's right. He once told me it was his bolthole. I reckoned he liked to get away from the family sometimes. Everyone knew not to disturb him there.'

'So you locked the back door, or merely checked it was locked?'

'I locked it. I couldn't trust any of the men to do it. Not when they'd been drinking.'

'But did you not think of checking to see if Sir Wilfred was in the garage?'

'For gawd's sake.' There was a brief flash of temper, quickly suppressed. 'He has his own set of keys. And like I said, it was more than my job was worth to go and interrupt him.'

'So was he still outside when you locked up?'

She pursed her lips tightly together. 'Well he must've been. Unless...' She hesitated. 'Unless he went out there later.'

Kite picked up his mug of tea and drank from it. 'From what I remember, I think you would be able to see the garage from the back door.'

'Yes.'

'So if he was in the garage when you checked the back door, I imagine there would have been a light on and you might have noticed it.'

'Let me get this straight,' she snapped. 'I didn't bother looking to see if Sir Wilfred might be in the garage. Why would I when it didn't matter to me? All I was concerned about was that the house was safely locked up. Is that clear? Besides, Lady Beatrice had let me borrow her copy of *The Lady* magazine, and I wanted to read it.'

Kite nodded, conscious of the stress which Rose was now displaying. Was that because being interviewed by a policeman was innately stressful or because he had strayed into uncomfortable territory?

'Anyway,' she said suddenly and defiantly, 'at this time of year, he'd shut the door of the garage to keep the cold out wouldn't he. So very little light would get out.'

'Good point,' Kite said, conscious that he was fast losing Rose's goodwill. Yet he couldn't shake off the feeling that she was being evasive. 'Can I ask if you bolt the doors as well as lock them?'

'Of course I do.'

'So how would Sir Wilfred get inside—?'

'Blimey! You don't half go on, don't you! There's a third door. Out the back of the study. Only he has a key to it. So obviously I don't lock that one up or check it's locked up. But he can come and go that way as much as he likes.' Rose stood up abruptly. 'Look, I really do have to take her ladyship her tea now.'

Kite held his hands up defensively. 'I am sorry for delaying you. Please do carry on.'

An uneasy silence descended on the room, even upon Sparrow, who seemed both alarmed and fascinated by the way things had gone. But as soon as Rose had left the room, he leaned forward. 'What does it matter whether she saw the light on? Whether the old boy was out there when she locked up or whether he went out there later?'

'Maybe it doesn't matter at all,' Kite said. Though actually he had a hunch that maybe it did matter. 'But Rose didn't seem entirely comfortable with my questioning, did she?'

'You wanted to speak to me?' The gruff tones of Frank Tomkin caused Kite to turn round. He had been staring out of the window, this time the study one rather than the kitchen one. If anything the snow had got worse, huge flakes falling relentlessly from the still skies.

'Yes, I did.'

'Well here I am.' His face seemed to be still clouded with the anger that had erupted the previous evening.

'I think we got off to a bad start last night,' Kite said.

'I didn't like your tone.' There wasn't a hint of apology.

'Sometimes, as a policeman, I have to ask awkward

questions.'

'You were doubting my professionalism, as a chauffeur, and as Sir Wilfred's right-hand man.'

Kite hesitated. He ought to just apologise to the man, openly and without reservation. But he couldn't quite bring himself to do that, even though common sense told him it was the best thing to do. 'If,' he said grudgingly, 'it seemed like that… then I am truly sorry.'

Tomkin said nothing, his mouth opened, but the only sound that came out was a growl, like a wild animal issuing a warning.

'I don't think your competence or indeed your loyalty to the family has ever been in question.'

Tomkin glared at Kite, suddenly uncertain about his adversary. Kite felt no such doubt. He knew what he was facing, because he had come across a number of such men in his career, men who served their masters with such intensity that any outsider became someone to be watched extremely carefully, viewed as a potential threat. And a policeman was an outsider of the worst kind, the representative of a larger external power which sought to challenge the monarchical and patriarchal society which a place like Crowthorpe Manor inevitably nurtured. In short, looking at Tomkin, Kite could see that he saw him as a threat.

Kite waited. Sometimes silence was the best way of extracting information and he sensed this was one such occasion. He had laid down some bait. How could Tomkin not want to talk about his loyalty to Sir Wilfred and the family? Get him talking and then see what comes out.

'I've worked for the Walkers since I was fourteen,' he said firmly. 'It was her ladyship herself who hired me. Just odd jobs round the house at first. Cleaning the stables, gathering and cutting wood, making myself useful. But it was fixing things I was best at: simple things like the children's pedal cars, bicycles, then the lights and the bell call system, machinery, you name it and I could fix it. That was why Sir Wilfred took me under his wing, because I was useful and because he knew I'd look after his car real well.'

Tomkin paused, apparently lost in memories and satisfaction at his own role in the household.

'I understand you had a good war too,' Kite added, not having finished with his flattery tactics.

He frowned. 'I'm not sure what you'd call a good war. It was hell at times. The main aim was survival. I served with Captain Alec. "Make sure he comes home safe and sound," Sir Wilfred told me. And I did. I was like a cat with nine lives, though he was less lucky. Caught a piece of shrapnel in his shoulder just as we were crossing no man's land. I pulled him into a shell crater. There were plenty of those, and plenty of mud and water at the bottom of them too. Anyway, I got him back to the lines, and after that it was back to Blighty for him. As for me, I got a generous allocation of leave. Someone must have pulled a few strings. I even got a medal.' There was pride in his voice.

'It sounds likes you deserved one.'

'I came back here for a few weeks, got well fed, but the captain – being an officer – was sent to Greystone

Manor while the medics sorted him out.'

'And when was this?'

'Early June last year. He was wounded on the day of his birthday, so it's easy to remember.' Tomkin carried on talking, mostly about the pleasures of eating fresh meat and vegetables newly dug out the ground while he was on leave, but Kite's mind was elsewhere.

'Sorry, Tomkin, I think I must have missed something.'

Tomkin looked up, rather irritated to have been interrupted. 'What do you mean?'

'Well, I don't want to tread on delicate matters,' he lied, 'but Elizabeth is with child, due to give birth early next month, so I was wondering how that might be the case if the captain was at Greystone Manor and she was here…'

'Ah!' Tomkin fell silent, though it wasn't the awkward silence which Kite might have expected. It was different. There was a barely concealed smile on his face, and he seemed in no rush to say more.

'Well?' Kite allowed his own impatience to show.

'Easily explained,' he said smoothly. For a man who had so easily lost his temper the night before, he was displaying a remarkable calmness. As if he knew this question might crop up and so had an answer all ready.

'That was one of my last tasks before I went back to the front line. I drove Mrs Elizabeth down to Greystone Manor to see him. It was a damned long way. God only knows why he couldn't have been somewhere closer to home, but you don't argue with the army, do you? We took rooms at the local hotel,

The George and Dragon, and she visited the captain each day, and well there you have it. I drove Mrs Elizabeth back to Crowthorpe, and the day after that I was heading south, on a train, destination the front line.'

'Thank you. And what about the captain?'

'What about him? He rejoined the regiment a few weeks later, and we saw the war through to the end together. I think you could say we were lucky. Not like so many other poor guys. But we did it proudly, for King and Country. Never let it be said we didn't.'

'Indeed, we are indebted to men like you and the captain.'

Tomkin nodded. 'Anyway I'd best be on my way. The light in Lady Beatrice's room is broken, so I'd better go and sort it out.' He turned to leave, but then turned back. 'I gather Captain Alec had a bit of a go at you? Not serving on the front line. The police wanting to strike.' He paused, as if not quite sure how to say what he had to say. Kite waited, acutely conscious of how what had happened privately in one room had quickly became a matter of common knowledge round the house. 'Don't take it personally. He's had it hard. And of course he has no idea what it is like to be short of money – not like us. And now his father is dead.'

'Of course. I understand,' Kite said. And he did understand, although there were things that he didn't. 'Thank you for your time and honesty.'

David Graves was waiting for Kite and Sparrow in the study as agreed, but there was no sign of Mary. It was ten o'clock, and Graves was sitting behind the desk, looking like he was the man in charge. He was studying some papers in front of him, and he continued to read them as if they were infinitely more important than anything the police might have to say.

'Shall we wait for Mary?' Kite said, trying to prompt Graves into some sort of response, but he continued to read, apparently determined to play the big man.

But Kite's patience was running thin. 'Mr Graves, do you by any chance know where your sister is?'

Graves looked up. 'Yes.' Then he looked down again.

Sparrow, who had moved his chair towards the corner in accordance with Kite's orders – 'I want them to forget that you are present, taking notes' Kite had told him – stood up. 'I'll go and remind her, shall I? If you tell me where she is, sir?'

Graves sat up, sighed theatrically and leaned back in his chair. 'She won't be joining us. She's in bed.'

Kite felt a flash of frustration. *What the hell?* He took a deep breath. 'Is she not well?'

'It's your fault, Sergeant. You upset her last night with your questioning. She slept badly and was in quite a state when I spoke to her this morning, so I encouraged her to take some of her pills.'

'What pills?' Kite snapped.

Graves smiled, the epitome of smugness. 'My sister sometimes has trouble with her nerves – when things are difficult, or when policemen come charging in and batter her with questions just after her employer has been murdered. She nearly killed herself a few years ago, taking too many pills at once. So now I look after them for her, keep them up high where she can't possibly reach, and when she needs them I hand them out.'

'I'm sorry. If I'd realised, if I had been warned…'

'… you'd have gone easy on her? I doubt it.'

'Perhaps later, when she is feeling better…'

'She'll sleep for half the day now. And be dopey when she does wake, so it's best you ask me the questions. Only I do hope it won't take long. Despite the sad circumstances, I have work to do.'

'So is the factory open today?'

Graves laughed. 'What do you think? It's January. Not exactly much fruit to process at this time of year.'

'But I imagine you have jam that needs distributing at this time of year?'

'In this weather?' he sneered. 'And may I ask exactly how this is relevant to your investigation?'

'I don't know. I can't possibly tell what is relevant or not until I get to the end of an investigation. Only then might I be able to tell you. Anyway, how is the Crowthorpe Jam Company doing at the moment?'

'The business is doing fine. Very well in fact. We survived the war and we've lots of plans for the future.' He waved his hand up at the various posters on the walls. 'New marketing campaign, new products, expansion of our territory. Now that I am back.'

'Back? From the front line?'

'No, from the munitions factory at Burton. Near Mansfield. The powers that be decided my management skills would be more useful there than as cannon fodder on the front line.'

'So who did your job here while you were at Burton?'

'Sir Wilfred was very active. But Maud decided she would get involved. All that women's rights stuff had gone to her head a bit. Thought she could do it better than the men.'

Kite smiled, seeing an opportunity to rile Graves. 'And did she do a better job than the men? Than you?'

Graves flushed red, but he didn't rise to the bait. 'Women can be very useful in certain roles in the factory, but when hard decisions have to be made, when the whip has to be cracked, when new strategies have to be developed…' He tailed off. 'I'm sure, as a man, you understand what I mean.'

'So the company is in a good state? Money in the bank? A solid customer base?'

'Yes, indeed.'

'If that is the case,' Kite said, savouring the moment, 'Maud must have done a good job in your absence? Perhaps even as good a one as you might have.'

Graves clenched his fists. Like many men who spend their lives ordering people around, he had a temper under the surface, and at the moment he was barely able to control it. 'You think you're clever don't you, Kite. But it's people like you that are the real fools. You think you know best. But remember this, pride comes before a fall.'

As threats went, Kite wasn't impressed. He turned to Sparrow. 'I'd really appreciate a cup of tea and a piece of Rose's fine cake. Perhaps you can go and see if she can provide that for the three of us.'

Sparrow stood up. 'Yes, sir,' he said dutifully, though Kite sensed he wasn't too happy about it. He was probably getting fed up with being used like an errand boy, but Kite didn't feel in the slightest bit concerned.

As soon as the door was shut behind him, he leaned forward.

'Perhaps you are right, Mr Graves. Perhaps I am a fool. But people tell me I am good at reading people, and I sense that maybe with my constable out of the room you might be able to speak more freely. I'm not taking notes, he's not present and recording what you say. So my question is, can you think of anyone who might have wanted to kill Sir Wilfred?'

To Kite's surprise, the question didn't seem to alarm or surprise Graves at all. Rather he seemed to give the matter some thought before finally replying. 'You have to remember, Kite, that Sir Wilfred was a pillar of the community. The Crowthorpe Jam Company provides work for most of the community round here. Without him, half the local families would be starving. From growing and harvesting the fruit, to making the jam – and pickles now – transporting it, all this puts food on the tables of the local families. So why would anyone want to kill him.'

'But the fact is that Sir Wilfred is dead, and was burned to death very horribly in his own car. So I think we can safely assume that someone, somewhere, disliked him very much indeed.'

'I disagree. I think it was an intruder, out to steal something. He panicked when he came across Sir Wilfred, probably clubbed him with a weapon of some sort, and then set fire to the place before making his escape.'

Kite scratched at his chin. 'I was thinking the

killer is more likely to be someone from within this household.'

'Your views are no secret, but I think you're wrong. You want the killer to be one of us because you despise us, don't you, for making a success of our lives and business here. You come from London with your big-city prejudices and you look for a reason to pin it on one of us.'

'I look for a motive. Who hated Sir Wilfred, or who might gain from his death?'

'That's not me! My interests were tied up entirely with Sir Wilfred and the success of his company. We saw the world in the same way, and he appreciated the work I did for him. There is no way Sir Wilfred's death benefits me. But if you want motive, why look further than jealousy: a ne'er-do-well who so resented Sir Wilfred's wealth that he wanted some of it and killed him when he got a chance.'

'What now, sir?'

David Graves had turfed them out of the study, rather pointedly, so they had retreated to the kitchen. Rose was nowhere to be seen. Sparrow helped himself to another piece of the cake that was lying on the dresser, but Kite was trying to focus. Ideally he would have liked a few minutes on his own while he thought things through, as he found Sparrow's restless energy disturbing.

'Sir?' The constable raised his voice, a child demanding attention.

Kite glanced at him before looking out of the window. He was pleased to see that it had nearly stopped snowing. 'I think we need to take a look under Mr Lamyman's tarpaulin.'

Sparrow laughed. 'I was afraid you might say that.'

When they got outside, they found themselves following a single track of footprints all the way to the crime scene. 'Someone was curious, a bit of a nosey parker,' Sparrow said merrily.

Kite felt a flash of irritation that his constable could be so flippant. This was serious stuff. He himself was focused on why someone would have come here so early. Was it merely curiosity? Or were they looking for something?

'Mind you,' Sparrow continued obliviously, 'the tarpaulin looks intact. Anyway, to judge from the tracks, it's someone with big clodhoppers. Frank, I'd guess. He's the one most likely.'

'Most likely, Constable? What do you mean?'

'The car was his baby, by all accounts. Look how aggressive he got last night when you queried how well he looked after it all. He probably wanted to snoop around to protect himself.'

'Maybe.' Kite was about to probe Sparrow's chirpy thinking further, but to his surprise he noticed there were two people walking across the yard. He didn't immediately recognise them, but they were huddled in coats, scarves and hats and apparently heading towards the house. Except when they realised that Kite was observing them, they switched direction and headed towards him.

'Who are these people?' he asked Sparrow quietly.

'Not a clue.'

They drew close, a man and a woman. 'You must be the detective sergeant.' The man's voice was hale and hearty. His face was thin, with hooded eyes, bushy eyebrows, a Roman nose, and bad teeth. He was, Kite estimated, in his early fifties.

'Detective Sergeant Kite, and this is Constable Sparrow.'

'I am the Reverend Justin Ransom, vicar of St Mark's in Crowthorpe village and of our little church of St John's, a quarter of a mile that way.' He waved his hand. 'And this is my wife Mrs Ransom.'

The woman bobbed her head and lowered her eyes, as if staring at men full in the face was against her religious principles. But then she spoke, and looked Kite full in the face. 'Please call me Jane.' Was this a hint of independence, Kite wondered, defiance even of her husband? She looked at least ten years younger than he did, but was almost as tall. She was undeniably attractive, a smooth face and clear grey eyes which assessed Kite as – perhaps – she might assess a new hat at a milliners, or a brace of pheasants hanging in the butchers.

'Such a terrible thing.' She waved her hand at the blackened remains of the garage. 'How could anyone?'

The Reverend Ransom placed his hand on her shoulder. '"Be sober, be vigilant," as St Peter tells us. "Our adversary the devil walketh about as a roaring lion, seeking whom he may devour." And so it is here. The evil one has come to Crowthorpe and devoured our dear brother Wilfred. We must pray against the Beast and implore God that our two gallant policemen will bring the killer to justice this very day.'

Kite nodded, temporarily uncertain how to respond.

But Ransom was warming to his task. 'Shall we do that now? I suggest a short silence as we gather our thoughts, and then I will say some prayers and perhaps at the end you gentlemen can join Mrs Ransom and myself in the Lord's Prayer.'

Kite nodded again. 'Of course.' What else was there to say in the circumstances?

And so Kite, who had several times in his life felt that God was nowhere to be found, bowed his head, and pressed the palms of his gloved hands together, and allowed himself to be drawn in to the simple ceremony which the vicar conjured up.

'Lovely, my dear,' Jane said at the end. 'As always.' She briefly laid a gloved hand on his forearm in an act of wifely devotion. 'And now I think we should go and offer our support to Lady Beatrice.'

'If you don't mind me asking,' Kite said quickly, 'where do you live?'

'In the village,' he said, pointing one way.

'Just over there,' she said at exactly the same time, and pointing back the way they had come.

'What my wife means,' the vicar said briskly, 'is that we are temporarily residing in the cottage by St John's church. Our vicarage in Crowthorpe village is currently being repaired and Sir Wilfred has very kindly allowed us to move into the cottage until such time as the work on the vicarage has been completed. Of course, it is not entirely inconvenient for me, because I look after St John's church here as well as St Mark's in the village. However, I do hope and pray that the snow has cleared by Sunday or I shall have great difficulty in getting to St Mark's for Matins.'

'Since you are currently living so close to the manor, then I would like to ask you some further questions.'

'It is very cold standing here,' Ransom said. 'And my immediate priority is to offer whatever support and spiritual guidance I can to Lady Beatrice and the family in their hour of need.'

'It would not take long,' Kite said, conscious that the vicar seemed distinctly unkeen to co-operate.

But it was his wife who intervened. 'Detective Sergeant, why don't you and your constable come to our cottage at one o'clock,' she said. 'I'll make sure the fire is blazing and you can ask all your questions in the warmth and over a nice cup of tea.'

'Could we not meet up sooner, before you return to your cottage?' Kite said.

'Oh no, I have a small stew cooking on the stove, so we can't delay. We shall be eating our meagre lunch at twelve o'clock, and after that my dear Justin likes to have half an hour with God. So you see one o'clock it will have to be.' She smiled obligingly. 'We will look forward to it.'

With that, the two of them turned and trudged off towards the house. 'She's much too pretty for him,' Sparrow whispered. 'And he's much too old for her.'

Kite didn't reply. Sparrow was probably right. But Kite was preoccupied with his own thoughts. Ransom and his wife were undoubtedly a somewhat unlikely couple, but Jane herself had shown herself to be a skilful manipulator of the situation – of both himself and her husband. She had expressed a willingness to co-operate with Kite's investigations, yet she had also ensured that she and her husband would have time to prepare for the inevitable questions. If they had stories that needed to be checked against each other, or lies that needed to be co-ordinated, then they now had the time to prepare themselves fully. Kite clenched his jaw in frustration. He had been played for a fool. And yet surely it couldn't matter. Neither a country vicar nor his wife were likely to be involved in such a brutal murder of their benefactor. Except – and this was the thought which continued to nag him as he saw them disappear inside the front door of Crowthorpe Manor – he knew only too well that killers came in all shapes and sizes.

Kite had himself been involved in the tracking down of Dr Crippen, and had been present when the police had finally found the dismembered body of Cora Crippen in the basement of their house. The case had been famous for being the first one in which wireless telegraph had brought a killer to justice, but Kite remembered it for another reason. He had encountered Crippen just once, and had been struck above all by his unimpressive presence. He looked like a nobody, and yet he had murdered his wife and cut her body into pieces just because he had become infatuated with another woman, Ethel Le Neve.

'Sir?' Sparrow's voice brought Kite back to the cold Lincolnshire day. 'Should we maybe carry on?'

'Yes, of course,' Kite said. 'I was just thinking.'

'Oh, oh, we've got more company,' Sparrow replied. 'Here comes Frank Tomkin to keep an eye on us.'

Tomkin was striding towards them with arms swinging. 'Can I help you?' he called while still at a distance.

'Shall I see him off?' Sparrow whispered. 'Don't want him tampering with evidence.'

'Thank you, Mr Tomkin, for your kind offer, but this is police business,' Kite replied firmly. 'However, since you are here, I would be grateful if you could just assist us to lift off the tarpaulin.'

When they had done that, they stood and surveyed the scene. The whole area was black, different shades maybe, but undeniably black. There was a thick covering of ash – the walls and roof structure Kite assumed – and there lay amongst it numerous pieces of broken slates, the bare chassis of the vehicle, twisted metal shapes which had once been beautifully engineered car parts, and the remains of wheels which would never turn again. The only things which were obviously missing were the bones of Sir Wilfred.

'Look!' Tomkin pointed. 'That's one of my petrol cans. And another over there, I reckon. With their lids off.' He turned and spat into the snow. 'The poor chap wouldn't have stood a chance.'

Tomkin gave a good impression of someone who cared about his boss. But did he really? Suppose Sir Wilfred had turned against him, threatened to sack him? Men with power often use it arbitrarily. Kite knew that only too well. And if Sir Wilfred had turned against him, then maybe Tomkin had decided to send him and his beloved car to hell together.

'Sir?' Sparrow was waiting for instructions. 'What are we looking for?'

Kite didn't answer because he had spotted something. It was much smaller than some of the twisted pieces of automobile which strewed the area, but Kite's attention was focused on it for a very simple reason: it looked so out of place amidst all the destruction.

He bent down and picked it up. He frowned, uncertain as to what he was looking at.

'Blimey.' It was Tomkin. 'Might I have a look at it?' Kite hesitated.

'I think I recognise what it is from.'

Kite handed it over and waited as Tomkin inspected it for several seconds.

Sparrow exhaled sharply and loudly. The two men looked at each other. It was Tomkin who spoke again. 'You thinking what I'm thinking, Constable?'

Sparrow nodded.

'What?' Kite was feeling left out.

'It looks to me a lot like the remains of a home-made bomb. If you'd been in the trenches, you'd recognise it. Some men made them out of the cans after they'd eaten the jam.'

'Jam? You mean Crowthorpe's jam.'

'Not Crowthorpe's, no. Ours never made it to the front line. Tickler's jam most likely. They had a massive contract with the Ministry. Not much bloody fruit in it. Beet pulp mostly I reckon, sometimes wood chips if they were pretending it was raspberry jam. Anyway, when we'd eaten the stuff, some of the men would while away the time making bombs with the tins.'

'Did you make them yourself, Tomkin?'

'Not me. The captain wouldn't have approved. To be honest, I couldn't see them being much use. When you're running like hell across no man's land, a dodgy homemade bomb is the last thing you need.'

'So is this a Tickler's jam tin or a Crowthorpe one?'

'Search me. What do you think, Constable?'

Sparrow shrugged. 'Hard to tell. I guess if you had a bit of the labelling, then you could tell, but in this inferno, well no paper is going to survive, is it?'

There was no arguing with that. Kite pushed the piece of twisted metal into his pocket and stood up. 'Thank you for your help, Tomkin.'

He shrugged. 'Glad to be of help to His Majesty's police force.' He had been dismissed – politely, but firmly – but he didn't go. Instead he began to hum, and then to break into a song.

'Oh, oh, oh, what a lovely war!'

Sparrow too joined in, suddenly come alive.

'What do we want with eggs and ham

When we've got bags of Tickler's jam!'

The two men looked at each other with grins stretched across their faces. Tomkin nodded at Kite. 'Don't you go telling them inside about this. It'll be more than my life is worth, singing about one of our biggest rivals. But it certainly brings back memories.' He touched his cap and trudged away towards the stables.

They watched him go and as soon as he disappeared round the side of the house, Sparrow turned towards Kite with a glint in his eyes. 'It could be him, sir.'

Kite didn't respond.

'I mean, the Tickler's jam bomb. Frank Tomkin was on the front line. He must have known how to make them.'

'And so must the captain.'

'So that narrows the field down, doesn't it.'

'Possibly, but there's no certainty that there was only one killer. In the circumstances, I am inclined to think there must be more than one person involved. Who is to say that Maud didn't ask Tomkin to show her how they were made.'

'You think so, sir?'

'Or you, you served on the Western Front didn't you, Constable.'

'Me, sir? Are you serious?'

'No, I am not. Sometimes telling jokes helps me stay sane.'

'Of course,' Sparrow said, his brain sparking into life, 'there must be several others living in the village who also served in the trenches and made bombs when they had finished their jam.'

'Indeed there must. But please don't mention that to the captain or he'll be turfing us out and sending us off there through the snow to interview everyone who fought. Anyway, let's get back to seeing if we can find anything else, and then we'll head back to the warmth of the house.'

They spent some half-an-hour poking around in the ash, getting cold, and finding not a lot else which interested Kite. A number of fragments of glass in one area ('he liked a glass of brandy didn't he?'), another scrap of metal from a jam tin ('the same or a different one?'), and a number of pieces of twisted metal which they agreed must be from petrol cans. When the snow started to fall again, large flakes out of a featureless grey sky, Kite was ready to call it a day when he spotted something that made him catch his breath.

'Look, Constable!' He bent down, put his hand down in the blackened debris and then pulled it out again. He stood up, his face gleaming in triumph, and holding his prize so that Sparrow could share in his excitement.

'The study key if I am not mistaken.'

'Is that important, sir?'

'That depends.'

'Depends on what, sir?'

'I'll let you think about that, Constable. But first, let's get this tarpaulin back into position and then get ourselves inside into the warmth.'

Kite was well aware that he and Sparrow were bound to be under scrutiny as long as they remained at Crowthorpe Manor, and that feeling was reinforced by the fact that they had hardly taken their coats off in the porch before they were buttonholed by Captain Alec.

'How's it all going?'

'Well—'

'Did you actually learn anything from grubbing around in the fire debris?'

'I think it may have clarified a few of my thoughts—'

'Such as?' The captain wasn't giving them any quarter.

'Actually, Captain, I need to report in to my chief constable in Lincoln. I wonder if I could use your telephone?'

'To tell him what?'

'Just to tell him what progress I have made.'

'You mean, none?'

'It's a matter of procedure, sir,' Sparrow said protectively. 'If Sergeant Kite doesn't report in…'

'Very well,' the captain snapped. He had made his spiteful point, but having done so he had no desire to go toe to toe. Kite wondered what sort of officer he must been in France. Unpopular at the least.

'You can ring from the study,' he called over his shoulder as he stalked out of the room.

Kite smiled. The study was precisely where he wanted to go. And when he got there, the first thing he did was head straight for the outside door and try and open it.

'There's two bolts, sir,' Sparrow said. 'Top and bottom.'

'Draw them back then,' Kite replied with barely concealed irritation.

Sparrow did so.

'Now try opening the door.'

This time the door swung open.

'It's not locked, sir!'

'So try locking it!'

Sparrow pushed the blackened key into the lock and turned it. There was a click. Sparrow pulled on the door. 'Locked, sir.'

Kite sniffed. 'So Sir Wilfred exited the house via this door, but left it unlocked. When he died, the key was in his pocket. Someone in the house later checked the door, realised the key was not in its usual place and bolted it for safety.'

'It could be any of them.'

'In theory, yes. But I surmise that it was very likely the killer. He – or she – would most probably have exited the house via this door, and later re-entered to the house the same way. The advantage of this was that they were less likely to be observed, because the other two doors were always checked and locked by Rose or Frank. After killing Sir Wilfred and returning to the house, the killer as a matter of course locked the door to keep out intruders.'

'So there was no spare key?'

'Maybe not. Or maybe the killer didn't know where it was kept.'

'I could ask around. I expect Rose might know.'

Kite frowned, distracted by a sudden thought.

'Shall I go and ask her, sir?'

'No. I need to make this phone call, and I want you to stay and keep out intruders while I do so.

Chief Constable Bostock sounded rather fuzzy over the telephone line. 'Ah, Kite, I was wondering when I might hear from you.'

'We only arrived here yesterday.'

'Have you arrested anyone yet?'

'No, sir.'

'But I gather you have managed to upset people.' Fuzzy line or not, Bostock sounded as acid and aggressive as usual, or possibly more so. Kite swallowed, uncertain how to defuse the situation. Someone – Lady Beatrice or Captain Alec he supposed – had already been getting in their complaints first. 'Cat got your tongue, Sergeant?' Bostock was giving no quarter. 'I thought you were ringing in to report your progress, not simper like a debutante at her first ball.'

'It's difficult here. There's a lot of snow—'

'And from what I am told you are focusing all your attention on Sir Wilfred's household. What about the people of Crowthorpe village? What about the petty thieves and poachers who haunt the countryside? In my experience, that's where you should be focusing your energies.'

In my experience. The words grated like chalk on a blackboard. Kite tried to stay calm. But it was becoming clear to him that Bostock and the Walker family had already agreed between themselves what his investigation should conclude.

'I understand what you are saying, sir,' he said, fighting hard to suppress his frustration, 'but it doesn't look like a local thug to me. I am sorry to have to say this, but it is my belief that is more likely that the killer is either one of the family or one of the other residents of Crowthorpe Manor.'

Bostock snorted violently. 'On what possible basis do you make that assumption? Lady Beatrice has allowed you to stay in the house because of the snow, and yet you seem to be making an art out of accusing and upsetting everyone you speak to.'

'The killing of Sir Wilfred was not the result of a chance encounter. It was not a random killing. On the contrary, based on my experience, I believe it was very carefully planned by someone in the household and—'

'Your experience!' Bostock bellowed, so loud that even Sparrow, hovering in the corner of the room, jumped. 'I have made some enquiries about you, Kite, and I am now regretting that I ever agreed to let you join the Lincoln police force. You have a reputation for distressing innocent people. For upsetting the apple cart. For making allegations which you cannot justify. Let me tell you something. You are lucky that the snow is so thick on the ground or I would by now have despatched one of my other police officers to take over from you, someone I can rely on to treat Sir Wilfred's family properly and to bring this unfortunate case to a satisfactory conclusion. So let me make myself absolutely clear. Sort it out. Stop upsetting Lady Beatrice and her family. Find the yokel who killed Sir Wilfred and bring him to Lincoln in handcuffs. Do I make myself clear?'

'Yes, sir.'

There was a click on the line, as Bostock terminated the call. Kite placed the telephone receiver gently back on its cradle, before suddenly smashing his fist down on the surface of the desk.

'Sir?' Sparrow, who had been standing with his back to the door throughout, looked alarmed.

Kite looked up. 'Tea, Constable. And cake. For crying out loud.'

Sparrow retreated to the kitchen. Kite was hard to read at the best of times, but it was his irascibility which Sparrow was finding most troublesome. He could understand why he might be annoyed with Bostock – few people in the Lincoln force had a good word to say about the chief constable – but that didn't excuse him for shouting at himself. What had he done wrong? He had got him here for a start, looked after him when he had collapsed in front of Lady Beatrice, and done everything that Kite had asked him to do, including all the running to the kitchen to get tea and cake. Sparrow paused in the corridor. That was what was bugging him. Half the time Kite was treating him like a servant, not like a police colleague. And that wasn't fair. He was a policeman, not a skivvy!

There was the noise of sudden laughter from the kitchen. This stirred him out of his self-pity and he moved towards it. Rose and Mrs Elizabeth were in the kitchen, both of them sitting down at one end of the table, cups of tea in front of them. They looked at him guiltily, as if he had stumbled into some secret conversation. Maybe he had.

'Speak of the devil!' Rose laughed.

'Everything all right, ladies?'

'Your ears burning are they, Constable?' Mrs Elizabeth smiled at him. For a woman who ought to be mourning her father-in-law, she seemed in remarkably cheerful spirits.

He nodded at them, holding the posture ever so slightly longer than he needed to. 'If it isn't too much bother, we've been outside, getting cold, so we'd love a cup of tea and the sergeant said he would particularly appreciate a slice of one of Rose's cakes.'

Rose giggled, and more surprisingly so did Mrs Elizabeth. They both stared at him, like two school girls eyeing up the young men at a dance.

'If you could bring it through to the study?'

'Ah,' Rose said, 'can't you carry it through yourself? Or is that too menial a job for you?'

Of course it is! That was what he wanted to say. He would also have liked to tell Rose to treat him properly. He hated being teased. He had hated it as a child and he hated it now. He pulled himself up to his full height. 'The sergeant told me not to waste time chatting.'

'In that case,' Lady Elizabeth said, 'we would hate to get you into trouble, so I am sure Rose will bring a tray laden with good things through just as soon as I have finished giving her my instructions for the day. I trust that will be satisfactory?'

'Yes,' he said, unaccountably embarrassed that a heavily pregnant woman could cause him to feel so… so uncomfortable.

When Sparrow finally returned to the study after a detour to the toilet, he was lighter of step and spirit. 'Cake coming up shortly!' he said cheerily as he pushed the door open, but Kite lifted a hand and motioned him to silence. He was on the phone again.

'Let me spell it out for you. That's G. R. E. Y. S. T. O. N. E.'

Sparrow moved towards the desk, and sat down to listen. There were some indistinct metallic noises from the telephone, but otherwise the only sounds were Kite's laboured breathing and the metronomic ticking of the Napoleonic clock on the mantelpiece. Outside the snow was swirling around. Which, Sparrow decided, was a damned good thing for Kite, because it delayed any possible arrival of reinforcements to replace him. And not just him. Sparrow was well aware that if Kite fell from favour, then so too might he. The only way to prevent that was to make an arrest that everyone was happy with.

Suddenly, there was a voice on the phone. Sparrow bent forward, in the vain hope that this would enable him to hear both sides of the conversation.

'Greystone Park. How can I help you?'

An indistinct reply.

'I wonder if I could speak to the person in charge?'

Sparrow shook his head in frustration.

Kite spoke louder and slower. 'I am a detective sergeant with the Lincoln police force. I am investigating a murder.'

There was a squeal from the other end of the phone. Sparrow could hear that. Then there was another silence and delay.

Kite leaned back, glanced at Sparrow and suddenly stabbed his finger in the direction of the study door, which was partially open. 'Shut it!' he hissed.

More silence, another hissed instruction: 'Notebook, Sparrow. What's got into you?'

Just as Sparrow had settled back down into his chair, the telephone crackled into life again. 'Hello. Would you mind speaking louder? I cannot hear you very well.'

This time, Sparrow could hear the woman. 'Miss Kempton.'

'Miss Kempton,' Kite replied, nodding at Sparrow, who began to write. 'I am Sergeant Kite. A member of the Lincoln police force.'

'And you are ringing about a murder of one of our patients?'

'Not exactly.' Kite tried to explain. 'It's about one of your former patients. Maybe you will remember him. A Captain Alec Walker. Came to you with a shoulder injury.'

'I will need to check our records.'

'Yes, do. I can wait.'

More noise, but this time it was the sound was muted and the tone so distorted that Sparrow couldn't understand it at all. But he began to write as best he could all of Kite's questions and comments, hoping that after the conversation Kite would fill the gaps.

'Yes, Miss Kempton, I am still here.'

…

'Yes, so Captain Alec was admitted on 4 June 1918?'

…

'And was with you for nearly three months? That seems a long time.'

…

'Aaah. I see.'

…

'Lots of officers did.'

…

'And do you keep a record of visitors?'

…

'Yes. Mrs Elizabeth Walker. That's right, she's his wife.'

…

'Oh yes. 12 June. Well, Miss Kempton, I must say I am very impressed with your record-keeping. And…'

…

'Oh, oh. Oh I see. I quite understand.'

…

'Absolutely. Well, thank you very much indeed. You have been most helpful.'

Kite placed the receiver back of the cradle of the telephone and leaned back in his chair. For some time he stared at the ceiling, mute and with eyes half closed. Sparrow waited. There was a knock on the door. Sparrow went and opened it. He watched Rose deliver the tray to the desk, his eyes keenly focused on her as she bent low in front of Kite. Despite his irritation with her, despite the way she had teased him in front of Mrs Elizabeth, he found it hard not to admire her bottom, pressed tight against her dress.

Kite emitted a grunt, and Sparrow quickly turned his attention to his notebook and the largely one-sided conversation which he had written down in it. He had left gaps, but until Kite told him what the woman had said, how could he hope to fill them in.

'Well, Constable, what are you waiting for? Get on and pour the tea.'

Sparrow moved forward with another stab of irritation. Kite was no better than Rose, treating him like he was the lowest of the low. But after the freezing temperatures outside and the wonderful odours of freshly cooked cake in the kitchen, he was more than ready to "get on with it". He poured tea for both of them, cut two slices of cake, and then retreated with his share to his chair. He sank his teeth into the sponge, savoured its cinnamon taste, and then found he could restrain himself no longer.

'So that ties it up?'

Kite gave up staring at the ceiling and instead looked at Sparrow.

'Ties up what?'

'You were checking up on the dates. That was Greystone Park, where the captain did his recuperation, and you wanted to check out Tomkin's story. Am I right, sir?'

'Yes.'

'Well the fact is I couldn't hear...' He paused and checked his notes. 'I couldn't hear what Miss Kempton said, but the dates, sir, they tie up. Mrs Elizabeth Walker told us she was about thirty-four weeks pregnant. I've got it written down in my notes from her interview. If I understand correctly what you have been told, she visited her husband on 12 June. By my arithmetic, that ties up beautifully. She slipped up to his room in Greystone, let him have his long overdue marital rights and Bob's your uncle.'

Kite made no comment, preferring to sip at his tea.

'So, sir, no skeletons in the cupboard there!'

Kite frowned. 'There's just one problem.'

'Is there?' Sparrow was genuinely puzzled. He knew about gestation periods. He had grown up in rural Lincolnshire. His mother had been a midwife. He could add up too.

'The problem is this. Captain Alec Walker suffered a shoulder injury as Tomkin told us. But that wasn't the whole story. He was also suffering from shell shock. And it was the shell shock which was the real problem. That's why he spent three months at Greystone Park before they sent him back to the front.'

'Why is that a problem? Sounds like we can rule him out. He's the last person to want to start blowing people up.'

Kite smiled. 'The problem, Constable, is this. His wife visited him on 12 June and indeed on 13 June and 14 June. As you so correctly worked out, this would fit in very well with her getting pregnant and now being six weeks away from giving birth. However, Miss Kempton told me that the captain was so unwell with shell shock that he didn't even recognise his wife. In fact her unexpected visit was all rather distressing to him with her claiming to be his wife and him accusing her of being an imposter. She stayed at a local hotel, and on three consecutive days she came over and tried to talk to him and each time he refused to have anything to do with her. So Miss Kempton then insisted that Mrs Walker return home as she was causing him unnecessary distress.'

Sparrow whistled. 'Well that's a turn up for the book. If the captain isn't the father of his wife's baby, then who is?'

'Indeed, Sparrow, that is the question.'

It was barely snowing when Kite and Sparrow trudged off to their meeting with the Ransoms. The few flakes which drifted gently in the air seemed like a promise that the worst was over, though clouds still hung heavy in the sky above, grey and unmoving. Several pigeons huddled on the roof of the stables, feathers fluffed and resigned to whatever might yet happen, and further away, across the fields, there was the sound of crows cawing their complaints.

The route to the church was through a small side gate at the back, and then straight on down a track which fell steeply away through a copse of oak and ash trees. As they came out of the far side, St John's church stood before them, pristine and white in the snow. The only other building in sight lay a couple of hundred yards to the east, a small stone-built cottage from whose chimney smoke spiralled.

'It looks like Jane has been as good as her word,'

Sparrow chirped. 'I wonder if she'll have baked some cakes to go with the cups of tea. I bet they won't be as good as Rose's.'

'I'd rather you focused on taking good notes of our meeting, rather than comparing their baking skills.'

'Don't you worry, sir. I won't miss a thing.' Sparrow was never short on self-confidence.

It was Jane who answered their knock on the door, and then led them into the small parlour. The fire was burning fiercely, and she soon returned with a tea tray. She poured cups of tea for them, and cut them each a slab of dark cake. Then she sat down opposite them and folded her hands on her lap.

'I'm afraid Justin isn't feeling very well. He gets these episodes sometimes, and then he has to go to bed until he is feeling better.'

'We just need to ask him a few questions.'

'Why don't you ask me?' She smiled, a butter-wouldn't-melt-in-my-mouth smile which immediately made Kite suspicious. 'I am sure I can answer on his behalf very adequately,' she continued. 'We are living in each other's pockets while we stay in this little house. And we don't have any secrets from each other. We are wedded to each other and to the church, so...' She lifted her hands and opened them up. 'So ask me your questions, Sergeant, and I will answer them if I can.'

Kite took another sip of tea and placed his cup down on the table. 'Where were you and your husband on the night of Sir Wilfred's death?'

'Here. Where else? Justin spent the day in Crowthorpe village attending to parish matters there, but he returned just as it was getting dark.'

'How does he get to Crowthorpe from here?'

'He walked there straight after breakfast. The weather was fine – the snow didn't come until the next day – but Frank Tomkin kindly gave him a lift back in Sir Wilfred's car.'

'And after he returned?'

'He had a cup of tea in front of the fire and fell asleep in the chair – the one you're sitting in, Sergeant, if you want to know every detail. We had supper about seven o'clock as usual. After that, I read my book and Justin went to the church to work on his sermon for next Sunday.'

'Why the church? Why not here?'

'Because he has no study here, and I am a distraction.' She emitted a single caustic laugh. 'Sometimes I would like to be more of a distraction. But he prefers to escape to St John's.'

'It must be very cold in there.'

'Actually it can be quite snug in the vestry, even at this time of year. There's a paraffin lamp. It smells a bit, but it soon warms the room up if you shut the door. He likes to light candles there too. He says it helps him to focus his thoughts on composing the message that the good Lord wishes him to pass on to his congregation. He is a bit of a perfectionist, writing and rewriting. I tell him he is wasting his time. It is not as if either of his congregations will care two hoots.'

'And how long was he in the church? When did he get back?'

She hesitated. For the first time, Kite sensed uncertainty in her voice and this puzzled him. After all, this was the key question – in effect, where was her husband at the time of the murder. It seemed improbable to Kite that she could possibly have been taken by surprise by it.

'The truth is, Sergeant, that I was feeling rather upset with him. I helped myself to a glass of wine – normally he controls that side of things – and then a second one because I was still feeling so cross that he was more concerned with his silly sermon than his own wife. And then I went upstairs and fell asleep in my dress. Rather shameful, I am afraid. Anyway, the result is that I am not sure what time he did return from St John's. I suspect that he will be cross with me because I didn't tell a little white lie, but of course as a good Christian wife I am required to tell the truth, and that is what I have done.'

'Thank you.' Kite nodded, then whispered conspiratorially, 'There is no need for your husband to know the full details of what you've told us. However, I would like to know what recent dealings your husband has had with Sir Wilfred.'

She smiled ruefully. 'You will have to talk to him about that – tomorrow, when he has recovered. All I know is that he was hoping that Sir Wilfred would make a contribution to church funds.'

'They discussed this did they?'

'As I said, Sergeant, you will have to ask Justin. I know nothing more.'

'But presumably you know when he and Sir Wilfred last spoke to each other.'

She gave a quick shake of the head. 'No, Sergeant, I do not. And if you have asked all your questions, I would like to go upstairs and see if my husband needs my assistance.' She stood up, reinforcing her point.

'Of course.' Kite knew he had no option but to withdraw with good grace. 'You have been most kind, Jane. We will go back to the manor and continue with our investigations. Thank you so much for your co-operation.'

'Not at all.' Her tone was brisk, and the atmosphere within the room had cooled sharply.

It was freezing outside too.

The two men started to stride up the hill, but Kite stopped and turned before they had gone far, looking back at the house just in time to see a face at the upstairs window before the curtains were drawn suddenly shut. Him or her? At this distance it was hard to tell.

'Blimey,' Sparrow said. 'She's not exactly a barrel of laughs is she. And as for her cakes, they're worse than my gran's, and let me tell you that's one hell of an achievement.' Kite didn't reply. Actually, he had been very glad to eat the cake, and had barely noticed its flavour or texture. They had managed to miss lunch at the manor, and as a consequence he had been feeling very faint again when they had entered the cottage. Faint and sluggish. The cake helped, but what he had really needed was a proper meal.

'And what do you think about the vicar not feeling well?'

'What do you think, Constable?'

'Very convenient I'd say. Or as my mother would have put it, it was all a load of hogwash.'

'Hogwash? Indeed.' A smile flickered briefly on

his face, but his mind was elsewhere. He continued to stare at the cottage, but if he was hoping for a twitching of curtains or the reappearance of that face, he was out of luck.

'A penny for your thoughts, sir?' For all his bravado and youth, Sparrow was no fool.

Kite turned and faced him. 'Well, Constable, this is what bothers me. On the one hand Jane Ransom is very protective of her husband and expresses concern about his well being—'

'Nothing wrong with that, sir.'

'If you'll let me finish, Constable.' Kite paused, waiting for his irritation with Sparrow to pass. 'On the other hand, you may have noticed that she failed to give him an alibi for the death of Sir Wilfred. If she had wanted to do so, if she was convinced that Sir Wilfred's death was nothing to do with her husband, then she could easily have said he stayed at home all evening—'

'But that would have been a lie. She was just telling the truth.'

'Like she was telling the truth by admitting that she had drunk rather a lot, so much indeed that she had fallen asleep on her bed in her clothes? Do you really believe that, Constable?'

Sparrow hesitated before replying. 'I suppose I do believe her,' he said. 'She's a vicar's wife. Why would she make up something that reflected badly on her? She convinced me.'

Kite grunted. 'I fear you are too easily taken in by a pretty face, Constable. And the fact that she has a husband who wears a dog collar does not mean she's a saint. She is, I think, a clever woman. Remember how she manipulated us this morning, protecting her husband from our questions, because he wasn't prepared for them. And now, again, he has avoided us. Let me remind you that we are investigating a very nasty murder.'

'You seriously think she could have killed the old man?' The scepticism in Sparrow's voice was obvious.

'Somebody did, Constable. I rule out no-one. Maybe it was him, maybe it was the two of them in cahoots.'

'But why would they do that?'

'Who knows! Money maybe. Money that Sir Wilfred was unwilling to hand over for their church. Or something else, some sin that the Reverend Ransom might feel was deserving of biblical judgement. Do you remember his prayer this morning, how he talked about the devil prowling around like a roaring lion?'

Sparrow did not reply for several seconds. 'You mean he thought the killer was the devil?'

'That is possible. But what I am thinking is this. Suppose he saw Sir Wilfred as the devil? In that case, he might see the killing of him as an act of divine punishment.'

'So you're saying the vicar may have killed him? But what's your evidence, sir?'

Kite smiled and patted Sparrow on the shoulder. 'Absolutely none at the moment. But something doesn't ring true. I can feel it in my bones.' He shivered. 'I can also feel the chill North Sea wind in my bones, so let's get back to the manor before I freeze to the spot.'

LATER THAT DAY

'WHAT NEXT, SIR?'

Kite waved his constable silent. He just needed some peace, some time to think, but that was proving hard to find. Sparrow, he decided, was more like a robin, constantly twittering. Robins did it to stake out their territory, but this investigation was his territory and Sparrow was at this moment just being a noisy nuisance.

Mind you, he wished he knew what was or should be next. There were too many thoughts running around in his head and he needed to get them into some sort of order.

'Call of nature, sir, if that's OK.'

'Yes, of course.' Kite watched him disappear and immediately stood up. This was his opportunity. He walked to the door and stood still. The house was, apart from Sparrow's receding steps, noiseless. He couldn't get used to being in such a big house, so many rooms and dark panelled corridors. What next indeed? Why not explore?

He turned right, towards the east wing, past the study and a room which (when he poked his head round the door) turned out to be a library. Where the men had retired to drink their port, and Maud too. Then on past the dining room where Sir Wilfred must have had his last meal, and opposite it another sitting room, much larger and grander than the one in which he had met Lady Beatrice (and in which he had fainted!). By this stage, he had nearly reached the end of the corridor. There was a single door at the end of it, closed but, as a slit of light revealed, not shut tight. And unlike all the other rooms he had passed, it seemed to be occupied. He stopped still. He could hear the sound of voices – one male and one female if he wasn't mistaken.

He hesitated, but only for a moment. Two people meeting here at the farthest reaches of the house suggested (to his suspicious mind) a secret meeting. So he braced himself and pushed the door open.

'What the devil?' The unwelcoming welcome came from David Graves. He had turned round from a conversation he was having with Maud and he looked furious.

'So sorry! I was looking for my constable.' Sometimes lies came out of Kite's mouth with disarming ease.

Maud Walker issued a paper thin smile, as calm as Graves was not. 'Unless he's hiding under the billiard table, I think I can safely say he is not in here.'

'Why on earth would he be in the billiard room?' Graves blustered. 'This is a family room. Out of bounds.'

Just for a fleeting second Kite wondered if he should point out that technically Graves wasn't part of the family either, but he thought the better of it. 'I expect he's got lost, a bit like me.'

'If I see him,' Maud said smoothly, 'I shall tell him that you are looking for him.'

'Thank you.' He turned to leave, then turned back. 'Actually, since I am here, Maud, perhaps I can ask you a question that has been bothering me.'

'You may.'

'I understand that you helped your father run the company through most of the war.'

'Only as a stand-in,' Graves butted in. 'When I was asked to go and use my management skills at the munitions factory at Burton.'

'Yes, you did tell us that, Mr Graves, and I can assure you that Constable Sparrow has made a note of it.'

'In that case, I don't see why you are asking questions about it again.'

'I haven't asked my question yet, Mr Graves.' Kite turned again to Maud. 'I do hope you will understand that what I am going to ask is aimed at trying to establish the truth.'

Maud nodded. 'And I hope that you will understand that I am in no way alarmed at the prospect of answering any question that you, or indeed any other man, might ask.' She stared defiantly back at him.

'I have been told, not least by Mr Graves, that you made a very good fist of helping your father run the company during the war, and so my question is this: will you continue to take a leading role in running the company now that the war is over? Or will you be handing the reins to your brother?'

Graves blustered in again. 'What on earth does this have to do with you, Sergeant – or indeed with discovering who killed Sir Wilfred?'

Kite ignored him. 'Maud?'

She straightened herself up. 'It is my belief that I am the only person who can ensure the future of the company.'

'Not your brother?'

'No. He has no interest in the company.'

'Or Mr Graves here?'

Maud paused and glanced briefly at Graves, whose normally flushed face was suddenly remarkably pale.

'I have…' he gulped, 'I have just asked Maud if she will do me the honour of marrying me.'

'And has she accepted your proposal?'

'She will need time to consider it, as is only proper.'

'David!' Maud's hard-set face told its own story. 'I shall not be marrying you. As I have just made very clear.'

'Oh dear, I have clearly blundered in at a very awkward moment…' Pretending to be sorry when he most definitely was not was also something that Kite could easily achieve.

'Damn you, Detective!' Graves snarled, as if Maud's rebuff was Kite's fault. 'Why don't you go back to London? That's where you come from, isn't it? Back to your cockney mates. Go and catch some of the pickpockets who lurk at every street corner there.'

Kite readied himself to take evasive action. The man's face was purple with fury and if he resorted to violence, then he himself was no longer fit or strong enough to deal with it.

'David.' It was Maud again, her voice low, yet controlled. 'You forget yourself.'

He looked at her, seeking some sign or hint of a softening, a change of mind, but he found none. He glared again at Kite, then swung round and swept out of the door, slamming it viciously behind him.

Maud and Kite stood still, frozen to the spot,

first looking at each other, then turning away, as if conscious that any communication between them, any blink or nod or even the hint of any facial movement, would be inappropriate in the circumstances.

'Well, Mr Kite,' Maud said eventually, 'you certainly have an impressive sense of timing. Impressively bad on this occasion, but impressive nonetheless. Though I sense that you may be feeling rather pleased with yourself.'

Kite tried to look surprised. 'Why do you say that?'

'Because you have accidentally forced into the open the fact that I am a major beneficiary of my father's death. And in your suspicious world that makes me someone with a motive for murder.' She paused, and when he didn't immediately respond. 'Well, am I right, Mr Kite, or not?'

'I suppose you are.'

'Of course I am.' She frowned, and then moved forward and touched Kite on the forearm. It was so unexpected that he flinched.

'Oh!'

'I am so sorry!' she said very quickly.

He said nothing. This was not the sort of situation he was accustomed to dealing with.

'I just wanted to implore you not to mention this to anyone. Not yet. Poor David will be frightfully upset and we will have to agree on a plan of what to say.'

'You mean whether to publicise that he proposed to you and you refused him, or just to keep it a secret between the two of you.'

'I suppose keeping it a secret would be kinder to him, but that may not be so easy to achieve in reality.

I suspect that he will have told Mary about his plans, and poor Mary is not the most discreet person. I fear she would find it difficult to keep entirely silent about it. And she may be upset too, because, of course, the marriage would have secured her future as well as his.'

Kite felt uncomfortable about what she was asking of him, even though there was not, as far as he could tell, any need on his part to spread the information. It would not assist his investigation. Besides, Maud had asked for his co-operation with such desperation that he found it impossible not to nod his agreement. 'If the information gets out, be assured that it will not be me who has spread it.'

She issued a half smile. 'That is very good of you. And now, if you will excuse me, I must hurry off and try to pacify him.'

Kite hovered in the billiard room for a couple of minutes. He told himself it was to allow Maud time to track down David, but there were other, less noble reasons: a mixture of envy, self-pity and anger. The full-size table was a thing of wonder – immaculate green baize, lights hung low over the top of it, and perfect red and white balls. These were positioned randomly on the table, as if a game had been suddenly abandoned. He looked around the walls. On the wall to the left was a rack of eight cues, of different lengths. He took one down and felt it, as if testing it for weight. He moved across to the table, settled down for a shot with the nearest white ball, trying to pot the red in the far pocket. He missed. He straightened up and, like a guilty schoolboy, replaced the cue. Eight cues. Was that one for each person in the household? Did the women ever play, or was this a male only domain? Except for Maud, perhaps, who didn't seem to accept the accepted rules.

Next to the cue rack was the score board. Again a thing of considerable craftsmanship. He scrutinised it for some time, and then frowned. The score was set at 32-15, so it was definitely a game that had never finished. Who had been playing? Hadn't Alec said David had challenged him to a game, and David had won 2-1 and then he had gone to bed. So why was there an unfinished game here? Had David hung around? Played a few practice shots on his own. Or had he met someone here? Did Tomkin like to slip downstairs and play a bit when the family were abed. Or Maud? Maybe it was as simple as that. Had she and David been playing a few shots until their conversation had turned difficult and he himself had turned up? Perhaps that was the most likely thing.

He looked around the room again, but this time his attention was gripped by the paintings grouped on one wall, all three of them portraits. In the middle was Sir Wilfred with his beetling eyebrows and hard stare, to the left someone in evening dress whom Kite assumed was his father, and to the right Alec, resplendent in his uniform. Kite scanned the rest of the room, pausing first on the grandfather clock and then, near the doorway, on the bell-pull lever which could summon Rose from the kitchen. He moved back to the portrait of Alec and stood right in front of it, taking in the supercilious smile on his lips. He felt the anger surging up inside him.

The painter, whoever he was, had captured the captain perfectly. He was a man born into privilege and money, and yet he had the arrogance to criticise Kite and his fellow policemen for wanting a pay rise. Damn him. Damn them all for their patronising sneers. All he wanted was to establish the truth and bring the killer to justice. Didn't the family want the same thing? Not all of them maybe. Not the killer, obviously. And yet… and yet it felt as though they were all deliberately doing their best to avoid helping him. It felt as if they were waiting for him to fail. It felt like a conspiracy. Not in the sense that they were all involved in the murder, but rather in the sense that none of them had any desire to see the killer apprehended.

There was something they were not telling him. The jam tin bomb. If it was indeed a Tickler's tin, what the hell was that about? To judge from the skull, Sir Wilfred had been clubbed over the head and then drenched in petrol. There was no need for a homemade bomb to make sure he died. An act of passion and hatred? But if you wanted to inflict the greatest pain, a bomb to speed up death made no sense.

Then there was the marriage proposal. Maud had been David Graves' guarantee of a comfortable life – and his sister's too. He had been relying on it. But now the old man was dead. Would he have ever countenanced Graves marrying his daughter and getting his hands on the business? Had Graves decided to take things into his own hands? Had Maud let him get the wrong idea, even encouraged him? Or had she taken things into her own hands? She was a very capable woman, capable of many things – including murder maybe. That would make sense. She was the only one who admitted to not being in bed at the time of the murder. She had been in the library writing one of her pamphlets until – supposedly – she fell asleep. Kite shook his head. How to find out what any of them truly felt about Sir Wilfred? How to identify the murderer before Bosworth sent some incompetent uniformed officer to take over from him?

'Sir, sir.' It was Sparrow's voice waking him from his reverie, and it was his boots that had beaten a tattoo along the corridor. He stood in the doorway, his face somewhat reproachful. 'What are you doing here, sir? I've been looking for you.'

Kite gave an enigmatic smile. 'I've had an interesting conversation with Maud. I'll tell you about it later. But first, let's get everyone together. We're being led up the garden path by someone, and I'd like to ruffle a few feathers.'

Sparrow frowned, possibly puzzled by his boss's sudden similes. But Kite didn't enlighten him. Instead he hobbled off, as fast as his knee allowed, back along the corridor. As he neared the larger sitting room, he paused. There were voices from inside, but the door was ajar, so he pushed it further open and put his head round the door. Elizabeth and Lady Beatrice looked at him with barely disguised irritation.

'I'm so sorry, but I have some new information, and I was hoping to gather everyone together.'

'Can't you just tell us?' Lady Beatrice said. 'We are perfectly capable of passing it on to the rest of the family.'

'I really would rather we had the whole household together.'

Lady Beatrice made an exasperated noise. But if she was going to say something too, a sudden cough intervened.

Elizabeth stood up, setting her hands under her bump as if the baby might be about to jump into action. 'In that case, perhaps you could ask Rose to bring us all something to keep us going.'

'Of course.' He nodded, bending slightly, a servant accepting instructions, before passing it on to his junior, in this case Sparrow.

It didn't take long for Rose to arrive, shadowed by Frank and Sparrow, each carrying a laden tray. Maud stepped forward to help distribute the cups of tea and slices of fruit cake. While she was doing so, her brother arrived, and so too did David Graves, whose face was set firm. He took up position in an armchair set some way back from where the family had settled near the fire.

'Well, Detective?' Lady Beatrice surveyed him from deep within her armchair.

Kite looked round, conscious that someone was missing. 'Where's Mary?'

'Lying down, I expect,' her brother said.

'Has anyone told her about the meeting?'

'For God's sake!' Alec jumped up from his chair. He stood there absolutely still. Kite suddenly saw him as one of those exhibits at the Madame Tussauds waxworks which his parents had once taken him to. Except that Kite could see that the man was trembling very slightly. With rage or what? 'Since nobody else will, I'll go and see if she will deign us with her presence.' And like a man pursued by a thousand demons, he raced out the door leaving everyone stunned into silence.

'The war,' Tomkin said quietly, though not so quietly that Kite couldn't hear. *The war*. Well, Tomkin had seen him at war. He was the one to know.

'We'll wait,' Kite said to the room at large. 'There's no rush.'

There was an unquestionable tension in the room. No conversations, only politenesses.

'Very nice cake, Rose.'

'What would we do without you, Rose.'

'Frank, would you mind throwing some wood on the fire.'

Kite surveyed them. How did they really get on with each other? Which of them was capable of murder? What was it Maud had said? That while sitting at the breakfast table she had realised that any of them might have killed the old man. But which of them had the depth of hatred and the ruthlessness to carry it through?

He slowly chewed his piece of fruit cake. Thank goodness he hadn't had another fainting episode. But he had had enough cake. What he could really have done with was a good filling lunch.

He finished his cup of tea, and almost immediately it was being refilled by – surprisingly – Elizabeth, as if she was presiding over a tea party of her friends. Except that there was no happy chatter, no gleeful gossiping such as Kite imagined normally took place at such events. It was an almost silent room throbbing with unease.

'How long does it take to see if Mary is coming?' David Graves uttered what most of them were probably thinking. Kite certainly was. He wanted to get the meeting started, stir things up and then see what happened.

He sipped at his second cup of tea and that was when he heard the sound. His first thought was that it was a sea bird, a black-headed or herring gull maybe, but the sound was quickly getting louder because it was getting closer. Someone was running along the corridor, feet thumping heavily, and then the door – which someone had pushed shut to keep out the draught – was flung open and there was Captain Alec Walker, eyes staring wide, red faced, gasping. He lifted his hands to his temples and then very suddenly was violently sick all over the small table on which Kite has just placed his teacup.

When Kite, closely followed by Sparrow, entered Mary's room, he immediately understood why Captain Walker had reacted the way he had. In his experience, people rarely look peaceful in death. That was certainly true of many of the murder victims he had investigated. How can anyone look peaceful when they have been stabbed with a kitchen knife or battered to death with a blunt instrument?

But Mary Graves' death was like no other he had encountered. He tried to summon up his experience and look at her and the crime scene dispassionately, but he felt like King Canute trying to hold back the tide. She was lying on the bed face up, arms flung out either side of her, her eyes fixed wide open as if she was trying to imprint her killer on her memory.

He bent down low over the bed and pulled Mary's hair away from the scalp. It was red and sticky. 'She's been struck very hard on the right-hand side of her head,' he said out loud, calm and clear, trying to set an example to his constable, but inside his emotions were churning. He glanced up, checking that Sparrow was paying attention and writing in his notebook, but to his horror he saw that his constable had opened the window and was leaning out of it as if he, like the captain, might be going to vomit.

'For crying out loud, Constable, snap out of it. You are meant to be making written notes on all of this.'

There was thud of heavy steps coming quickly up the stairs.

'And we don't want anyone in here.'

David Graves pushed open the door and stared down at his sister. 'What in God's name?'

'Out!' Kite ordered at the top of his voice. He could feel his own tenuous grip on the situation slipping. But his outburst seemed to be exactly the jolt that Sparrow needed, because the constable advanced quickly across the room.

'Mr Graves,' he said, holding out a warning hand. 'We really do need you to go back down to the sitting room and stay with the others. Best not to say anything more about it. You can see that we need to look for any possible clues. And when we have, we'll come down and report to the whole household.'

Kite waited for Graves to leave and for Sparrow to

shut the door firmly behind him.

'Thank you, Constable. Now, would you please take notes. Detailed and precise.' He paused, then took a deep breath. 'Mary was hit over the head. There is a dent and swelling and dark bruising to testify to that. And blood of course. We're looking for something pretty heavy, I would imagine. If we can find it, there will very likely be some debris on it. Blood, maybe hair.'

He looked up again to check Sparrow was indeed taking notes.

'I suggest the weapon used was dense, relatively small, most likely metal. If the killer came to the room with the deliberate intention of killing her, then he or she will have wanted to keep the chosen weapon concealed, in a bag or pocket.'

Kite tried to put himself in the shoes of the killer. Someone who knew the house well, someone with a clearly defined plan. Methodical and swift, silence and surprise essential.

'I've got all of that down, sir. Anything else?'

'Mary did not die immediately. Look here, Constable.' He pointed, allowing Sparrow to approach and get a better look. 'There are marks around her throat. Her scarf has been pulled tight round her neck, but if we release it, like this… what do we find? Clear evidence that she has also been strangled. The killer wanted to be sure and didn't have time to waste.'

He paused as he now forced himself to focus on another aspect of her death, unquestionably the most gruesome one. He surveyed it with intense concentration. He wanted to be able to recall all the details. If the snow relented, he might be able to get a photographer to come the next day and record what had happened, but he might have the devil of a battle with Lady Beatrice and David Graves over that. And that would become another reason why calls would be made behind his back to Chief Constable Bostock.

He took a deep breath and continued. 'As you can see, Constable, a tin of jam has been forced into Mary's mouth.'

'While she was alive, sir?' Sparrow spoke softly, as if by so doing he might reduce the horror of what they were witnessing.

'No, thank God. Look, her mouth is too small, so it looks as though the killer has cut the corner of her mouth. You will note that there is some blood, but not as much as I might have expected. This suggests to me that her heart was no longer pumping when this took place. The order of events is: she was struck over the head, then strangled until she was dead, and only then was the jam tin forced into her mouth. We can be confident that – mercifully – Mary was already dead when this grotesque final act took place. As for the jam tin, there is no doubt about its provenance this time. As the label says, it's Tickler's plum and apple.'

'Whoever did this must be a lunatic.'

Kite ignored the comment. Focus on the job in hand. The evidence, the detail. 'One more thing to note down, Constable. There is still some body heat and there is no significant stiffening of the limbs, so we can assume that Mary has been killed recently. Certainly within the last two hours, probably more like one.'

When Kite and Sparrow descended to the ground floor, it was to find that the household had decamped from the sitting room to the kitchen. Kite wondered if that was because it was nearer the stairs which led up to Mary's room.

'The kitchen is the warmest room in the house,' Lady Beatrice said defiantly, as if she could read Kite's thoughts.

There was a bottle of deep purple liquid in the middle of the long table. Everyone seemed to have a glass of its contents in their hands. 'Sloe gin,' she continued. 'My speciality. Though I confess I need some help with the picking now. I decided we all needed something to fortify us. Would you and your constable like to join us?'

He nodded. 'A small glass please.' He could certainly do with a bit of fortifying.

He waited until he had had a sip before he spoke. 'I can confirm that Mary is dead. A brutal attack, as two of you have already witnessed. We have not attempted to move her. But I have locked the door to prevent anyone going in. I need to make a phone call to the station in Lincoln.

'But you can't just leave her there,' David Graves said, and immediately drained his glass.

'Of course not. But I am afraid we will have to leave her there for a few hours at least. I suggest we try to contact Mr Lamyman. But would he really want to come here in these weather conditions? Perhaps tomorrow if things improve, but in the meantime the door is locked and we have left the window open to ensure it remains cool in there.'

'Have you… have you removed the…?' Graves couldn't bring himself to say the words.

'I have deliberately left Mary exactly as we found her. I am afraid that in the circumstances that is the correct thing to do.'

'But it is grotesque! Utterly grotesque.'

'There is nothing I can say to make this better for you, Mr Graves. However, I can assure you that Mary's death would have been very quick. My belief is that she would have known very little about it.'

Maud stood up. 'I'll come with you to the study, Sergeant. After you have reported in to your chief constable, we can make that call to Mr Lamyman.'

No-one objected. Alec himself was silent, staring at the floor. He was letting his sister take charge. No attempt to insist on his seniority as the male sibling. The confident swagger of the previous day had disappeared. Broken by what he had seen upstairs, and perhaps still traumatised by what he had experienced in the trenches. Kite suddenly realised that he felt sorry for him.

As soon as they entered the study, Maud shut the door behind them. 'David told me about Mary. Alec wouldn't say anything. It's as if it all brought back the horror of the war.'

'You mean the shell shock,' Kite said, and then immediately regretted it.

Maud stared at him. 'What do you mean?'

Kite cursed silently. She knew what he meant. He could see it in her eyes. She knew about her brother's trauma and the real reason for his prolonged stay at Greystone. And now, because of this one slip of his tongue, she knew that he knew.

'Not something any of you talk about, I expect,' he said trying to brush it off as unimportant to himself. 'Too difficult for those who suffer it and those who care about them. Best to keep quiet.'

'Who told you?' she said, looking him straight in the eyes.

'It doesn't matter. I won't include it in my report unless it turns out to be relevant. You can trust me on that.'

'Can I?' she said. But she didn't wait for an answer. She walked over to the desk and sat down. 'Perhaps you should make your telephone call now, and then I will ring Mr Lamyman.'

Kite followed her over and picked up the handset. He put it to his ear and tapped the receiver. Nothing. He tapped the receiver. Still nothing. He tried again. 'I'm not sure that it is working.'

He handed the handset to her. She tried the same routine herself, listened, then a second time and then she gave up. 'As you say, it's not working.'

'Does this often happen? Is there another telephone in the house?'

'No. To both questions. I can't recall when we last had a problem.'

Kite walked over to the window and looked out, as if to reassure himself that he hadn't imagined the snow. White flakes were still falling, albeit not as heavily as earlier in the day, though the wind had got up and was spinning and whirling them around like fairies at a winter ball. In other circumstances it would have been an entrancing sight.

Maud moved across the room and stood by his shoulder. 'Do you think the snow has caused a problem? Perhaps it has caused a tree to collapse across the telephone line.'

'It's possible,' Kite said, still gazing out across the unfettered snow, stretching out into the distance. 'But I think we need to investigate.' When Kite said 'we', he wasn't thinking of himself. 'I gather that Tomkin is a very practical man. Perhaps he and Sparrow could go on a reconnaissance for us.'

'If that's what you'd like, Sergeant, then of course Frank will co-operate fully.'

Tomkin and Sparrow trekked out through the snow, sinking up to their knees at every step. They followed the line of the telephone wire, stretched up high on poles, down the invisible road and out towards the village of Crowthorpe. They had walked some half a mile when, as if by common agreement, they stopped.

'Not sure this is getting us anywhere.'

'No.'

'If the line has been brought down, it could be anywhere between here and Lincoln.'

'And if it has come down, how can we fix it? We know it's not working. So what good will us finding the broken line do?'

'I think he wants to know the cause.'

'Why?'

'I think he must be worried that it might have been sabotage, rather than an act of God.'

There was no reply. For at least a minute, they stood still and silent, looking out into the far distance where the telephone line disappeared from view.

'Of course,' Tomkin said eventually, pulling his scarf tighter round his neck, 'it's always possible that the fault is inside the house. I mean if someone wanted to sabotage the line, especially in this weather, it would be much easier to do it in the house.'

Sparrow grunted. 'In that case, let's go back before my balls freeze off!'

'This is nothing compared to the trenches,' Tomkin replied. Secretly he reckoned Sparrow wasn't as tough as he made out.

As they reached the gateway, they noticed the hunched figure of Kite standing in the front porch. He was doing up his coat, though his gloved fingers didn't seem to be doing a very good job of it. They increased their pace, and it was only as they drew near that Kite looked up.

'I was beginning to worry about you,' Kite said.

'Can't see any problem with the line. Maybe it's nearer Lincoln.'

'It's not the line,' Kite said. 'It's the handset.'

Sparrow and Tomkin looked at each other.

'Sorry to have sent you off on a wild goose chase. After we had checked all the wiring inside the house, Maud dismantled the telephone for me. She's a very capable person. Also very observant. She noticed some scratches underneath it. New, she said. Someone had been fiddling around with it. Anyway, the wires inside had been cut, and by the looks of it various other bits have been removed.'

'Maybe I can fix it,' Tomkin said.

'You're welcome to try, but I fear that without the missing parts it will be beyond even your famed skills. Anyway, you'd better get inside and warm up. I'm going for a walk round the yard before it gets dark. Just in case there's something we missed.'

But it wasn't a walk round the yard that Kite went on. Instead he first made his way round the back of the house, pausing outside the back entrance to the west wing. Then, satisfied, he made his way across the yard to the back gate and out. He was in search of the elusive Reverend Justin Ransom. If someone had asked him why, he kept that as a secret from Sparrow and Tomkin; he would have had trouble explaining honestly. The longer he had been at Crowthorpe Manor, the more suspicious he had become of everyone. He had even found the cheery-chappy persona of his constable at odds with the seriousness of the situation. And right now, he didn't want to have to share his thoughts and theories even with him. Kite had also decided that Sparrow was the sort of man who talked too freely, that while chatting with Tomkin or with Rose in the kitchen or even the disturbingly flirtatious Elizabeth, he might let something slip. 'A loose tongue brings no good' his mother used to say, and Kite had taken it to heart.

The snow was still lying thick and undisturbed out in the fields. In the yard, there had been plenty of tracks criss-crossing the yard, covered but not entirely obscured by relentless falling of snow. One set led to the stables where Maud kept her horses. Another set, along which someone had toiled to and fro several times, led to a building which housed a substantial supply of wood, all cut and chopped neatly into different sized logs, presumably to fit the different sized fireplaces in the house. Kite had noted that there were fresh footprints as well as old ones near the tarpaulin which marked where Sir Wilfred had met his end. No surprise there. Had someone come out to observe the scene of crime again, to pray for the old man or maybe to silently celebrate his death?

As Kite made his way down towards the church, he noted that there were no fresh footmarks on the track, none perhaps since he and Sparrow had tramped down it and then back up it some three hours earlier. He felt cheered by that, and he needed a bit of cheer. That meant that if the elusive Reverend Ransom was not in the cottage, the chances were he would be no further than the church, communing with the Almighty away from the dangerous distractions of his wife.

Kite continued trudging down the track. The snow crunching under his feet was the only sound except for his own heavy breathing, the birds having apparently all taken a vow of silence in protest at the cold. He marched on through the canopy of trees and then out into the open where the church and cottage came into full view. There was movement outside the latter – Jane Ransom to judge from the long skirt. She had what Kite assumed to be a bundle of firewood in her hands, and she glanced up at him, pausing for a few moments, before pushing the front door open, entering and then slamming it shut behind her. He had no doubt that she had seen him. He shrugged. He'd try the church first. He was curious to look inside it, and if the Reverend Ransom Justin was there he would have him cornered.

As he reached the lychgate, he paused, allowing himself to take in the church's structure. He hadn't spent long in the county of Lincolnshire, but he had already been despatched to investigate several minor rural crimes – theft mostly, with the exception of a dead body found in a ditch with a knife wound to the neck. The dead man had a reputation as a troublesome drunk and no-one was willing to admit that they knew anything about it. ''E won't be missed,' was the most charitable comment Kite heard. It seemed that every village in the county had a church in it, and this was no different from most: it was built of grey stone, a solid tower with spire on top, Gothic windows, some adorned with stained glass, and the building itself surrounded by a sizeable churchyard. People died and everyone expected a plot of earth where they could be lain and remembered. Kite reckoned that in the spring, with the daffodils bursting into life and the sun streaming down, this must be a lovely place to come if you were seeking some peace and solitude.

But there were no signs of new life yet. Like everywhere else, the churchyard was white and, in its own way, very beautiful. Kite scanned it all, wondering rather ludicrously if the vicar was hiding from him behind one of larger gravestones or – more likely – one of the large rectangular chest tombs that lined the right-hand side of the pathway in front of him. Family graves he assumed, as he made his way towards them, pausing only to brush some snow off his trousers. The writing underneath was worn but still visible, a George Walker who had died in the 1851, aged 77. A predecessor of Sir Wilfred very likely, his grandfather maybe.

Kite straightened up. Time to try the church door. It was clear that the vicar had indeed come to the church in the last couple of days. There were footprints in the snow which revealed that, though quite how recently was harder to tell. It was possible he had been inside the church for some hours or maybe he was skulking in the cottage. Kite moved forward. Now he was so close, he might as well try the door and see if it was open. He turned the handle, but the door refused to open. It was locked. He banged on the door. Might Ransom have locked himself in? It seemed unlikely. Unless he had some reason to be afraid. The thought took Kite unawares. Could Ransom be afraid? Of what, or rather of whom? And then he saw something else that caught his attention. There was a trail of footprints across the snow around the south side of the church.

Unlike the path to the church, this was not a well-trodden track. The prints had been made by a single person, going one way and then back. Who? The vicar he guessed. Or was it someone else? Kite's curiosity was aroused. He would follow them and see where they led, and after that he would head for the cottage.

Where they led was along the side of the church building, under a spreading oak tree and beyond until they came to a stop in front of a gravestone by the graveyard wall. Kite knelt down to get a proper look. There was a thin covering of snow and he brushed it off. This revealed a simple inscription: two names, a date of birth and a date of death. Kite had knelt down to get a good look, but as he stood up and scanned the rest of this the area, he realised that all these gravestones were modest compared with the grand ones at the front of the church. This was where the locals and the servants were laid to rest.

'Sergeant Kite!' The Reverend Ransom's voice sounded across the churchyard. Kite looked up and saw he was standing near the porch on the southern side of the church, where Kite had been banging on the door only a few minutes earlier.

Kite raised his hand in acknowledgement and walked as briskly through the snow as he could.

'I expect you've been looking for me.' Ransom was still bellowing like a drill sergeant even though the distance between the two men had closed.

Kite pressed on until he was only a few yards away. 'You're an elusive man,' he wheezed.

'Like the Scarlet Pimpernel!' He beamed, much more animated and cheerful than Kite was expecting. 'They seek him here, they seek him there!'

'Are you fully recovered, Reverend?'

'Oh yes, fully. And do call me Justin. Except if you were you to come to a church service of mine, then Reverend would be more appropriate.'

'I am not anticipating being around here for too much longer.'

Ransom looked up and sniffed the air. 'I wouldn't be too sure. This snow hasn't finished yet. Or perhaps you feel you are close to catching the culprit?'

Kite shrugged. The fact was he didn't feel close at all, but he had no intention of admitting it to Ransom – or indeed anyone else.

'Personally,' Ransom continued, 'I think you're

barking up the wrong tree. I find it quite inconceivable that any of the inhabitants of Crowthorpe Manor could have killed Sir Wilfred. He was so important to them all. He was the backbone of the family and the business. Much more likely it was a random attack, a scoundrel looking to steal something, and when he discovered Sir Wilfred there in the garage, he panicked and attacked him and when he realised he had killed him he set fire to cover his tracks and ran away.'

Kite frowned and scratched at his cheek. It was the same theory that he had heard from the others. It suggested some degree of co-operation – they were all singing from the same unconvincing song sheet. But it also presented Kite with an opportunity, and he seized at it with casual alacrity. 'In that case, Justin, how do you explain Mary's death?'

Ransom's mouth opened and then shut. Not a sound escaped except a gasp of shock. He stared at Kite, his face a picture of disbelief. 'What in God's holy name are you saying?'

Kite paused. Either the vicar was a consummate liar and actor, or he knew nothing about Mary's death. 'We found her dead in her bed earlier today.'

'You mean… I mean… what did she die of? A heart attack or something?'

'She was strangled.'

'Strangled?' Ransom gulped, as if short of air. 'You're certain?'

'Oh yes, I've seen a few such cases in my time in London. First the poor woman was violently attacked and then she was strangled with her own scarf.'

Kite didn't say any more. He had no intention of mentioning the jam tin. Instead he waited to see what Ransom said. But Ransom said nothing. Instead he started to sway on his feet, stretched out a hand to steady himself, misjudged the distance to the wall of the porch and fell to the ground.

'Damnation!' Kite bent down. Ransom's head had glanced against the stonework as he fell, and there was a trail of blood down the side of his face. For a moment he panicked. Ransom's eyes were shut. 'Justin,' he said sharply. He pressed his thumb on his wrist, and was relieved to feel a pulse of life. 'Justin,' he snapped again. 'Open your eyes. Look at me.' And much to his relief, after several seconds had passed, the vicar did precisely that.

When Kite arrived at the cottage supporting the bloodied Justin, there was a short period of domestic pandemonium as Jane clucked over him like a mother hen – sitting him down, washing his face clean, making him (but not Kite) a strong cup of tea with three spoons of sugar, then moving him to his favourite armchair in front the fire, which she refreshed with wood which she instructed Kite to bring in from outside. Only when that was all done did she escort Kite to the front door and question him, her voice low and intense.

'What on earth has happened? He was muttering something about Mary.'

Kite decided to keep it simple. 'I'm afraid Mary is dead.'

Just as her husband had, she expressed shock. When

Kite explained that she had been murdered, she too gasped, but there was no dramatic collapse to the floor. Instead she straightened up, no longer leaning towards him.

'When was this?'

Kite ignored the question. 'I wonder if you can tell me if you've seen any strangers around here today?'

'No, I am sure I have not.'

'Maybe you went out for a walk and saw someone you didn't know, or indeed someone you did know.'

'We have not been abroad,' she said flatly. 'Look at the weather. Justin didn't even go and sit in the church. The only time he's been out today was when he saw you walking down the hill and then going towards the church. I said you were probably looking for him, so he went out to find you. I wish I hadn't said anything, because then he wouldn't have come home covered in blood.'

'A bit of blood,' Kite snapped. He felt anger swelling inside him. It wasn't his fault. He could hardly not have told Justin that Mary had been murdered. What was it that Sparrow had said about Jane and her husband? 'She's far too pretty for him.' A pretty face maybe, but it was very much odds with the sharpness of her character.

'Anyway,' she said, 'I hope you asked him all your questions before you caused him to collapse, because he's in no state to answer any more today.'

'Of course not,' Kite said, knowing he had lost another battle with her. 'I hope he is feeling better very soon.' Kite nodded and went out into the biting cold. He had nothing more to say. He was feeling deeply frustrated. The blood on the man's head was pretty trivial he reckoned, the damage superficial. But the bottom line was, whether by chance or design, the Ransoms had managed to evade his questioning again. It felt like a failure.

And yet, as he walked back up the hill, he found himself dwelling on something else, and by the time he had emerged from the other side of the trees and the house had come into view, he had come to the conclusion that maybe it hadn't been a totally wasted trip after all.

Kite was brushing the snow off his coat and boots in the porch when Sparrow appeared. 'Thought you'd got yourself lost, sir. I was looking for you.'

'Nothing like fresh air to clear the mind,' he replied.

'And is your mind any clearer?'

'I don't know about that, but I am damned cold. Where is everybody?'

'Most of them are having tea together. That seems to be all they do at this time of year. Not Rose and Frank, of course.'

'Perfect, let's go and join them.'

The hum of chatter led them directly to the bigger sitting room, but as soon as Kite walked in silence fell, though whether that was because they had been talking about him or about something they didn't want him hearing, he didn't know, nor indeed care. He was just glad that he had got them corralled in the one room like sheep in pen.

'I do hope I'm not interrupting something.' He surveyed them all, noting the irritation and, in some cases, the barely concealed hostility on their faces. Only Elizabeth offered a genuine-looking smile.

'You must have a cup of tea, Detective Kite.'

'Thank you.' He moved further into the room, establishing himself with his back to the big bay window. He wanted to have a clear view of everyone and experience had taught him the wisdom of not standing with an open door behind him.

As he took a first sip at his tea, Rose and Tomkin appeared, bearing not cakes, but scones.

'Fresh out of the oven,' Rose announced proudly. 'And a choice of Crowthorpe's jam to go with them.'

Kite waited for his scone, opting for the blackberry and apple jam which always reminded him of his childhood. He devoured half of it before he stood up, cleared his throat and called for everyone's attention. Despite the frowns on some faces, it was clear that they were all keen to hear what he had to say. Even Rose and Tomkin hung around, and no-one told them to go.

'I have interviewed all of you separately, some more than others. Constable Sparrow has made a note of all the important points. But the fact is that I still don't feel I have a clear idea of what exactly happened – and when – on the evening of the death of Sir Wilfred. I also feel bound to tell you that there are some discrepancies in what different persons have told me. Indeed I believe there have been some untruths told.' He waited for his words to sink in, sensing rather than seeing the disquiet in them. If he had been asked to list with his hand on the Bible what untruths he had discovered, he would have had to remain silent. But he was convinced that Crowthorpe Manor was a house teeming with lies and half-truths. What he intended to do now was probe and goad, and then to wait for the cracks in the family facade to appear and the truth to slip out through them.

'Which of us are lying?' The captain stared at him, his Adam's apple bobbing as he spoke. 'We have done our utmost to accommodate you, and yet here you are drinking our tea and eating our food and insulting us.'

Kite clasped his two hands together and held them defensively against his chest. 'Can I remind you, sir, that I am investigating two deaths, one victim being your father and one being his secretary. I am not yet able to separate the wheat from the chaff, the truth from the untruths, but Mary's dreadful murder has clarified one very important thing.' He paused, conscious that he now had the attention of the whole room. 'The killer of both Sir Wilfred and Mary lives within these walls.' He paused. 'I think, Captain, that you will now have to agree on that?'

'I have no intention of giving you the satisfaction of agreeing that you are correct. The house is not locked during the day. Someone could have entered the house by the door at the back of the west wing and gone up to Mary's room without being observed.'

Such as the vicar, or indeed his clever wife. That was what flashed across Kite's brain, but what he said was different. 'We have checked for footprints in the snow. I saw no trace of any fresh tracks leading to that door.'

Alec stood up. 'Right from the outset, you have refused to examine the possibility – indeed I would say the probability – that the killer is a disgruntled employee—'

'Enough, Alec!' Lady Beatrice had taken hold of her walking stick and now banged the metal ferule hard on the floor several times. Mother and son glared at each other, the only sounds in the room being the crackle of the fire and Lady Beatrice's heavy breathing. Eventually he sat down, and she turned her face towards Kite.

'What exactly is it that you want to know, Sergeant?'

'Lady Beatrice, I was wondering what you talked about during the evening meal on the night of your husband's death?'

'Is that all?'

'I'd like to start there. Can you remember?'

She frowned. 'Let me think.' It took her some time to think. Kite was expecting someone to jump in and 'help' her. But to his surprise, no-one did. Was that because no-one dared interrupt or were they waiting for her lead?

'The food of course.' She looked up at Kite. 'Lamb stew and a very nice apple and blackberry crumble. The meat was rather tough, but everyone was polite enough not to mention that. Instead people thanked Mary for her work in the kitchen, which had enabled Rose to have the afternoon off. Of course, we talked about the weather, don't we always! Maud told us about her horse which had become lame. Oh yes, I also mentioned that I had had a visit from the Reverend Justin Ransom. He is the vicar of St Mark's in Crowthorpe. He also looks after our little church of St John's. I think you may have met him. He calls in whenever he needs an injection of money, or a cup of tea and a slice or two of one of Rose's famed cakes. Of course he is living in our farm cottage near St John's currently, so he's not very far away.'

'So was it money or cake this time?'

'Not beating about the bush, Sergeant!' She laughed. 'He asked me if we would support a fund-raising effort to repair the roof of St Mark's. Of course, by "support" what he meant was would we fund it entirely ourselves. Then he wouldn't have to bother to drum up his ladies in the village to do lots of good works. He is, I am afraid to say, a rather idle man of God.'

'And what did your husband have to say about that?'

'Very little indeed.'

'So he didn't agree to it.'

'He left it to me to make the decision. Of course, now my husband is dead, we shall as a family be sure to mark his life with a suitable donation to the church, but to be spent on a memorial in St John's, not the roof of St Mark's. There are other households in Crowthorpe who are sufficiently well off to make contributions. I don't see why we should pay for everything.'

'Is there anything else you remember talking about at dinner?'

'No,' she said firmly. 'Nothing.'

He looked around the room. 'Has anyone else anything to add? Perhaps Lady Beatrice has forgotten some conversation that others might remember?'

No-one responded. The only sound which Kite imagined he could hear was that of the shuffling of feet as the members of the household closed ranks.

'And what about after supper, when the menfolk and Miss Maud gathered for a chat over their port and cigars.'

'Actually,' Maud said, 'just for the record – perhaps Constable Sparrow can write this in his little notebook – I drank crème de menthe. I hate port.'

'And what did you talk about while you were drinking your… crème de menthe?

'I wanted to talk about women's suffrage, but of course the men weren't interested.'

'Why do you think that was?'

Her brother jumped in. 'Because she's always talking about it.'

Maud turned and glared at Alec. 'Because they know I am right. But they hate the prospect of having to admit it to me. So they laugh and jeer and fill up their glasses with even more port.'

'Your father jeered as well, did he?'

Maud's face froze. She half opened her lips, but no sound came out.

David Graves stepped forward from his position against the far wall. 'What the devil are you playing at, Kite?'

'Not playing, Mr Graves. I am deadly earnest. As I said earlier, I have had several conversations with members of the household about what you all talked about after dinner. Horse racing, the weather, a refusal to discuss the politics of women with Maud, all your accounts agree on these points. But there are three matters which are bothering me.'

He paused and picked up the plate on which half his

scone still lay. He bit off a small piece, then set the plate back down. He held up his right hand and raised the index finger.

'First, in all of your accounts, none of you talked about Sir Wilfred. None of you have said how he was or what he wanted to talk about.'

Kite raised a second finger. 'Secondly, I assumed that after dinner with all the key persons sitting together relaxed in the privacy of the library that you might have discussed the family jam business, but no. Maud told me quite specifically that you did not, that she strongly disapproved of talking business with men who had been drinking heavily.'

Maud laughed. 'When do men not drink heavily if there is alcohol within reach?!'

Another of Kite's fingers went up. 'And thirdly, I am faced with another peculiarity. That when I asked poor Mary what was discussed at supper on that fateful night, she too mentioned horse racing and the weather and Maud's fury when her attempts to discuss women's suffrage were laughed down. Not after supper, please note, when the men and Maud were ensconced together, but at supper. She insisted that all this happened round the dining table.'

Kite nibbled another piece of scone and surveyed the room. It felt very much as though there was a secret which they all shared, but were unwilling to reveal. Who, he wondered, might be the first to crack?

Alec cleared his throat noisily. 'I think it would be fair to say that we often discussed racing, and the weather and Maud certainly likes to push her own ideas, so a degree of overlap is not so surprising.'

There was a murmur of agreement and a nodding of heads.

Kite felt a heavy sense of despondency. It was as if Alec had established the line of defence, and everyone else was eager to follow it.

He sighed audibly. 'So just to be clear, at no stage was there any discussion of the Crowthorpe Jam business. Even though David and poor Mary had been asked to join the family for the evening meal. I am bound to say I find that very strange.'

'There is nothing strange about it at all.' Lady Beatrice snapped the words out. 'I won't tolerate business talk over dinner, Sergeant. They can save their business claptrap for the working day.'

The meeting broke up after that. People drifted away to do whatever it was they wanted or needed to do, and Kite soon found himself alone in the room with Lady Beatrice and Sparrow. 'You're excused now,' he whispered to Sparrow. 'I need a private word with her ladyship.' Sparrow opened his mouth to say something, but Kite hissed 'private word' and he went out, shutting the door with an unnecessarily loud bang.

'Well, Sergeant?' She fixed him with an eagle eye.

'Mary told me that there had been a substantial theft of money from the safe.'

'Ah.' Lady Beatrice took a handkerchief out from her sleeve and dabbed at her nose. Playing for time, Kite reckoned. Caught off guard. Which is what he had hoped for.

'It was a misunderstanding.'

'What sort of misunderstanding?'

'Just a misunderstanding. Sir Wilfred told me about it, and we quickly dealt with it. That is all.'

'So why had Mary not been told?'

'I imagine because my husband forgot or – actually this is more likely – he could not be bothered to put her at ease about the situation. Anyway, it is all over and done with.'

'Could I ask—'

'No.' Lady Beatrice was as sharp as a butcher's knife. 'This is a private matter, nothing to do with you, and I would ask you to exclude it from your enquiries, which should be focused solely on my husband's death – and, of course, Mary's. Now, I would be grateful if you would leave me in peace and shut the door behind you.'

It was nearly eight o'clock, and Kite and Sparrow were sitting in the kitchen eating supper with Rose and Tomkin. Kite was feeling refreshed after an hour of snoring on his bed. He knew he had snored because Sparrow, who had woken him up, had told him so. 'Like a herd of pigs,' he quipped, 'if you don't mind me saying so. No disrespect intended.'

Sparrow had let it pass, and instead splashed water on his face, brushed his thinning hair and made his way down the stairs.

It was when Alec had come in to ask if they had another bottle of the red wine warming in the kitchen that Kite had taken his chance.

'Would it be possible for Constable Sparrow and I to play a game of billiards? When we've finished eating that is. It would be such a great opportunity for us both. It's a long time since I've played on a full-sized table. And the balls and cues are of the highest quality.'

Alec couldn't have been more stunned if a troupe of circus performers had walked in through the door.

'Of course,' Kite continued, 'if you and David are planning to play after you have finished your meal, then that is your prerogative and Sparrow and I shall instead enjoy the warmth of the kitchen and the good company of Frank and Rose until we are ready to turn in.'

Rose had got up from her chair and she removed a bottle of wine from the back of the cooking range and gave it to Alec. 'Don't worry, sir. I'll give 'em hell if they mess it up.'

He nodded. 'Very well.' Though he didn't give the impression of being at all happy with it.

'I'm beginning to regret that I suggested we have a little wager on this.' Sparrow, normally so cocky, had just missed a shot, and he was discovering that Kite was a very good player.

Kite smiled. 'My uncle used to make the tables. Sometimes, when the boss wasn't around, he'd let me have a go. He was a damned good player himself, so it was a case of learn fast if I wanted to stand a chance of competing with him.'

Kite tried an ambitious potting of the red at the far end of the table, but missed. 'Blast! It must be the beer.'

'You only had one, sir.'

'Even so.'

They fell silent as Sparrow compiled a substantial

break, and then missed what should have been an easy pot. Instead the red ball hovered around the pocket, but refused to drop.

'I hope you're not letting me win, Constable, to curry favour.' Kite settled down over the table and then potted both the red and Sparrow's white ball to secure the points he needed for victory.

'Damn!' Sparrow was not, it seemed, a gracious loser. 'How about another game? Double or quits?'

Kite tried to smile but ended up yawning. 'The fact is I'm tired. Let's call it a day.'

'I'll let you have your winnings when we are back in Lincoln,' Sparrow said. 'I didn't think I'd need money on this trip.'

'You can buy me a pint when we get home.'

They both returned their cues to the rack. Then Kite wandered over to the three portraits, and stood in front of Sir Wilfred. 'We don't really know that much about him, do we. Liked his horses and his posh car. Not to mention his brandy and cigars. No doubt he was a tough businessman. Tough on his family too maybe.'

Sparrow came and stood next to Kite. 'A bully you mean?'

'Look at his eyes, Sparrow.' Kite pointed at the portrait. 'You can tell a lot from people's eyes.'

'It's just a painting.'

Kite ignored the comment. 'Maud told me she realised any of them could have murdered him. Which suggests that he was indeed a bully. Unlike the others, she didn't assume the killer was a local ne'er-do-well trying to pilfer a few things from the outbuilding. On the contrary, she had her suspicions that it was someone in the household who killed Sir Wilfred.'

'And you do too? Even though Mary may have seen someone near the gate?'

'Most certainly. Poor Mary may well have seen the killer. Maybe even recognised him or her, but couldn't believe her eyes, thought she had seen a ghost.'

'But even if you believe in ghosts, sir, you can't believe that they kill people.'

'Indeed I don't.'

'And now Mary is dead.'

'Yes indeed. And a hellish death it was too. But...' Kite paused for several seconds as he assembled his thoughts. Then he delivered his conclusion. 'But in killing Mary the murderer has made a mistake.'

'Sorry, sir.' Sparrow's surprise was writ clear across his face.

'Well, for a start it confirms what I always assumed, that the killer is living in this house. Secondly, it confirms the connection to Tickler's Jam. First a bomb, and now an even more hideous use of one of their jam tins. So the question is why Tickler's Jam?'

'They are a rival. And during the war a more successful rival. I guess Sir Wilfred was very jealous of them.'

'Exactly. But I think the use of the jam rammed into poor Mary's mouth had a very clear purpose. It was a warning – to everyone else in the house to keep their mouths shut.'

'You mean... I mean... are you saying that everyone in the house knows who killed Sir Wilfred and Mary?'

'No, not necessarily. But some people in the house know or have very strong suspicions, I am certain of that. The problem is to work out who.'

'So how on earth do we do that?'

Kite didn't answer the question because his mind had moved on to another matter, one about which he felt somewhat guilty. So he made his confession. 'Constable, I need to tell you something. After you and Tomkin returned, I didn't just go for a walk, I went down to the church to try and track down the Reverend Ransom. I found him eventually, but I have to admit that it didn't go well. The fact is that I didn't get any clear statement out of him about his movements, either on the night of Sir Wilfred's death or earlier today when Mary was murdered.'

'He must have said something, sir!'

Kite grimaced. 'When I told him about Mary's death, he collapsed on the floor, cutting his head on the porch of the church, and as a consequence that was the end my interview.'

'Blimey.' Even Sparrow was silenced.

Kite yawned. He was exhausted. 'I think we should go to bed.'

'But do you suspect the vicar, sir?'

'It's possible. They live close enough.'

'But he's a vicar, sir!'

'Constable, if you think a vicar is incapable of killing someone, then I suggest that you are very naive. Anyone can kill if the circumstances are right and they have a strong enough motive. Plenty of young men like you, in the trenches, fighting for King and Country and for their own lives, killed Germans without a second thought. Suppose our vicar sees his role as being God's instrument on earth, punishing a sinner – there really is no difference.'

Sparrow looked appalled. 'With respect, sir, I would say there is a very big difference. I was doing my duty as a soldier, whereas whoever killed Sir Wilfred and Mary was wreaking murder.'

'Or vengeance or justice.' Kite paused, waiting for his words to sink home. 'Perhaps I have gone a little bit too far, Constable. I don't mean to cast aspersions on the bravery and sacrifices made by many men like you, but I wanted to make a point. That anyone who felt wronged or cheated by Sir Wilfred might, if presented with the opportunity, have taken it and killed him. Rule out nobody. Old or young, man or woman, chauffeur or a man of God. Who knows what goes on in their heads and hearts.'

'You say chauffeur. Do you mean Tomkin is your main suspect?'

'No,' Kite snapped, betraying his irritation and tiredness. 'I suspect everyone. Anyone and everyone.'

'I see, sir,' Sparrow replied, though his tone of voice was uncertain. 'So may I ask how we are going to catch the killer?'

Kite ignored the question. 'First and foremost, I suggest you lock your bedroom door tonight if you can. If you don't have a working lock, then I suggest a chair rammed under the handle. Because for all I know, one of us may be next on the killer's list. Second, in the morning we must try again to make contact with the outside world and get some help.'

THE THIRD DAY

DESPITE BEING DOG tired, Kite had slept intermittently. He had risen and passed water three times, and since that third occasion he had been unable to settle. When he had finally given up trying to sleep, he had pulled on his jacket and trousers and opened the door, and that was when he had caught the smell of food being cooked. He padded quickly, but silently down to the kitchen. If Rose was there on her own, it gave him an opportunity to talk to her without being overheard or interrupted.

She was bent over the stove, and didn't even turn when he said 'good morning'. Merely waved at the teapot on the hot plate. 'Only just made it.'

Kite helped himself, added milk and sugar and sat down on the far side of the table facing her. She was still stirring the pot vigorously.

'You seem to have a lot of responsibilities in this house.'

She turned and looked at him. 'I did have a girl to help. Kay. Nice and willing. From the village. Came in every day.' She frowned. 'Then she caught the influenza. She was dead within a week. Poor little Kay. She didn't have the strength for it.'

'I'm sorry.'

'Anyway, after that Sir Wilfred decided I could manage on my own, with Mary and Frank helping out. The last thing he wanted was Elizabeth getting ill. Worried about his grandchild, you see.'

She turned back to the saucepan and redoubled her

stirring. Kite paused, preparing himself. What he had to say next wasn't going to be easy. He took a deep breath. 'Tell me about your brother,' he said.

Rose didn't respond. Indeed Kite might have assumed she hadn't heard his question if she hadn't stopped stirring whatever food it was in the giant saucepan. She didn't just stop moving, she froze. Even the strands of hair which had escaped from under her white cap seemed to go rigid.

Kite raised his voice. 'Rose, I saw Paul's gravestone.'

She turned very slowly. Her face was pale and her mouth pursed. She pushed back one of the loose strands of hair.

Kite gestured towards the chair in which she always sat, at the end of the long kitchen table. 'Sit down if you prefer.'

She sat down, carefully resting her hands on her lap. Kite waited, but she showed no sign of speaking. He knew from experience that pressing someone too hard could be counter-productive, but he gave her a nudge nevertheless.

'I followed some tracks in the snow and they led me to the grave. When I saw his name, I decided that the footprints must be yours. And then I noticed too that it was the first anniversary of his death.'

'What do you want to know?' she said eventually.

'How did he die?'

'What does it matter to you?'

'Please…'

'It was at the factory. He climbed up a ladder and fell into a vat of hot jam.'

Kite jumped, so much so that hot tea spilt down

onto his trousers. He swore, then apologised, but Rose showed no sign of noticing.

'He was…' She hesitated and frowned, searching for the words, pain etched across her face. 'He was different. That's how I saw it, but people aren't kind to people who don't fit in. Six pennies short of a shilling they would say of him. Or other nastier things, like village idiot. But he wasn't an idiot. He was just slow. He needed guidance. Needed to be told exactly what to do and not do. Then he was fine.'

'And you weren't there?'

She shook her head.

'You were back here in the house I imagine.' Even as he said these words, Kite felt a shiver of self-disgust. His words were a trick, an attempt to trip her up, to see if she had something to hide. In terms of doing his job or trying to track down a murderer, there was nothing wrong in this, but nevertheless it felt anything but right. How could he stoop so low? What was he becoming?

'I was working at a munitions factory in Burton,' she said, passing his test in a single sentence. 'I was one of the canary girls. Mr Graves had been seconded there to help in the management, and he had to find some more workers, and so he wrote to Sir Wilfred and Lady Beatrice.'

'But weren't you needed here? By Lady Beatrice.'

'I suppose I was, but at the time it seemed important to me that I should do my bit for the troops, and Lady Beatrice promised she would look after Paul.'

'But couldn't Mr Graves have hired local women from Burton easily enough?'

'I think most of the unmarried women were already employed. But there was another reason. He wanted someone in the workforce he could trust. Be his eyes and ears. Things were going missing, and he needed my help. So, God forgive me, I went there and left Paul behind.'

'I am truly sorry about Paul, but I don't think you should blame yourself. Accidents happen. I saw too many men and women dead in factories during my time with the Metropolitan Force in London. Often the result of poor safety regulations.'

'When did you move to the Lincoln police?'

'In November.'

'So you took part in the strike in London?'

The conversation had taken a sharp turn. 'Yes,' he said. He didn't want to go down this path. He still had questions for her. Yet she was sitting waiting for him to say more and she seemed a sympathetic audience, unlike Captain Alec had been. He suddenly realised how much he craved the opportunity to put his side of the story to someone who was genuinely prepared to listen. So he continued.

'We weren't the money-grabbing traitors that the newspapers and politicians claimed. All we wanted was a fair wage, and a pension which would keep us alive when we retired, and pensions for our wives. The fact is that unskilled labourers were earning more than police constables with many years of experience.'

'Do you have a wife?'

The question caught Kite unawares and he felt his chest tighten. 'She died of the influenza. Like your girl Kay.'

'That must have been hard for you.'

There was silence then, as Kite tried to calm himself. Rose seemed a kind woman, and as if to prove it she leaned forward and rested her hand on his. He flinched, just as he had when Maud had placed her hand on his arm.

'Oh, oh I am so sorry. I shouldn't have, I—'

'It's fine. You were just being kind.' He was flustered. 'I wasn't expecting it. You took me by surprise.'

'Even so, I'm very sorry. I know what it is like to lose someone.'

She stood up, went over to the range, gave the big saucepan a stir and returned to her seat. 'So why did you move to Lincoln?' she said.

'I wasn't very popular with my inspector.'

'Because of the strike?'

'I was quite active in supporting it and he didn't like that at all. And after the prime minister agreed a deal, my inspector decided to make life difficult for me. So in the end I decided to leave the Metropolitan Force and apply for a job in Lincoln.'

'And how are you finding life in Lincoln?'

Kite laughed. 'Maybe it'll seem better in the summer, but right now it feels like jumping out of the frying pan and into the fire.'

'It's no fun being at the bottom of the pile. I look at the lives that the Walkers have, and I sometimes think they don't know they've been born.'

Kite and Sparrow were in the yard looking out across the snow. Sparrow's motorbike was propped up

163

between them, and Sparrow himself was all dressed to ride it. The overnight change in the weather had opened up an unexpected possibility. The temperature was now noticeably above freezing. Water was dripping merrily from the roof of the manor house, and in a few places even from the unheated outbuildings. And, encouragingly, the road which led to Lincoln was now visible. There was still plenty of snow on it, but its outline was apparent.

'Do you really think you'll get there in these conditions?'

Sparrow grinned. 'I'm used to driving in bad conditions. Not that this bike is as handy as the one I drove in the war, but even so I fancy my chances of making it.'

Kite felt uneasy. It had been Sparrow's idea, one which he had agreed to with alacrity, but now that he assessed it in the cold light of day, he was having his doubts.

'I need you to give the letter to the chief constable yourself. If he isn't at the station, go and knock on the door of his house. We have a very dangerous killer here, and I need armed police.'

'I do understand, sir.'

Sparrow pulled his goggles down, pulled his leather gauntlets on and gave a jaunty salute, like a lanky schoolboy off on a daring escapade. He gunned the motorcycle into life and with a wild spinning of the wheels headed towards the gates out and beyond. Kite watched for some time, observing how the motorbike slid from side to side, and wondering again how on earth Sparrow could possibly get all the way to

Lincoln. But if he could get as far as Crowthorpe, and if the phone line from Crowthorpe to Lincoln was operative, maybe he could ring from there. Or enlist the help of Lamyman.

Kite shrugged and turned back towards the house. Up on the first floor, a curtain twitched. He saw the figure of Elizabeth looking out. She lifted a hand in acknowledgement. Who else had seen Sparrow drive off? Rose knew because she had been in the kitchen while they had discussed it. She had given him a thick sandwich of meat and pickle for later. And no doubt by now she had taken a cup of tea up to Lady Beatrice and gossiped the latest news.

He was conscious that if he hadn't been before, he was himself certainly the centre of attention now. Every move he made was likely being observed and being discussed around the members of the household – at least one of whom was a murderer. In the meantime, he himself was on his own until Sparrow returned with reinforcements.

Kite was tempted to go back inside and warm himself up with a cup of tea, but he felt guilty about doing that while Sparrow was out there battling the snow. Instead he decided to go and walk round the boundaries of Crowthorpe Manor again. If, his thinking went, Mary had seen someone near the gate, then that person could easily have been someone from the house, and if so they would have been trying to get away from the scene, and then reappearing from the back of the house as if they had just been woken up by all the noise.

He started with the main gate, deciding to walk

clockwise, along the ha-ha which stretched right across the front of the house. When it ended and was replaced by the tall garden wall, he continued, stopping only when he reached a green gate set in the wall. He tried the handle and was surprised when the door opened. When Sparrow had checked it out on the first day, it had been locked. But now it wasn't. Had someone been using it? The killer? He went in and shut it behind him. There were two bolts and he debated whether to slide them shut. In the end he decided against it. There were tracks across the snow towards the house, but they were relatively fresh, made last night maybe, so could hardly be relevant to Sir Wilfred's murder.

But what about Mary? Might someone have entered the house from here in order to see her? Getting in via the door at the back of the west wing, sneaking in, up the stairs, killing her, down the stairs and out again, before re-entering the house via the front door.

Kite shivered and pulled his coat tighter around his body. The wind was still bitterly cold, even if the temperature had risen slightly. He turned and surveyed the trail of his own steps. If the door was only locked at night, anyone who knew this and was familiar with the layout of the house could have crept in and gone up to Mary's room and killed her. Maybe he had been wrong to rule out an outsider. And yet an outsider would have been at considerable risk of being noticed when coming in or going out. But not all outsiders. He had a sudden thought. Suppose the intruder had been the vicar or his wife? If they had encountered someone, they could easily have excused their presence in the house under the pretence of paying a pastoral visit. But wouldn't someone have mentioned this to him? Or did the whole household know more than they were letting on? Were they all secretly glad that Sir Wilfred was dead? Had they agreed what they should and should not say? Or was that too fanciful?

Kite shook his head in frustration. He needed help, that much he knew. And sooner rather than later. Anxiety was gnawing away inside him because a killer who had struck twice could very easily strike again, and there was no knowing who that third victim might be. Indeed the closer he got to the truth, then the more likely it became that he himself might be the next one on the murderer's list.

When Kite got back inside, it was to discover that Rose had rustled up some fatty bacon, eggs and bread, and a fresh brew of tea. He, she and Frank Tomkin sat at the kitchen table enjoying the spread and barely speaking until Tomkin casually asked him about Sparrow's expedition. Kite wasn't surprised by the question. Almost certainly Rose would have mentioned it.

'I've sent him back to Lincoln,' Kite said, offering nothing more than that. But his words sparked in Tomkin several gloomy observations: 'The road will be damned treacherous in these conditions'; 'I reckon we haven't seen the last of the snow'; and 'Sir Wilfred's barometer is dropping again.' But Kite concentrated on his food and asked for a refill of tea.

'Don't be so miserable, Frank,' Rose said. 'By all accounts Constable Sparrow was quite a motorcyclist on the Western Front. I dare say he can look after himself.'

'By his account, he was,' Tomkin said sharply. 'There's plenty of soldiers out there in the trenches who would have swapped their job with his at the drop of a hat.'

Kite looked up and found Rose gazing hard at Tomkin. Then she glanced across at Kite and rolled her eyes before returning her focus to Tomkin. 'Plenty of motorcyclists died out there too. He was a dab hand at motorcycling before the war, so it made sense for him to be assigned to those duties.'

Tomkin grunted, but he said no more.

Kite sipped at his tea and complimented Rose on the breakfast. She nodded her thanks and stood up. 'Perhaps you men can clear the things away for a change. I'll go and take a cup of tea to her ladyship.' She busied herself with a tray, and soon was gone.

'She's in a bit of a mood this morning,' Tomkin muttered. 'Why can't she clear the table herself when she comes back. I have plenty of my own jobs to do. If you ask me, Maud's been giving her dangerous ideas about the role of women. It's all very well for the women to do the men's jobs in the war, but now we're back, she should stick to the kitchen and the house, and I'll stick to my duties.'

Kite almost asked him what his duties were, now that there was no Sir Wilfred to chauffeur around, indeed no car in which to chauffeur anyone else around in either. But he resisted the temptation – Tomkin was in a miserable enough mood as it was. Instead he decided to take another tack.

'I guess it must have been difficult for you in the trenches.'

'It was difficult for everyone on the front line. The bombing, the mud, the not knowing when you might be going over the top, into the barbed wire and German machine gun fire.' His words petered to a halt. Bad memories flooding back Kite imagined. He saw Tomkin twitch, then shake his head as if trying to free himself of some unspoken horror.

'But you rescued the captain.'

'He got hit by a piece of shrapnel. I got him into a shell hole and kept him safe there until the worst was over. So he got sent home to recuperate, and I got rewarded with some time off too. Not as much as him, but more than many.'

'And you didn't suffer from shell shock?'

'No.'

'Bad dreams?'

'I still get them occasionally. Don't always sleep very well.'

'What about the captain?'

'You'll have to ask him. But I don't suppose many of us who survived sleep like babies anymore.'

Tomkin stood up. There was the sound of footprints approaching. 'Sounds like Rose returning,' he said. 'Best be getting on with it.' He began to clear away his things. Any thoughts of rebellion in the kitchen had dissipated like the morning mist. As she re-entered the kitchen, he brushed past her without a word.

'He's a sullen sod sometimes,' she said without emotion. 'Still, I guess after fighting in the trenches, you can't expect him to be a cheerful Charlie all the time.'

'Is he ever a cheerful Charlie?'

She frowned. 'He used to be.'

Kite was poised to get up, but Rose sat down opposite him and leaned forward. 'He's not the same man as he was before the war. He got a medal for saving the captain. But when he came back, it was like part of him had gone missing. He used to be… well, not the life and soul of the party, but up for a bit of fun. But since the war he's only seemed at peace when he's been cleaning that damned car, or tinkering with the engine, or driving Sir Wilfred here, there and everywhere. And of course until they buy a new car, he won't be able to do that. And as for buying a Rolls-Royce again, I can't see Lady Beatrice allowing it. She kicked up a real stink when Sir Wilfred bought that one.'

'Why was that?'

'Too extravagant. Sir Wilfred had a tendency to splash the money around, but she has always been much more careful. "It doesn't grow on a tree, Wilfred," she'd say, and he'd laugh. "In our case, my dear, it grows on trees and bushes and in the fields".'

'Does Frank talk about the war?'

'Not much. The Rolls-Royce, the weather, the horse racing, but not the war. Who does? Mostly it's them that never fought as far as I can see.'

Kite made his way back upstairs with heavy legs. He needed to use the toilet and after that clear his head. He had a headache coming on. Not unusual for him, and he had had the foresight to pack some powders.

A dose of them and he would soon be feeling better. And all being well, Sparrow and some reinforcements would be back by that evening. He had asked for a couple of constables, armed with rifles. Being stuck out in the back end of Lincolnshire, cut off by the snow, made him feel all too acutely the precariousness of his situation. A man who had killed Sir Wilfred and Mary in such horrific ways was a man to be feared, for surely it had to be a man, not a woman. Or was that being naive?

When he was a fresh-faced new policeman, his sergeant had regaled him (on several occasions and at considerable length) with the story of how he had arrested one Mary Pearcey for murdering Phoebe Hoggs, the wife of her lover Frank Hoggs. But she hadn't killed only Phoebe, but the wretched woman's eighteen-month-old daughter too. The clinching evidence, bloodstained knives, had been found in the woman's kitchen in Camden Town. Women were less likely than men to commit murder, Kite acknowledged to himself, but women were also capable of the most horrendous acts. What about the baby farmers Amelia Dyer, Amelia Sach and Annie Walters? They had each been paid to look after babies who they then slaughtered (poison and strangulation were their favoured methods) before disposing of them in the River Thames? Quite how many defenceless innocents had been killed by them no-one knew, but at least those three women had, like Mary Pearcey, breathed their last at the end of the hangman's rope.

Kite sat down on his bed. He was shivering. He didn't know why as it wasn't excessively cold inside.

Maybe it was nerves, the case 'getting to him' as his mother would have said. Or maybe it was the sense of morbid doom which had risen like a monster from the deep and begun to wrap its tentacles around him. The snow, the sabotaged phone line, two brutal deaths, and the lies and deceits which had spread through the household like the Spanish influenza. But if there was one thing which most disturbed him, it was the hideous image of Mary Graves, eyes wide open with the can of Tickler's jam rammed into her mouth. The very thought of it made his gorge rise. Suddenly he was up on his feet and beating a path to the toilet, arriving just in time to vomit up his eggs and bacon into the bowl rather than all over the floor.

He made his way back to his bedroom and opened the window, sucking the cold air into his lungs. He spat, trying to rid his mouth of the foul taste of regurgitated food. He looked out across the fields, still largely pristine white. There were tracks all around the yard, and of course tracks leading out of the gates onto the road which led all the way of Lincoln and…

Kite gasped. In the distance on that half-hidden road was a figure. He stood and watched for a couple of minutes. If Kite's eyesight wasn't deceiving him, that person was heading towards the manor. And, Kite was almost certain, that man (surely it was a man) was pushing a motorbike.

Wrapped up in his coat, hat and gloves, Kite trudged as far at the gate and then stopped. He would rather have lain down on his bed for an hour, but that would have been absurd. He ought to keep walking and meet Sparrow out on the road and find out what on earth had gone wrong, but what was the point? He would know soon enough and whatever else he needed to do, he needed to preserve his energy and not collapse again. So he stood there, leaning against the gate and watching Sparrow get closer and closer.

The first thing Sparrow did when he arrived was push his motorbike over into a drift of snow that had piled up by the western side of the entrance. He turned and faced Kite, arms on hips, breathing heavily. His face was red and despite the cold it was damp with perspiration.

'What happened?' Kite tried to sound calm and unflustered, but he doubted that Sparrow was taken in.

'I'm not sure.' Sparrow bent forward, taking in deep breaths of air. 'It started coughing when I was about a mile down the road and then it just came to a stop. There's plenty of fuel in the tank. I filled it up myself last night.'

'What's happened?' The voice of Tomkin boomed out behind them. He was hurrying across the snow.

'There's a problem with the motorbike.'

'In that case why don't I take a look. Your constable looks like he could do with a sit down and a mug of hot tea.'

While Sparrow headed off towards the house, Kite followed Tomkin across the yard, now rutted with frozen snow and ice. Though the clouds were higher than they had been on previous days, the air seemed colder, whipping in from the frozen north and cutting deep into Kite's fallible frame.

Tomkin settled the motorbike in one of the farthest

sheds. 'Got all my tools here,' he said cheerfully. 'With a bit of luck I should be able to fix it.'

'I do hope so.'

'It's a lovely motorbike. A Lincoln Elk 6 hp Twin Model A if I'm not mistaken.'

'Sparrow seems to like riding it.'

'He's a lucky chap. Very new, made in Lincoln of course.'

'I'm not much into the technicalities. At least it got me and Sparrow here before the snow set in. Mind you, it wasn't that comfortable riding pillion.'

'I'm surprised they didn't buy a sidecar and stick you in that.'

'Money I expect.' Which wasn't exactly the whole story. Kite knew he wasn't the most popular man in the Lincoln force. His involvement in the previous year's strike in London, being an 'incomer', a man from London who knew nothing about how things worked out in the shires, all these things weighed against him. A sidecar was a luxury that the chief constable would never have allowed. Kite felt like a lepper every time he was in the station or working alongside any of the others. Which was why Sparrow had, for all his gung-ho characteristics, been a much better colleague than he could have hoped for. He had a reputation for insubordination, but that had not been Kite's experience of him.

'This would cost a pretty penny.' Tomkin had already started to wipe the bike down.

Kite didn't respond because he wanted Tomkin to focus on the job. Instead he went and sat down on a wooden trunk pushed up against the wall. The room was well ordered, with tools hanging from nails and hooks on the wall, and a long trestle table holding boxes of different sizes. Kite wasn't surprised. Tomkin was clearly much valued for his practical skills and it would have been striking if he didn't run a neat and tidy show inside this, his personal domain. Kite sat still and silent, and even closed his eyes, waiting for Tomkin to pronounce.

'My guess is that something has got into the fuel,' he said loudly. Kite sat up with a start, embarrassed that he may have fallen asleep and – even worse – that Tomkin had noticed.

'What makes you think that?'

'Firstly because there is no obvious physical sign of damage, nothing missing or out of shape.' He frowned, then began to unscrew the fuel cap. He put it carefully down on a white cotton sheet which he had laid on the ground, then ran his finger slowly round the exposed entrance to the fuel camp. Then he sniffed his finger, touched his tongue with it very briefly, and then wiped his finger on the white sheet.

'Well?' Kite was suddenly impatient.

'I thought maybe someone had doctored it with sugar, but I don't think so. You look on the sheet there.' He waited while Kite moved over and squatted down to take a look. 'That looks like sand or something like it. I reckon if some of that had got into the fuel tank…' He paused. 'What I'm saying is that if enough of that got sucked up into the carburettor, it would cause the engine to cough and splutter and then die.'

'So you're saying this looks like sabotage?'

'That's for you to decide. Maybe your constable,

for all his fine talk, doesn't look after his machine as well as he might.'

'He's hardly likely to drop a lump of sand or soil into a fuel tank.'

'Like I say, that's for you to decide. All I will say is that if it was me and I was going to cripple his motorbike, that's how I would do it. Only I'd clean round the fuel cap when I'd finished.'

'Do you think you could get it working again?'

'I would certainly hope so. It'll take an hour or two, maybe more, but all being well—'

'What about fuel? Did you lose it all when Sir Wilfred was murdered?'

'No, I've got some in reserve. I never knew if and when he might want me to drive him somewhere.'

Tomkin's comment was for Kite like a wake-up call. How could he not have asked Tomkin about this before. How had he failed to do so. 'So where did you take him in the days before he died? I suppose mostly to the Crowthorpe Jam factory, but did you drive him anywhere else. Anywhere unusual?'

Tomkin considered the question. Whether he was struggling to remember where he might have gone (unlikely Kite reckoned) or was wondering whether he should keep quiet about it, only Tomkin himself knew. In the end he was quite precise.

'About three weeks ago I took him to Lincoln. I dropped him off at the White Hart in Bailgate, up near the cathedral. You may know it. The best establishment in the city. Got there about eleven thirty. He had lunch there and I drove him back home in the afternoon.'

'And who did he have lunch with?'

There was a pause before Tomkin replied with a chuckle. 'Not with me. He gave me some money and told me to go to the pub up the road.'

'Do you have any idea who he was meeting?'

'No.' There was no hesitation this time.

'Male or female?'

'I didn't see them.'

'Did he often meet people in the White Hart?'

'It wasn't his usual place for doing business in Lincoln if that's what you mean.'

'So it was a business meeting?'

Tomkin leaned forward. 'I really don't know, Sergeant,' he growled. 'You can ask me as many times as you like, but the answer will remain the same. I don't know!'

'Sorry!' Kite held up his hands defensively. 'Old habits. I'm a bit like a ferret chasing a rabbit sometimes. But maybe I can just ask this other question. Did you get any impression as you drove him home as to whether it had been a good lunch meeting or a bad one?'

Tomkin ran a hand through his hair. He smiled. 'Actually, now I think of it, I'd say he was in a very good mood. So whatever it was, it had gone well.'

'And how often did you drive him to Lincoln?'

'Three or four times a year.'

'Just him, or did Lady Beatrice sometimes accompany him?'

'Sometimes she did. But not always.'

Kite considered this. There might be, he felt, something significant about this trip to Lincoln. It wasn't Sir Wilfred's preferred place to meet in the city. So had someone else invited him there? Was it they who were calling the shots? The alternative was that it was nothing to do with business, but something more personal. Was he meeting a woman? Was he having an affair? Whatever it was, one thing was clear. He had not wanted Tomkin to know who he was seeing.

'Is that it?' Tomkin said, bursting into his thoughts. 'Because if you want me to fix this motorbike, then I need to concentrate.'

'Actually, there is one thing more. Before the phone was sabotaged, I rang Greystone House and spoke to a Miss Kempton, who seems to be in charge there.'

Kite looked up and saw that Tomkin had a wary look on his face.

'The interesting thing is that she remembered the visit which Mrs Elizabeth made to Greystone to visit her husband. You drove her there of course, and you stayed nearby in a hotel.' He paused, curious to observe Tomkin's reaction. Tomkin half-nodded, but his mouth was tightly closed. 'This was the occasion when Mrs Elizabeth and Captain Alec conceived the baby – or so I was told. But by the time I had finished speaking to Miss Kempton, it was clear to me that that could not possibly have been the case because the captain was very ill, not with a shoulder injury as I presume you are aware, but with shell shock. So ill, in fact, so out of his mind that he didn't even recognise her, let alone want to sleep with her. Miss Kempton had to ask her to return home since her presence was very distressing for him.'

He paused, letting this sink in, before he asked his killer question. 'Frank Tomkin, I have to ask, are you the father of Mrs Elizabeth's baby?'

Kite and Sparrow found Elizabeth in the library with her sister-in-law Maud. They were sitting at the circular table in the middle of the room, heads lowered as they studied a newspaper. There was a fire burning in the small fireplace – it seemed comforting to Kite rather than significantly warming. Both women looked up at the same moment, rather guiltily he thought.

'Oh, it's only you,' Maud said. 'Thank goodness for that.'

Kite half smiled. 'That's not what people usually say when I interrupt them.'

'Alec doesn't like me giving Elizabeth what he would call "dangerously subversive ideas".'

'You mean votes for women?'

'Not just votes. Ideas about the role of women in what is a world dominated by the male of the human species.'

'I see.'

'They expect us females to do their every whim.' Having got an audience, Maud had no intention of letting the opportunity to argue her cause pass by. 'To go through the hell of childbirth in order to produce their babies of course, or to be more precise produce male babies who can be their heirs. To look after those children. To run the household while dressing to please those men. To sit quietly at dinner and agree with everything they say. Why should we put up with all this? So I am encouraging Elizabeth not to succumb to these intolerable ideas.'

'And did your father hold these same intolerable ideas?'

'Indeed he did.'

'Yet he encouraged you to help him run the business during the war, did he not?'

'He permitted me to help. That is very different from *encouraged*.' She flared with indignation. 'I kept insisting I could help, but it was only when David was seconded to go and work at the munitions factory that my father gave way.'

'Yes, Mr Graves told me about that.'

'They built a huge one at Burton on Trent. They needed lots of people there. David was there in some sort of managerial role for the best part of two years – telling the women what to do and when; of course, they probably knew the job better than him. He even persuaded Rose to go and work there too for a while. Mother was furious and blamed David for dragging her away. She tried various different women from the village to take Rose's place, but they were all sent packing after a few weeks. Finally she managed to pull a few strings to get Rose back because she couldn't cope without her. And of course when she arrived at the front door, she was yellow.' Maud laughed. 'No wonder they called them the canary girls. Wasn't she a sight, Elizabeth?'

Elizabeth nodded, glancing at Maud as she did so, but avoiding looking at Kite. 'She was indeed. But she went back to normal soon enough, thank goodness.'

Kite waited in the corridor, pretending to admire the hunting prints on the walls. Killing foxes for fun didn't appeal to him. He had seen too many people brutally murdered to take any pleasure in a chase which ended with the tearing to pieces of a cornered or exhausted animal. He moved slowly from one to the next wondering how long he would have to wait, and wondering too if what he had in mind was very foolish. Maud had gone to see her horses and Elizabeth to the toilet.

He heard the noise of water being flushed away, and of taps being turned on, and he stood very still. He dawdled in front of a racing print – a blue and gold liveried rider driving his horse to victory, left hand lifted high as he prepared to bring his whip down on his steed's flank. He turned as the door opened and Elizabeth appeared. She stopped and for a few moments they stared at each other.

'Sergeant Kite, I wasn't expecting to see you here.' She laughed, though it seemed to Kite more like a nervous laugh than anything else.

'I need to speak to you,' he whispered.

'Again? I thought you had asked all your questions.'

'Not here, somewhere quiet where there is no risk of us being overheard.'

He saw alarm flicker across her face. 'Why?' she said. Her voice had dropped to a whisper too.

'Let's try the billiard room. I don't suppose anyone will be there at this time of day.'

She paused, as if about to disagree with his plan, but then shrugged, turned around and began to walk down the long corridor. Kite followed, and when they had both entered the room, he shut the door quietly behind him. She sat down on one of the four chairs ranged on the far side of the room. He took hold of one of the others and positioned it opposite her.

'Well, what is this all about?' She spoke briskly, as if this was an irritation to her programme for the day.

'Yesterday, before the telephone was sabotaged, I spoke to a Miss Kempton at Greystone.'

'Miss Kempton?' She frowned. 'The name rings a bell.'

'She is the matron there. You would most certainly have met her when you visited your husband at Greystone.'

'I suppose I must have.' She put on a display of struggling to remember. Kite waited unimpressed. 'Let me see. Steel grey hair, overweight, and a rather sharp manner. Would that be her?'

'I wouldn't know that as I haven't met her. But certainly a firm manner. One thing I do know with great certainty is that it was she who had to tell you to go home because your attempts to talk to your husband were upsetting him a great deal.'

'It wasn't like that.'

'I also know he wasn't in there just for his shoulder injury. He had shell shock, so badly that when you visited him he didn't know who you were.'

She shifted in her chair and placed both hands over her bulging stomach as if to hold it in place. 'What exactly are you trying to say, Sergeant?'

'Elizabeth, what I am saying is that to judge from what Miss Kempton told me, your husband could not possibly have impregnated you during the three days you tried to see him at Greystone. So I do therefore have to ask you who the father of your child is.'

She stood up suddenly. Her face was a mask of fury. 'How dare you! I only have to ask, and my husband will horse-whip you out of this house.'

Kite stood up too. 'But you won't ask him and he won't do it. Because you and he have to believe that it is his baby.' He paused, taking in a deep breath before continuing, in a calmer tone. 'Mrs Walker.' He was pleading now. 'I need to know the truth. I need to know it so that I can prevent anyone else in this house being murdered like poor Mary. I am convinced that your secret is at the centre of this murderous mystery. But that does not mean it will have to be revealed in court or indeed to anyone else. I understand the shame you would be subjected to, and let me assure you I will protect your secret if I possibly can.'

She stepped forward and before Kite could react she swung her right arm and slapped him hard on the side of his face. He almost yelped.

'You know nothing about what it is like to be in my shoes. You know nothing about what it is like to be a powerless woman. You think you are a good man, but in reality you want to ruin our family. You want to make an arrest, and you don't care what damage you wreak on the rest of us.'

'I seek only the truth.'

'You sound like that wretched Reverend Ransom. "I seek only to do God's will on earth." That's what he says when he comes knocking on our door. When actually what he wants is my father-in-law's money, not to mention a free meal and as much wine as he can drink.'

'Please, Mrs Walker. I will ask you again. I beg you to trust me. Who is the father of your baby?'

She looked at Kite and said nothing. Then it was as if all the fury and blood had been drained from her face until it was as colourless and cold as the sky outside.

'Is it Frank Tomkin?' he said softly.

Again she said nothing.

'Because David Graves was away at the Burton munitions at the time. So it couldn't have been him. So if it wasn't Tomkin, then there are not very many possibilities left. In fact—'

'It was him,' she hissed, before turning away and exiting the room, one hand protectively cradling her unborn child.

Kite sat down. He wished a hole would open at his feet and he would disappear deep into the earth. What was he doing? Why had he forced the poor woman to answer his appalling question. What sort of man was he? And what had been the point? Because the fact was that he didn't believe her. Not for a minute.

'Ah, there you are,' said Kite.

Rose turned round. He had been searching for her round the house, and had finally found her in the large sitting room. Her face was red and she was holding a cloth in her left hand. She looked flustered. And her response to him wasn't welcoming. 'Detective Sergeant Kite. It's you again.'

'It's me again. Turning up like the bad penny.'

'I am rather busy.'

'I need to ask you something.'

'I really can't stop now or I'll have Lady Beatrice to answer to. Or if not her, then Maud.' She turned away and began to rub hard at the large dresser.

'Well, I do have one query.'

'Oh yes?' Her left hand was working like a piston.

'I seem to remember you saying that from about half past nine on the night Sir Wilfred was killed, you were in bed reading a magazine – *The Lady*.'

'That's correct.'

'I don't suppose anyone can corroborate that?'

'Corroborate? What are you talking about?' She had paused in her dusting, but now returned to it with a vengeance.

'Your brother was killed in a factory owned by Sir Wilfred.'

'Everyone knows that.' Her dusting became even more ferocious.

'But everyone was careful not to mention it to me. But that is by the by. My understanding is that Paul only started working in the factory after you went to work in the munitions factory.'

She didn't respond, but she did stop polishing, and stood very still.

'And that it was Sir Wilfred who insisted that Paul go and work in the factory.'

She turned round. Her face was taut. 'I wouldn't know. I wasn't here.'

'Didn't you ask around? You had expected him to be looked after and—'

'Yes, of course I expected him to be looked after. Paul could be useful as long as he was properly supervised. He was a help round the house for me, getting firewood and coal, carrying the laundry and anything heavy. But the women they hired to take my place were fussy old women who made no allowances for him. They were horrible to him. And they complained to Lady Beatrice and Sir Wilfred and that is why he was moved to the factory. Because of them. The accident was very unfortunate, and I was very angry about it at the time. But it was the war and I can see now that Paul had to do something.'

'And I can see that it might give you a very strong motive to kill Sir Wilfred.'

Rose twisted the rag in her hands, tighter and tighter, as if it was wet and she was determined to squeeze every last drop of moisture out of it. Her mouth opened, but no words came out. Kite waited. He was in no rush.

'I did *not* kill him,' she said finally, her voice hoarse and breathless. 'How could I when I was in my room?'

'You say you were in your room, but I only have your word for it. As far as I can see, you could easily have slipped down the back stairs in a dressing gown and night clothes, out the back door, circled round to the garage where Sir Wilfred was sitting in his car, and killed him, before retracing your steps. Then when the car exploded, you just joined everyone else in the confusion as they rushed down to find out what had happened.'

'Couldn't any of the others have done just that? Why pick on me?' Her voice had reached a startling pitch. 'Because I'm a servant and I'm an easy target? Is that it? You'll arrest me and everyone will be convinced that I must have done it. How could one of his own family have killed him, they'll say. Much more likely to be his slatternly slut of a maid servant.'

'Rose, it is my opinion that you have a very powerful reason to want to kill him. Above all, I cannot think that it is merely coincidence that he died on the anniversary of your brother's death. I can imagine how much that must have gnawed away at you until you reached the point where you just had to take revenge for Paul.'

'You think you're so clever don't you.' The words flew fast and furious from her lips. 'You think you're the big detective from the Metropolitan Force in London. Except that they couldn't wait to get rid of you after the strike. And now you're not too popular in Lincoln either. Which is why you're desperate to catch Sir Wilfred's murderer, to prove to your new boss how good a detective you are. And if you can't actually discover who did it, you'll pin it on someone, anyone – and that anyone is me.'

Kite found himself reeling under her assault, and he found himself doubting his own judgement too. Perhaps he had got it wrong. Sir Wilfred was clearly a man who could make enemies in his sleep. What about that secretive meeting Lincoln? And how did the pregnancy of Elizabeth fit in? Had Sir Wilfred discovered that Alec couldn't possibly be the father? Had he threatened to expose the lie, or maybe disown her and get Alec to divorce her? And why did the killer use Tickler's jam as his *coup de grâce* in the killings of both Sir Wilfred and Mary? Kite was sweating, but he felt a sudden chill too, not through fear, but something equally elemental: his body's need for food. If he didn't have some soon—

'I can prove I didn't kill Sir Wilfred,' Rose said quietly.

Kite didn't register what she was saying because he was struggling to stay on his feet. Rose repeated her words, more forcefully this time. 'I said, I can prove it wasn't me.'

Kite looked at her, trying to focus on what she had to say. 'What do you mean?'

'I was in my bed from about half past nine until the moment the car exploded. Lady Beatrice had let me borrow *The Lady* magazine. But I was not reading it. Frank will confirm that, because he was in bed with me. All of that time too.'

'He was?' Kite's head was beginning to spin. He forced himself to his feet. 'Can I have a glass of water?'

Rose hesitated, studying him as if he was some unusual garden insect that she had come across in her kitchen. He could imagine her squashing any such intruder without mercy in order to protect her.

'Of course,' she said. She moved swiftly to give him a glass of water fresh from the tap.

He drank it greedily. He would have liked something to eat too, a sandwich rather than yet more cake, but unusually he could see no sign of bread or cake anywhere. In any case, he told himself, he needed to speak to Tomkin.

He made his way to the front door, pulled his coat on, and was just buttoning himself up when the door opened and in stepped Sparrow.

'Where have you been?' Kite wasn't particularly concerned, but he felt he should say something.

'Just been talking to the captain.'

'Well I need to talk to Tomkin. And I want you there.'

'Yes, sir. Any particular reason why you want to speak to him?'

'Of course there is,' Kite snapped. 'I wouldn't be going out into the cold unless there was a damned good reason.'

'I merely meant…' Sparrow started to speak, but then thought the better of it.

Kite was aware that he was being unreasonably irritable, but that was the least of his problems. He had almost convinced himself that Rose was the person most likely to have killed Sir Wilfred, and yet when confronted with the accusation she had rolled out proof that it couldn't have been her. Or at least an alibi that he would have trouble breaking – unless Tomkin denied he had been in bed with her.

'Constable,' he snapped, 'did you happen to see Frank Tomkin while you were chatting to the captain?'

'No, sir. Not since I brought the motorbike back.'

'Ah, the motorbike. Well that's where he'll be. Trying to fix it, I hope. Let's go and find him.'

They made their way across the yard in silence except for the crunch of ice and snow underfoot. The clouds were dark and low. Kite stopped and looked up. 'More snow soon if I'm not mistaken.'

'That's what the captain said.'

'Anyway,' Kite said, as he resumed his steady plod, 'what exactly were you and the captain talking about?'

'The war mostly. He was telling me he wants to write a book about it.'

'A book?'

'Telling everyone what it was really like fighting in the trenches.'

'Did he by any chance mention his time at Greystone?'

'No, he didn't.'

'Did he admit to having shell shock?'

'No. I asked him about his shoulder, and he merely said it had taken time to get right. Then he started asking me questions about my time in France.'

'Did you ever see him while you were on the front line?'

'Once, from a distance. He was giving someone an earful. I stayed clear. Besides, I was looking for his colonel. I had some despatches I needed to deliver.'

Kite grunted. They were approaching Tomkin's workshop. The doors were closed against the cold, but when they got there and Sparrow pulled them open, there was no sign of Tomkin.

'Is this the right place?' Sparrow said.

'Of course it's the right place. Look at it!' He swung his arm in a wide arc. 'What do you think it is? A ladies millinery store?'

'And you left him repairing the motorbike? Because it's not here either.'

'I have noticed that, Constable.'

'Maybe he's taken it out for a test run.'

'How long were you out here talking to the captain? Didn't you hear anything?'

'We weren't talking here. The captain wanted to go and see the Reverend Ransom about his father's funeral, so I went along with him in case I could learn anything useful.'

'And did you discover anything useful?'

Sparrow frowned. 'The problem was that the captain wanted to talk to him in private. They walked across to the church, and I was left in the cottage with his wife. She made me a cup of tea, so I reckon I got the best deal!'

'So you didn't learn anything useful from either of them?'

'No… I mean it was clear from what she said that neither of them liked Sir Wilfred, and she was fed up with being in that tiny house with just him to talk to. He's rather old for her and I—'

'We are trying to catch a killer, not entertain the ladies, Sparrow.' He stamped his feet on the hard ground, as frustration took a grip of him. 'Let us go and see if we can find Tomkin. Maybe he fixed the bike and it's broken down again.'

'Yes, sir. Of course, sir. I hope he has fixed it because otherwise I'll have the chief constable tearing my ear off for failing to look after police property.'

Kite sighed loudly. 'I dare say it will be me who gets the blame. Not you.' He knew how these things worked. He was, after all, top of Bostock's *persona non grata* list.

Outside it took very little time to establish that the few motorbike tracks headed out towards the main front gate. It was clear from the footprints where Tomkin had trudged to his workshop with the broken bike. A fresher set of tyre tracks were roughly parallel, also towards that same gate.

They stopped after a short while, and Sparrow squatted down. 'To judge from these footprints, he was pushing the bike, not riding it at this point.'

Kite frowned. 'Maybe he was trying to avoid attracting attention.'

'What do you mean?'

'Can you hear the sound of a distant motorbike anywhere, Constable?'

Sparrow looked around, staring into the distance towards Lincoln. 'No.'

'Tomkin has driven off on the motorbike and, if he hasn't broken down, that means—'

'He's ruddy well scarpered!'

'Yes.'

For several seconds, they were both silent. Then Sparrow spat out his thoughts: 'Bloody hell, he's the killer, ain't he! He killed Sir Wilfred and Mary. Not only that, he's now done a runner on my ruddy motorbike.' He made it sound as though the theft of the motorbike was a worse crime than a double murder.

Kite scratched at his chin. 'I'm not so sure.'

'Why not, sir? It stands to reason.'

'Unfortunately he has an alibi.' Kite let his words hang in the stillness of the winter air.

'What on earth are you talking about, sir?!'

'At the time that Sir Wilfred was murdered – from half-past nine until the time the explosion took place – he was in Rose's bed.'

'What? Him and Rose? But I'm sure she said she

had been reading a copy of *The Lady* magazine. I bet it is in my notebook.'

'That is what I remember her saying too. But I needed to put some pressure on her because I thought she was not being entirely truthful, so I accused her of killing Sir Wilfred. Of course, she denied it at first, but then she told me that she could prove she hadn't because Frank Tomkin would vouch for the fact that they were in bed together in her room.'

'And you believe her?'

'I know what she said. Whether she is lying... well, that's the reason I need to talk to Tomkin.'

'So... so why has he done a runner if he didn't do it?'

'I really don't know, Constable. I wish I did.'

'But what made you think that Rose had killed Sir Wilfred?'

Kite began to walk again, up as far as the gate and then beyond until he could see where Tomkin's footprints disappeared, where he must have started the motorbike and headed off on the Lincoln road. He stood and looked around at the landscape still white and flat as far as he could see. Above the sky was an uninterrupted expanse of lowering grey cloud. He wondered if they were due more snow that night.

'Penny for your thoughts, sir.' Sparrow was like – Kite smiled at the thought – Sparrow was just like a sparrow, hopping around seeking out tit-bits to keep his curiosity satisfied.

He shivered. 'Let's get inside.' He trudged back to the house, desperate to get into its shelter. He fumbled at his buttons, heaved his coat off and hung it up, then leant against the wall.

'Sir?' Sparrow was persistent as well as curious.

Kite took in a deep breath. He was feeling dreadful. 'There is one reason why Tomkin may have set off on the bike and then decided not to come back.' He paused, he needed to sit down, he needed—

'What's that, sir?'

'If he was the father of Elizabeth Walker's child.'

And then Kite collapsed.

'Are you all right, sir?'

Kite opened his eyes. It took a few seconds for him to work out that he was lying on the floor. Someone was leaning over him, but he couldn't work out who it was. It was all a blur.

'Sir?' That must be Sparrow.

He sensed that somewhere in the background there were others observing his embarrassment. Someone was giving orders, though quite what those were didn't break into his consciousness. A woman's voice. It might be Maud, he decided, leading from the front. He hoped so. He felt safe in her hands.

'He's not looking too good.' Not Sparrow. But he really couldn't work it out.

'It's a shame that we cannot contact the doctor,' someone said. Female.

'Yes indeed. But with the phone being out of action—' Male.

'And the motorcycle gone—' Male.

'And I am certainly not risking my horse in the snow.' Female. That was surely Maud.

Kite wanted to open his eyes, to push himself up and tell them all that he would be all right in a little while. Food and drink and a short rest, that was all he needed.

But he couldn't, and besides they seemed to have made a decision on his care because Kite felt hands grabbing him under his armpits and legs, lifting him to the side, and then lowering him back down again. He was still on his back.

'Let's get him upstairs to his bed.' He had given up trying to work out who was saying what. What did it matter? He just needed some sustenance and sleep and then he would soon be feeling better.

'One, two, three!' came the order and then he was being lifted. He was, he realised, on a stretcher. He managed to open his eyes a crack, but only for a moment or two. He could see the back of the man at the front – that looked like Sparrow in his police uniform – but he didn't know who was holding the other end immediately behind him. Not Tomkin, obviously, so maybe David Graves or the captain or possibly the vicar, except that if it was the vicar, wouldn't he have been spouting prayers over him?

Kite gave up trying to open his eyes. If he wasn't going to be fed, then he would settle for a nice long snooze. He felt himself being moved. The stretcher bearer in front swung left. Was that towards the kitchen? He wasn't sure because he couldn't remember where he was when he collapsed. His guess was that they were taking him to his bedroom, so through the kitchen and then up the stairs two flights. He hoped to hell that they didn't drop him. But Sparrow was strong. He must have carried a few injured soldiers on the front line, even though to judge from the way he talked he had constantly been on his motorbike, almost single-handedly winning the war.

THAT NIGHT

IT WAS JUST past nine o'clock when someone tapped on the solid green door of the Bostock household. Brenda sat up abruptly in her armchair. She had been trying to darn one of her husband's socks and had drifted off into the land of not-quite-asleep.

For a moment she wondered if she had imagined it. She certainly wasn't expecting anyone. None of her friends would call unannounced at this time of night. And even her husband's cronies rarely risked doing so. Early on in her marriage, she had established the house rules, and one of those expressly ruled out drunken colleagues calling round without very good reason. But now that her husband had risen to the heights of chief constable, it had become harder to enforce her rules if he took exception to them. 'I won't be told what to do at work,' he had said once after returning home very much the worse for wear, 'and I'll be damned if I'm going to be told what to do in my own house.'

She stood up and went to the window, but before she could draw the curtain back there was another much louder knocking on the front door. She peered out and was just able to make out a man in heavy dark clothing accompanied by one of the uniformed policemen from the station, a new constable she thought. She would have to put him straight, but first she needed to answer the door before one of them knocked it off its hinges.

'One moment,' she called as she entered the

corridor. She cocked her head, but there was no sign of her husband appearing from the small room at the back of the house which he called his study. It was, in reality, more of a private space into which he retreated after supper to drink his whisky. That was rather an extravagance in her eyes, but she had discovered the hard way that sometimes it was necessary to make concessions in order to maintain some sort of control of a man. Her mother had taught her that, and she had learned her lesson very well.

She advanced on the front door, unbolted it and pulled it open. 'Constable,' she snapped, 'do you have any idea what time it is?'

The man blanched. He was very young and skinny and looked distinctly alarmed. Perhaps he had already been warned about her reputation, and if so she was well pleased. But most likely the sergeant on duty had deliberately sent him on this task as a joke. Well, he would soon learn that calling on her was no laughing matter. And she would find out too who the duty sergeant was and make sure he never tried this trick again.

'You... you... you are Mrs Bostock?' the man stammered.

'Yes I am. But what is your name and rank?'

He shivered. 'Con... Constable Light, ma'am. I was hoping I might speak to your husband.' The words stumbled out of his mouth. 'This erm... this gentleman needs to impart some information to the chief constable most urgently.' He glanced back at the man behind him, who now advanced a step into the light. A tall man, well built, neat moustache, filthy coat. Forty or so she guessed. Ex-army to judge from his bearing, but then who wasn't these days? She prided herself on weighing up people. She was better at it than her husband.

'What is so urgent that it cannot wait until the morning?'

The man stepped forward another pace, gently easing the constable out of the way. 'It concerns a case of murder.'

'Murder? But of whom. When?'

'Your husband is already aware of it. I am a messenger from his detective sergeant. I have been despatched by the sergeant to deliver some information about these events to Chief Constable Bostock with the utmost urgency.'

'My husband has gone to bed,' she replied tersely. 'But if you give me this information then I will pass it on as soon as he is awake in the morning.'

'I am afraid I must insist on speaking to the chief constable myself. It is a very grave matter and any unnecessary delay may cause further deaths.'

Brenda Bostock considered this. She was intrigued. She knew that she would have to let the man into the house, and after she had got him settled she would have to winkle her husband out of his study and hope that he wasn't too drunk. But she was as nosey as the next person when she sensed a secret to be sniffed out. Besides her friends would be fascinated by the inside story on a murder. But there was something else, something familiar about the man. She could swear that she had seen him before, quite recently in fact, and he had been looking a lot smarter then than he was now.

'What exactly is your name, sir? You can hardly expect me to disturb my husband if I don't even know who you are.'

But the man merely shrugged. 'This is very sensitive official police business, so I am sure that a woman of your status will understand if I say that I am reluctant to take up your very kind suggestion.' Another apologetic shrug. He was, Mrs Bostock could see, a very self-confident and smart operator. 'I will impart everything – including my name – to the chief constable, and then he may tell you as much or as little as he sees fit.'

Brenda Bostock drew herself up to her full height. With the advantage of the doorstep, she was fractionally taller than the man, but she knew that she had lost her battle with him. She was not used to being outmanoeuvred, but she realised with some surprise that she didn't mind too much on this occasion. In fact she rather admired the man for standing his ground. Besides he was an attractive looking fellow too, and if she hadn't been yoked to her wretched husband, maybe in another life… maybe…

'Mrs Bostock?' He smiled, demonstrating that he could be a charmer too. 'I do appreciate that my appearing unannounced at this time of night is most inappropriate and unsettling, but believe me when I say that the circumstances are both critical and urgent.'

There was a moment of intense scrutiny as each of them looked at the other. Then she yielded ground. 'Come in, sir.'

She let him pass, but stepped across in front of the bemused constable. 'Not you. You go back to your station. And let me make something clear, Constable Light. This conversation between myself and this gentleman is not to be discussed with anyone at the station.'

'Yes, yes, ma'am.'

'One word from me to my husband, and your career in the police force will be over. Do I make myself clear?'

He nodded nervously, backing away into the street and almost slipping over on the ice.

She smothered a smile and shut the door firmly behind him.

'So,' she said, 'Mr Man-with-no-name, I expect you would like a cup of tea.'

'It's been a long day.'

'How about a piece of cake too, then?'

'Who the devil are you?' The voice belonged to Chief Constable Bostock, who had emerged from his lair at the back of the house in trousers and collarless shirt.

'Detective Sergeant Kite sent me,' he said quickly. 'He insisted I call on you however late it was.'

'Did he now?'

'I was going to make him a cup of tea and give him some food,' Mrs Bostock said. She was determined to be part of whatever it was that was unfolding.

Her husband gave a harsh laugh. 'Probably prefer a whisky, I imagine.'

'He's hungry,' she insisted. 'He's had long day…'

'Very well. Bring him something to eat. We'll sit in

the parlour.'

Mrs Bostock laid a tray of tea and cakes and scones and jam in half the time that it normally took her, and then carried it through to her parlour, barely pausing as she knocked on the door and entered. But if she had been hoping to catch them in the middle of some revealing secret conversation, she was disappointed. Both men, she noted, had glasses of whisky in their hands. Yet she was not disappointed, because alcohol loosens the tongue, as does feeding a hungry man.

'Thank you, Mrs Bostock,' the man said, and there was something in the way he said it, in the turn of his head and the wariness in his face that convinced her that she was right – that she had seen him before.

'I'll say goodnight then.' She nodded, though more to the man than to her husband, and then she shut the door behind her and trudged her way upstairs with heavy feet, and into her bedroom. She changed into her nightwear then padded silent as a fox out of the room and across the landing to the bathroom. She pulled the door to, then sat down on the closed toilet seat. And there she sat for several minutes. The sound of the two men talking was muffled much of the time, but when either of them raised their voice she found – as she had often had found before – that snatches of conversation rose up through the inadequately boxed-in pipework with reassuring clarity. So when, some fifteen minutes later, her husband showed the man out of the house, she was satisfactorily informed about the key elements of the conversation. And she realised too that she had indeed recognised the man from an incident some three weeks earlier.

By the time her husband came stomping up the stairs, she was back in her room, sitting on her chair, a Bible open in her hands. His footsteps stopped outside her door. She was trembling, and praying that he didn't come in.

The prayer did not work. He pushed open the door, and for several seconds he stood framed against the dull light of the lamp in the corridor. She looked up after a few seconds, only too aware of his eyes on her.

'Still awake are you?' His voice was gruff and slurred.

She stood up.

'Good. Take your nightgown off.'

She shivered, knowing what was coming. 'Your visitor seemed a bit of a rum character,' she said as she started to undo the buttons at her neck.

'Hurry it up,' he growled. 'I haven't got all night.'

She tried to make her fingers move faster, but they were fumbling over their task. Even so she was determined to have her say. 'Who was he? I really don't like men turning up on our doorstep at this time of night – and unannounced too. He kept hammering on our front door until I answered it. And then he refused to tell me his name and—'

Bostock moved forward and, where her fingers were fumbling, his pulled hard at her gown, sending buttons flying and ripping the material.

She squealed. 'Now, look what you've done!'

'I've barely got started,' he snarled, his breath heavy with alcohol.

'Please don't!' she wailed.

It was a last and futile attempt to restrain him. The

next moment she felt an explosion of pain as his hand cracked against her head, so that she fell to the floor. She tried to get to her feet, whimpering with pain. 'Quiet!' he snarled, as he grabbed her arm and pushed her down on her bed. 'One more squeak out of you and by God you'll regret it!' he said, as he dropped his trousers and pants to the floor and clambered on top of her.

Long after her husband had left her and gone to his room, Brenda Bostock lay rigid and naked on her bed, as if terrified that any movement might provoke his return. Only when she could hear his stentorian snoring through the thin wall which separated them did she feel able to scrabble in the darkness and find her ruined nightgown and pull it over her and then lie down under her bedding and sob quietly.

It wasn't the first time her husband had hit her – or indeed forced himself on her – but this felt worse. And shuddering under her blankets, fighting the urge to howl like a whipped dog, she came to a sudden and shocking realisation: she couldn't take it anymore. No, not couldn't, but wouldn't. She had been driven to the edge of the precipice and there was nowhere else to go. There was a choice – to surrender permanently to her vicious bully of a husband or fight back. She thought of the small group of women she had been meeting at Agnes' house over the last year. They were such a support, and had opened her eyes. She knew what they would say. Don't put up with it. Stand up to him. But how?

Her thoughts drifted back to earlier in the evening,

before her husband had brutalised her. The insistent banging at the door and the stranger on her doorstep. Except that he wasn't a total stranger. She had seen him before. She didn't *know* him, but she did recognise him. When he had stepped inside, he had looked at her warily, as if aware of her recognition. Had she studied his face for too long? Had she shown too much interest in him? At the time it had been merely a matter of curiosity to her: who on earth was he, this man who had turned up unannounced on her doorstep, and where had she seen him before?

But things had changed as she had sat in the toilet and caught snatches of the conversation the stranger had had with her husband. She learned that the stranger's name was Tomkin. He was Sir Wilfred Walker's chauffeur. And the murdered man was indeed Sir Wilfred. He had been killed two or three days previously. That surprised her. Her husband had known about the death and sent a detective to investigate, and yet he had never told her. Why? He liked to brag to her about the important cases his men were investigating, and what could be more important than the death of a knight of the realm? And then Tomkin had said that there had been another death. Whereupon, her husband had hushed him and their voices had dropped, and the conversation had become almost impossible to follow. But Mrs Bostock's thoughts had drifted to the woman he knew to be Sir Wilfred's daughter: Maud Walker. Who had come to two of their meetings at Agnes' house and given them rousing speeches on the rights of women and the right to vote. Suppose the dead woman was her? It was a horrific thought. Suppose? Suppose? Suppose? Mrs Brenda Bostock had knelt down on the floor of the toilet and strained to catch whatever else she could of their conversation. But all in vain.

Kite lay on his back. It was still very dark, impossible to tell what time of night it was. He was feeling better for his sleep – erratic and dream-ridden though it had been – but he was absolutely parched. He needed water badly. He got up, pulled back the curtain in the hope that it would allow some light in, and then fumbled his way to the door. He twisted the handle, but the door refused to open. He tried again, but it refused to budge. Either it was jammed or he was locked in. He felt for the lock, but there was no key in it. He turned round. His eyes were getting used to the darkness, and he made out a glass on the table by his bed. He shambled across. It was full. Someone must have left it for him. Thank God for that. He picked the glass up and drank from it so greedily that some of it dribbled down his chin. He ran his fingers across it, desperate not to waste a drop, and it was only then, as he licked his lips dry, that he noticed a strange aftertaste. As if it had been sitting there for far too long. Or maybe something had got into the water supply. Better to stick to tea if he got the chance, but he had been so thirsty.

He sat down on the side of his bed, trying to summon up the energy to walk back over to the door and try again, but his legs were refusing to do anything. Sleep was engulfing him like a London pea-souper and in the end he rolled over onto his side, pulled his legs up into his stomach and tried not very successfully to pull his bedding over him. He needed to sleep the sleep of the dead. Surely, in the morning, he would feel better. His eyelids closed. Somewhere not so faraway he could hear noise, steps, voices whispering, a rattle at his door. He ought to shout out and tell them he couldn't get it open. But it didn't really matter. He had no desire to urinate. In the morning he would make a noise and get help, but right now all he wanted to do was sleep.

THE FOURTH DAY

IT WAS BREAKFAST time in the Bostock household. Brenda had already been up for an hour after her night of dread and disturbed sleep. She had dressed carefully and applied her make-up to try and hide the bruising. It wasn't perfect, but she thought that in the dingy light inside the house, it would do. It didn't do to 'flaunt it' (his words, not hers). The last thing she wanted was to provoke her husband anymore. Best to behave as if nothing had happened, as if the violence of the previous evening was 'one of those things', all part and parcel of being married.

By the time she heard him stomping down the stairs, she had his porridge simmering on the stove and the kettle just coming to the boil.

'Good morning, dear.' She attempted a smile to match the cheerful, forgiving sound of her voice.

He grunted back.

She quickly placed a bowl of porridge in front him, next to the small bowl of jam which he liked to add to it. Next she produced a mug of strong tea and a small rectangular package wrapped in paper and string. That was his lunch of bread and cheese sandwiches.

Another grunt, and a slight nodding of the head. That was the closest to an apology that she was going to get.

She sat down with a mug of tea and sipped at it, wondering how much she dare say.

He glanced up. 'Are you not eating?'

'I've already had something, thank you.'

'I prefer it if we eat together.' He had paused and was surveying her face.

'I'm sorry. I was very hungry.'

He took another mouthful of porridge. Silence, apart from the sound of him and his breakfast.

'I was a bit alarmed last night.'

He carried on as if her hadn't heard her.

'So late. And without any warning. He was a big man, and of course I had no idea who he was or whether I could trust him even though there was a rather nervous looking constable with him. And then he talked about there being a murder, but refused to tell me anything about it or even what his own name was.'

He grunted again. She had the funny thought that if she was to shut her eyes and then opened them again, he would turn into a pig. She almost giggled.

He ladled another spoonful of porridge into his mouth. 'I see the thaw has set in,' he said, changing the subject.

'Indeed it has, my dear,' she said with insincere sweetness. She watched in fascination as he ate. He really was like a pig at a trough. She waited until he had come up for a gulp of air and a slurp of his tea.

'So what was his name?'

'What does it matter? It's police business, all of it.'

'I am your wife, Henry, and I had to deal with a strange man turning up on my doorstep at nine o'clock at night. He might have…' She paused for dramatic effect. 'He might have murdered me, Henry. I think the least I can expect is for my husband to explain to me who on earth he is and for what reason he came round to my house and nearly scared the living daylights out of me!' Her voice reached a crescendo by the end of this speech, but all it did was provoke.

Henry Bostock scraped the last of the porridge out of his bowl and pushed it away from him. 'Woman,' he said, glowering at her, 'I will tell you who he is and the details of the case as and when I choose – and not before! This is men's business and I am dealing with it. Do you understand?'

He stood up and pulled his braces up over his shoulders. 'Well, do you understand or not?' His voice was a low, ominous growl. 'Sometimes you push me beyond all reasonable limits.'

'Oh yes,' she said, through pursed lips. 'I understand fully.'

He turned away and stomped out of the room and back up the stairs.

Brenda was shaking slightly. She shouldn't have pressed him. What was the point? She had known he wouldn't tell her anything in his present mood. But she had felt the ridiculous wifely need to give him one last opportunity to share with her what was going on. And of course he had refused.

Her mind was made up. She hurriedly cleared the table. The last thing she was going to do was leave a mess behind. It would be five minutes at least before he came down, and by the time those had elapsed she had donned coat, scarf, gloves and hat and slipped out of the front door, quietly clicking it shut behind her. There was no going back now.

Agnes' house was a good fifteen-minute walk from

Brenda's home, but she reached it in record time, striding out as if the devil himself was pursuing her, fuelled by both anger and fear. Anger with her husband and yet fear of him too, in case somehow he had divined her plans and was even now following her and would catch her up and stop her. None of her fears were realised, yet when she found herself on Agnes' doorstep, she froze, suddenly consumed by anxiety. Suppose Agnes was out, suppose she couldn't help, suppose she didn't want to help. Oh dear God! She banged on the door before she could be overwhelmed by her thoughts.

There was a delay, a considerable one in which the demons of doubt assailed her, and then the door swung open and there was Agnes. 'Brenda, what on earth are you doing here? Is everything all right?'

Brenda burst into tears, and half turned to go. But Agnes grabbed her elbow and steered her inside. Agnes was younger than her and poorer than her and yet they had already established a firm friendship. They had first met at Dot Bretherton's house. There had been a dozen or so women there, who were all passionate about the role and rights of women. Downtrodden wives like herself mostly. On this occasion, there was a guest speaker, a Miss Maud Walker, and she had spoken at length about the campaign to establish votes for women. 'We want women to vote for our members of parliament, and once we have done that we want women to get elected as members of parliament too. And when we have done that, one day I want to see a woman as prime minister.' They had all roared their approval, and afterwards Brenda and Agnes had left together and by the time they had reached Agnes' house, they had agreed that they should meet for tea the following Saturday afternoon.

Agnes was in her mid-thirties with one teenage girl, Elsie. Her husband Tom had died at Arras. His twin brother Ralph had survived with barely a scratch and was now Agnes' lodger. Brenda had only met him once and he had announced very early in their conversation that he had promised his twin brother that if anything happened to him, then he would look after Agnes and Elsie. Brenda had wondered what exactly 'looking after them' entailed, but didn't ask. He seemed a nice enough man and as long as Agnes didn't appear with a bruise on her face, she wasn't going to intrude.

'Brenda, I'll ask you again. What is the matter?'

'I need your help.'

Agnes nodded. 'Why don't you take your things off?' It was hot in the kitchen, and Brenda peeled her coat off and removed her hat.

'What about the scarf?'

Brenda hesitated. Agnes leaned forward and unwrapped it from around her neck. She frowned. 'He's been hitting you again, hasn't he?'

'That's not why I am here.'

'I see.' Agnes sat back in her chair, as if this gave her a better perspective on her friend. 'But you want my help?'

'To get to Crowthorpe.'

Agnes frowned. 'Crowthorpe? But why?'

'It's where Maud Walker lives.'

'Yes, I believe you're right.'

'Her father has been murdered.'

'Really? Sir Wilfred?' She sat up, alert and intrigued. 'Is Maud all right?'

'I don't know. Maybe.'

'When did this happen? I haven't heard about it.'

'Three days ago. It hasn't got into the newspapers yet. All the snow and that.'

'So,' Agnes said with a deep frown on her face and scepticism in her voice, 'you want to go all the way to Crowthorpe to see if she is all right?'

'There's been a second murder at Crowthorpe Manor.'

'You don't mean Maud?' This time there was alarm in her voice.

I don't know who, but…'

'I do hope not. She's such a wonderful woman. But even so, isn't this something that you need to let the police deal with? Two murders.'

'My husband is being very evasive.'

'Perhaps he doesn't want to alarm you…'

'I know my husband better than you do, Agnes. Trust me when I say that something is wrong and my husband is in the middle of it. Last night we had a very late unannounced visitor, and the man refused to tell me who he was, and this morning when I asked my husband he refused to tell me too. Yet I know he was Sir Wilfred's chauffeur—'

'How do you know?'

'I thought I recognised him from somewhere. Then I overheard some of their conversation. Not all of it, but enough. And as I lay in bed last night, it came to me. I saw him a few weeks ago outside the White

Hart near the cathedral. He was driving a very smart Rolls-Royce.'

'Brenda, that's as maybe. Now I am very fond of you, but I feel I must speak candidly. You do seem on edge and perhaps your hatred of your husband is affecting your judgement.'

Brenda flinched. The word *hatred* was a strong one, but she couldn't deny it. 'I don't know about my judgement,' she said carefully. 'You may be right, but I have no-one else to turn to for help. Only you.'

Silence descended between the two friends. The only sound was the creaking floorboards above them – someone moving about upstairs. 'Is that Elsie?' Brenda said.

'That's Ralph,' Agnes said very quickly. 'Elsie is filling in at the bakery. It's good for her, and an early start too.'

Brenda said nothing for some moments, suddenly aware that her unexpected arrival had caught her friend unawares. She also became conscious of the small clock on the dresser, ticking away relentlessly, a reminder that time was passing and she hadn't achieved anything yet. She leaned forward. 'Agnes, I want you to drive me to Crowthorpe. This morning.'

'You what?'

'On your brother-in-law's motorcycle. You drove when the war was on, and I saw him driving it with you in the sidecar just before Christmas.'

Agnes' mouth hung open.

'Well, yes or no?' Brenda demanded. She had no time to waste, and no other options.

'He's not going to let me take it for a joyride.'

'It's not a joyride. It's a very serious matter. Anyway, I am pretty sure that he'd do anything for you.'

'Would he indeed!' The voice was male and came from just behind Brenda. She turned to see Ralph standing in the doorway. 'Good morning, Mrs Bostock. This is a surprise.'

'Ralph, you are just the man I was wanting,' Brenda said briskly. 'I need to borrow your motorbike.'

'Can you drive a motorbike?' He gave her an amused smile.

'I was asking Agnes if she would drive it, while I sit in the sidecar. That way you will know that it is in safe hands.'

'I don't lend my motorbike out to ladies who want a bit of fun.'

Brenda stood up and advanced closer to him. 'But if it was two men wanting a bit of fun, that would be all right would it?' He was a head taller than her, but she stared at him fearlessly. 'Anyway I need it for police business.'

'As far as I can tell, you are not a policeman.' He laughed, pleased at his own joke, still not taking her seriously. But this was like poking a hornet's nest with stick and then standing still to see what happened.

'Oh, I am only a woman, is that it? And even though I am married to the chief constable of Lincoln, I don't count for anything. Is that what you think, Ralph Taylor?' She paused, but so briefly he had no chance to respond. 'I came here to see Agnes because she is my only hope. I came here to ask for an act of kindness. I came here to try and save the life of a very dear friend. And you have the nerve to laugh at me.

To mock me. I look at Agnes and I look at you and I wonder how your brother would feel as he looks down from heaven and sees you…'

'Please, Ralph!' Agnes moved forward now, standing right next to Brenda, slipping her arm through hers. 'I will drive very carefully. I promise you. And you know I always keep my promises.'

He stood there, arms on his hips, silent, his mouth clenched, stubborn as an ox.

'If my dear friend is brutally murdered because I fail to arrive in time,' Brenda said, taking up the cudgel, 'I shall make sure that everyone in Lincoln knows that it was because you refused my pleas for help.'

He looked from the hard-edged glare of Brenda to the please-please soft-hearted appeal of Agnes, and he caved in. 'Very well. It seems I have no choice.'

Agnes threw herself forward and hugged him. 'Thank you, Ralph. You won't regret it.'

For a briefest moment his own arms enveloped her, and then they both stepped back hurriedly, as if they had been struck by lightning.

There was something between them. That was as clear as a bump on a log to Brenda, but she pretended not to notice the flushed face of her friend. 'You are so kind, Ralph,' Brenda said, suddenly purring like an overfed cat. 'I will make sure you are fully recompensed for your fuel and your kindness. I will even put in a good word for you with the chief constable if you wish.'

He nodded. Expecting him to say 'Thank you' was perhaps asking too much, but Brenda was content. She had got what she wanted.

'And how far might you be going, Mrs Bostock? Conditions still aren't good.'

'Saxilby,' Brenda said, jumping in before Agnes could. She was aware that if she said Crowthorpe, then he might have second thoughts about such a long trip.

'In that case, as long as you are very careful—'

'Of course we will be,' Brenda replied. 'With Agnes in charge, what could possibly go wrong?'

Half an hour later, they were ready to leave. Ralph had left for work – but not before he had checked Agnes was able to start the bike, and given her several tips on how to control it. She had borne this with very good grace, something Brenda wasn't sure she could have done had she been in her shoes.

'He's very protective,' Brenda had said as they watched him stride off to work.

'He's caring,' Agnes had replied.

Silence.

'Are you…?' Brenda started, then stopped. More silence. The question hung unasked in the air, but begging for answer.

'It's hard, being on your own with a child.'

'I can imagine.' Brenda felt something clutch at her heart. She would have given anything to have been on her own with her child. She took a deep breath, pushing away her own lurch of grief.

'Agnes, he is obviously very fond of you. So you're in the driving seat, but only for now. As I have learnt to my cost, once people marry, things change. So this is the best opportunity you'll ever have to tell him how you want things to be. You'll regret it if you don't.'

'Maybe.'

'There's no "maybe" about it.'

Agnes retreated upstairs to change, but reappeared a few minutes later to find Brenda making up bread and cheese sandwiches, and brewing tea for a flask.

'Brenda, before we go, can I ask you something?'

'Of course.'

'What do you think you can achieve when we get to Crowthorpe. I know you don't trust your husband, but surely the police know best. And if there is a killer loose there, what on earth can you do to catch him?'

'Him? It might be a woman.'

Agnes' face tightened with irritation. 'But what exactly is your plan? I mean why exactly are we going there?'

'The last thing my husband said to this Tomkin fellow was not to tell anyone at the police station what they had discussed.'

'Why would that be?'

'But the one thing which alarmed me more than anything was when Tomkin said that the detective Kite was asking the family a lot of awkward questions.'

'Isn't that what he should be doing?'

'Exactly. But my husband said – and these were his precise words – "don't worry, I'm sure we can put a stop to that". And they had both laughed.'

'But you still haven't told me what your plan is. Please tell me you have one.'

'I want to check that Maud is safe. Whoever else is involved in two murders, I can't believe she is. So she will be my ally. Then I think we need to warn

Detective Kite.'

'But once your husband is there, how can you do that?'

Brenda smiled, then giggled.

Agnes was surprised. 'What?'

'He may well be delayed.'

'What do you mean?'

'I am not sure his breakfast will agree with him today. Loose bowels can be such a problem sometimes.'

The two women looked at each other. Smirks turned to wide grins and then to out-loud laughter.

'Time to be going,' Brenda said eventually.

'Absolutely,' Agnes replied.

Chief Constable Bostock made it to the police station in Monks Road, but only just. The walk from his house was little more than a ten-minute stroll. Other people in his position might have insisted on transport, but he liked to be seen striding the streets of Lincoln, resplendent in his uniform, in charge and yet a man of the people. He thrived on the deferential nods and 'Good mornings!' of clerks and manual labourers, of shopkeepers and mothers with children. And when he was offered a pie warm from the oven or a freshly baked loaf by one of the local proprietors, then he accepted it with a nod of acknowledgment, as being his due recompense for keeping the city safe.

But on this particular morning, which was cold and overhung with dank, featureless cloud, he found his pace quickening and his civility lessening the further he got from home. He even turned down an offer of some very desirable bananas as the discomfort in his bowels grew. Normally he would have paused to admire the cathedral, but not on this occasion. By the time he reached the White Hart, he had slowed down again. He wanted to hurry, but the fact was he needed to clench his buttocks tight to prevent a very nasty accident occurring. This conflict of need meant that an urgent walk turned into an embarrassing waddle. He gritted his teeth and carried on as quickly as he dared, head and eyes cast down so as to discourage anyone from striking up a casual conversation. The last thing he wanted was to be delayed by anyone. It was a case of avoid eye-contact and fight the urge to evacuate his bowels.

When the station finally came into view, he felt a surge of relief. He was glad to see that there were no officers hanging around outside, but as he approached the entrance, Frank Tomkin appeared from within and blocked his way.

'Good morning, sir! I was beginning to wonder if you—'

Bostock pushed past him, colliding shoulders as he did so. 'Out the way, man.'

Inside he afforded the same treatment to three or four others, before he reached the toilet and slammed the door shut behind him. And there he stayed for some considerable time.

When Bostock finally exited the toilet, the first thing he did was snarl orders at the unfortunate Constable Light. Then he made his way cautiously to his office, shutting the door firmly behind him. Even so, he had barely sat down before Tomkin was tapping on his door and then pushing round the door.

'Everything all right, sir?'

Bostock growled.

'It's just that last night…'

'We'll go when I'm ready,' he snarled, as pain flashed through his guts.

'Of course, sir.' Tomkin remained there, half in and half out of the room, unwilling to withdraw and yet uncertain how to proceed. 'Can I get you something, sir?' he said, and immediately regretted it. It was already the talk of the station that the chief constable had a serious bowel problem. He was hardly going to want anything to eat.

'For God's sake, man, leave me in peace!'

Tomkin flushed, and bobbed his head. 'Of course, sir. Sorry to bother you, sir.'

He began to back out of sight, but Bostock hissed him back: 'Just keep an eye on Constable Light.'

'Yes, sir. I will, sir.' Don't you worry, sir.'

As the door closed firmly behind the retreating Tomkin, Bostock leaned back in his chair and closed his eyes. What the devil had caused such a problem that morning? It wasn't the first time, but this was unquestionably the worst he could remember. Was it his breakfast? The jam had tasted a bit… different. Was it Brenda, taking revenge on him for claiming his marital rights? Because if it was, by God he'd make her wish she hadn't been born. But that was for later. Right now he had a more serious problem, namely the damned Detective Sergeant Kite. He had been a trouble-maker in London and now he was doing it in Lincolnshire, upsetting the Walker family by digging up the dirt on them and failing to focus his attention on the village of Crowthorpe. It wouldn't be difficult to find some ungrateful wretch there with a motive to kill someone as wealthy as Sir Wilfred. Thank God Tomkin had brought the matter to his attention. The only problem was: how to deal with Kite and solve the murder in a way that would keep everyone happy, especially Lady Beatrice and her son Alec.

These were the things which bothered him, but it wasn't until he had made two more uncomfortable visits to the toilet that he finally began to feel that he might leave the station safely. He wondered about the wisdom of leaving arrangements to Constable Light. He had already marked the young man down as barely competent. But the young man was desperate to please, and in the circumstances that was an advantage. He could be counted on to do exactly as he was told. When he was told to keep his mouth shut, he would hopefully do precisely that. And, Bostock's thinking continued, if things went wrong, then the best thing about Light was that he was dispensable.

Dispensable? He pondered the word as his stomach churned away. *Dispensable* covered what the vicar of his church would have called a multitude of sins. But sins were part of life, and sometimes choices had to be made and decisions acted upon. Constable Light would never rise very high. He had been raised in an orphanage. He was indeed dispensable.

In the end the motorbike trip from Lincoln to Crowthorpe proved largely straightforward. Agnes drove with remarkable skill, only once giving Brenda a scare when she skidded on a downhill stretch of road and barely avoided ramming the sidecar into a very solid-looking oak tree. Brenda squealed in alarm, but Agnes merely laughed and let out a 'haloo!' as if she was out hunting and the fox had come into view.

Some miles behind and (obviously) unknown to the two women, Chief Constable Bostock, Frank Tomkin and Constable Light were progressing less successfully. Within five miles, they had to make an unplanned stop at Bostock's urgent request. Neither of his fellow travellers were stupid enough to say anything, and when he returned from the bushes, Tomkin was regaling a wide-eyed constable with tales of his time in the trenches. A little later and more seriously, on the self-same hill which Agnes had had her alarming skid, the lorry in which the three men were travelling skidded on the same patch of ice. The wretched Constable Light wrenched at the wheel to try and avoid disaster, and almost managed it, but he was not able to avoid a glancing collision with the sturdy oak which Agnes had narrowly avoided.

Bostock was the first out of the cab, turning the air blue. Light, who had been driving, looked at if he had had all his blood drained from him. It was Tomkin who got down on his hands and knees to examine the damage. 'Could be worse,' was his only comment, which merely drew a further tirade of invective from the chief constable. He ignored it, asked Constable Light if he would kindly bring him the toolbox, and took off his coat.

When Agnes brought the motorbike to a halt outside Crowthorpe Manor, both women were splattered with mud from head to foot. No-one was outside to greet them (why should they have been?) and as Brenda brushed herself down as best she could, she was conscious of how quiet it was. The only sounds were of melted snow dripping from the eaves and trees, and just occasionally the cawing of crows in the distance.

'Well,' she said to Agnes, adjusting her hat on her head, 'we'd better go and see what's what.'

She found herself banging hard on the door twice before she heard any noises from within: a muffled voice and the heavy tread of shoes on a wooden floor and then the door opened.

The woman who greeted them looked surprised and unwelcoming. She ran her eyes up and down their muddy coats. 'Who are you? Do you have an appointment?'

'We are friends of Maud's.'

'Is she expecting you?'

'No, but I am sure she will be glad to see both of us.'

The woman seemed unconvinced and maintained her stance across the entrance. 'The household is not taking visitors at the moment. We are in mourning.'

'We have come all the way from Lincoln and we are in need of sustenance and... other things.'

Brenda waited, but Agnes had had enough. 'Do you want me to pull up my skirts and piss on your doorstep, or what?'

Brenda held her breath. The woman looked like she could give as good as she got.

Then, suddenly, there was the sound of more steps

approaching, and like an angel from heaven there was Maud, dressed in black with a tweed jacket against the cold and with an expression of amazement on her face.

'Brenda, and… and…'

'Agnes.'

'Yes of course. How could I possibly have forgotten? Please, you must accept my apology, Agnes.'

Agnes nodded, conscious that Maud was looking at her with great interest.

'Let's get those filthy coats off you. Rose will brush and dry them off in the warmth of the kitchen. Do come in.' And she took both women by an arm and led them in past a tight-lipped Rose.

'We were very sorry to hear about the death of your father,' Brenda said softly. They were in the smaller sitting room, a tray of tea and cake in front of them.

'Thank you. It was a terrible shock.'

'It must have been.'

'And we were very worried about you, Maud. As our friend.'

'And inspiration,' Agnes added.

They fell silent, sipping tea and chewing hungrily on the Victoria sponge that Rose had produced. Now that they had reached Crowthorpe Manor and reassured themselves about Maud, Brenda wasn't quite sure how to proceed. But proceed she had to do.

'Do you want to talk about your father's death or would you rather not?'

'It was in his car,' Maud replied. She described what had happened in simple and unvarnished terms.

'I understand there was another death, a female. We

were concerned it might have been you.'

Maud carefully placed her cup and saucer down on the table. 'You know about that? I didn't think…' Her words came to an uncertain halt. She seemed surprised that news should have leaked out so quickly and far.

'A Mr Tomkin came to see my husband last night and—'

'Frank, the chauffeur? He went to Lincoln?' Her eyes opened wide, and her hand flew to her mouth. And the surprise in her voice was convincing. 'We… we thought… we all thought that he must have been the killer because he disappeared very suddenly on Constable Sparrow's motorbike. Running away we thought.'

Brenda frowned. 'Tell me, Maud, who was the woman who died?'

Maud was silent for several seconds, her face draining of colour. 'It was awful. Mary Graves. My father's secretary. Wouldn't say boo to a goose, and yet… and yet she was most brutally murdered. It makes me feel ill just to think of it.'

'But everyone else is all right?'

She nodded.

'So where are Detective Sergeant Kite and Constable Sparrow?'

'You know about them? Gosh, you are very well informed.'

'My husband tells me everything,' Brenda lied. She wasn't sure why she was lying. Why not admit that she had eavesdropped? She wasn't sure she knew why. Surely she could be honest with Maud, but somehow it felt necessary.

'I can't say that I have seen them this morning. I was late rising. It has all been very sapping.'

'Perhaps someone else knows. Rose perhaps? Or your brother?'

'Yes, of course, I'll go and see.'

She returned with Rose, who stood near the door, as if to say she had too many things to do, and didn't want to be answering questions longer than absolutely necessary.

'I don't know where they are,' she said firmly.

'But they ate breakfast did they?'

'Yes. Not that I spoke to them. After all that has happened, I was given some extra time in bed, as no-one wanted to be up early. I came down about half-past eight to get things started, but to judge from the dirty plates they had both eaten some of the pie I was keeping back for later.'

'You didn't hear or see them go out?'

'No.'

'So you don't know where they've gone?'

'No I don't. I didn't see or speak to them. But if I was to guess, maybe they decided to try and walk to the village and ask questions there.'

'You may be right, I suppose.'

'Is that it? It's just that I have lots to do and…'

'Of course,' Maud said, cutting across. 'We are sorry to have inconvenienced you, Rose.'

With that, Rose turned and left the room.

'I am sure they will be back soon,' Maud said firmly. 'I expect they are out there looking for clues. Perhaps they have gone and arrested someone. It would be a great relief if they had.'

'It would be a much greater relief if they would return to Lincoln and never come back.' The words were those of a man. He was standing in the doorway, hands on his hips. 'All that damned Kite has done is cause trouble.'

'Ah, you must be Maud's brother.'

'*She* is my sister,' he snapped. 'I am Captain Alec Walker. I don't know who you are, but we are a house in mourning and I would ask you to leave and return to wherever you came from.'

'I am Brenda Bostock.' She lifted her chin, determined not to give ground. 'I am the wife of Chief Constable Bostock, and I am here on his behalf to pass on some vital information to Detective Sergeant Kite.'

He glared at her. He had small bullet-like eyes, and hair that was longer than would have been tolerated in an officers' mess. His Adam's apple throbbed, betraying anxiety. 'I find that hard to believe.'

'Which bit of it do you find hard to believe? That I am Brenda Bostock? That my husband is the chief constable? Or that he should entrust me, a woman, with an important task relating to your father's murder?'

He opened his mouth to reply, but seemed to think the better of it. He twitched slightly and opened his mouth again, but it was Maud who spoke. 'Alec, I can vouch for Brenda. And for Agnes. I know both of them.'

He glanced at the two women, intruders in his house, and then back at Maud.

'Part of your cabal of frustrated women, are they?'

And with that, he turned on his heel as if he was on the parade ground and marched back to wherever in the house it was that he had come from.

The three women were silent as the sound of his steps dissipated into silence. Brenda took another piece of cake and noticed that her hand was shaking. To hell with the man.

It was Maud who broke the tense atmosphere. 'Brenda, dear, why are you so insistent on seeing Detective Kite?'

'We can't tell you,' Agnes said, bursting in. 'We promised.'

'Really?' Maud stared at her.

'Not yet anyway. Maybe when we've spoken to him.'

'Well I am sure he and Constable Sparrow will be back at some point. Most likely by lunchtime or when they are hungry.' She laughed softly. 'Don't you think?'

'But where do you think they might have gone?' Agnes was not to be distracted. 'You know the area well.'

'It all depends on why they went out,' she said. 'I suppose they may have been looking for clues.'

Brenda felt a surge of anger at her condescending manner. There was, quite clearly, a gulf of class, money, and education between Maud and Agnes, but she hated to see her friend treated like that. She looked again at Maud. There was, of course, a class difference between Maud and herself too, but not so pronounced. She had the sudden realisation that perhaps she had misjudged Maud, seen only the women's rights side of her and not the upper class side, with all the privilege that went with it and the presumption of superiority.

'Who else lives nearby?' she said, sharply.

'Only the vicar and his wife, the Reverend Justin Ransom and Jane. In the cottage near the church.'

'They know about the two deaths?'

'He came and prayed over…' She paused, suddenly choked by the memory. 'He said prayers where my father had died, and paid a visit to my mother. But as for Mary's death, I am not sure.'

Brenda stood up. 'Well, there's nothing to be gained by sitting here. We'll just have to go and look for them ourselves. Perhaps you can tell us the way, Maud. If you would, please.'

'Of course. But if I may say so, I wonder if Rose might not be correct, that they have gone to the village to investigate there. That's where most of our workers live, and my father was, I have to admit, rather strict at times, so someone there could have held a grudge against him.'

'Of course. But I think it's easier if we start here. If they don't turn up, we'll try the village.'

'In that case,' Maud said, 'you need to go out that gateway at the back, and keep going down the hill and through the trees. You can't miss it.'

Brenda hoped not. She and Agnes collected their coats, thankfully warmed through and cleaned, and then headed off. Initially they walked in silence, out beyond the manor and its surrounding buildings, and down the lane which had now turned into a treacherous track, a mixture of snow, slush, ice and mud which demanded that they paid attention to where they placed their feet.

They had reached a slightly more reliable patch of ground when Brenda placed a hand on her companion's arm and stopped. 'Tell me, did you find it odd that no-one admitted to having seen either Kite or Sparrow this morning, or knew where they had gone?'

Agnes frowned, her face puckering up like that of a small puzzled child. 'I suppose I would have expected at least Rose to have seen them, if she is required to prepare breakfast for everyone. However, if they had decided they needed to go to the village and they had to walk, well that would explain them getting an early start.'

'I admit that is true. But it puzzles me that both the captain and Rose suggested they had gone to the village even though neither of them had spoken to them or even seen them this morning.'

'Why are you puzzled? I don't understand. If the jam factory is based there and—'

'I am puzzled because of what I overheard last night. The killer was someone in the house. Detective Kite was convinced of that and the family didn't like that. He was rocking the boat by asking them too many questions. And my husband didn't like that either.'

'But if Kite catches the killer then—'

'My husband doesn't want him to catch the killer.'

'But if Detective Kite has evidence to prove it…'

'You don't know what my husband is capable of.' She spat the words out with a venom which caused Agnes to step back in alarm. 'He knows Sir Wilfred and Lady Beatrice.'

'Really? You're sure.'

'Oh yes. He likes to boast of his social connections. It makes him feel big. He brought some Crowthorpe jam home once. "A present from Lady Beatrice" he said. "We had lunch together." He was so pleased with himself!'

'But… but surely if Detective Sergeant Kite can prove who the killer is…' Her words tailed off.

Brenda didn't notice. She was oblivious. She had turned round and was looking back up the hill, to where the clock-tower on top of the house was just visible. She remained rigidly still for some twenty seconds or more before she shivered. 'I have a bad feeling,' she said. She lifted her hand and carefully felt the bruise on the side of her face. She needed to be reminded of what her husband had done. She needed anger to force her on, but alongside anger there marched fear. How long would it be before he turned up? Perhaps even now he had arrived and was knocking on the front door of the manor. What would he do when he realised that she was here? It didn't bear thinking about, especially if her additives to his breakfast had had the dire consequences she had hoped for and he had worked out that she was to blame. In fact, he would be sure to blame her. And when they got home that night, out of sight behind closed doors, God only knew what he would do to her. Worse than the previous night, worse than ever.

'Brenda?' Agnes was staring at her. 'Is everything all right?'

Brenda tightened the scarf around her neck and

pulled her hat down further. 'Perhaps this whole enterprise is a big mistake… my big mistake, and I have dragged you into it and—'

'And maybe it is not.' Agnes slipped her arm through her companion's. 'I want to be here with you. Come on, let's go and see if the vicar has seen him anywhere. Or perhaps Kite has confided in him.' And with that they continued their trudge, down the treacherous track, through the trees and beyond, both lost in silence and in their own thoughts.

When they knocked on the door of the cottage near the church, there was a long delay and a variety of noises from within before the door opened. The woman who had opened it was flushed in the face and looked at them with ill-disguised dismay.

'Who are you?' she demanded.

'I am Mrs Bostock, the wife of the chief constable of Lincoln.' Brenda didn't normally use her husband's status as an opening gambit, but this was not a normal situation.

'Really?' The woman exuded disbelief as she swept her eyes up and down her unexpected visitor, as if she expected to find some insignia attached to her coat – still somewhat mud-splattered from the motorcycle ride despite Rose's efforts – which would confirm her outrageous claim.

Brenda pressed on. 'You must be Mrs Ransom. I was hoping that you or the Reverend Ransom might be able to help me. I am trying to find Detective Sergeant Kite.'

'I do know who you mean, but I cannot say I know

where he is. Quite the contrary.'

'What about the police constable. Sparrow is his name, I believe.'

'Sparrow.' She smirked. 'Quite a character is Constable Sparrow, but I haven't seen him this morning either.'

'Is your husband in? Or…' She paused. 'Or is he ministering to his parishioners?' She made that activity sound rather insalubrious, but if she was trying to gain Mrs Ransom's assistance, she failed. The woman straightened herself up, pulled the most dismissive of faces and pointed imperiously towards the church.

'My husband will no doubt be in there, praying for the soul of Sir Wilfred. Or perhaps you will get lucky and find Detective Sergeant and Constable Sparrow in there, on their knees, being shriven of all their sins.' Then she banged the door shut and slid a bolt loudly into place.

They looked at each other, suppressing the laughter that had risen to their lips.

'Who are his parishioners out here, except for the inhabitants of the manor?' Agnes said. She giggled as she started to walk towards the church.

But Brenda did not respond, because they had barely covered half a dozen paces when she stopped and stared at the ground. The snow near the house was anything but pristine now. Of course they had themselves made their own marks upon it. There were their own footprints , leading from the track and to the cottage. But there were at least two other sets. She looked across the snow towards the church. One set led there. That was surely the vicar himself. But the other ones were a different shoe and a little bit bigger. They were the prints of a man who wore boots such as a working man might wear. She looked back at the cottage and realised that these led only one way. To the front door. The man that had made them must be in the house. She smiled. No wonder Mrs Ransom had been so sharp. She had a visitor.

Agnes tugged at her sleeve. 'What's the matter, Brenda? We need to find your detective.'

'Sorry, I was a bit distracted.'

They resumed their walk towards the church. The snow lay thicker down in the hollow, and the path the Reverend had taken was clear enough.

The footsteps led to the church. The double doors were shut, but to their relief not locked. They eased their way in and paused, allowing themselves to get accustomed to the lack of light. As churches went, the windows were small. Ivy or some other creepers were further limiting the entrance of light. It felt unwelcoming and uncared for.

'Hello!' Agnes' voice echoed round the space. 'Reverend Ransom?'

There was no answer.

She called again, but Brenda was interested in something else. She moved forward down the aisle, following a trail of water, mud and snow that had not yet melted. 'Someone has been here this morning.' She followed the tracks down past the pews before swinging left, past the lectern and then right. They ended at a closed door. Brenda paused, tapped on it and pushed her way in.

There was a man sitting in the corner, his face flickering disturbingly in the light of a single guttering candle. His eyes were open and alert, but it was hard to know if he was studying them or was lost in his own imagination.

'Reverend Ransom?' It wasn't much of a guess, given that he was wearing a dog collar.

He frowned, but said not a word.

'We're looking for Detective Sergeant Kite and Constable Sparrow? Have you seen them this morning?'

Again Ransom failed to respond.

She raised her voice, in case he might be deaf. 'It's very important that I speak to them. It concerns the murder of Sir Wilfred.'

'Sir Wilfred!' The name seemed to spark a strong reaction. He lifted his hands to his forehead, rubbing his fingers hard on his temples as if in distress. A low moan came from his barely open mouth and his whole body began to quiver. 'No! No! No!' The words were like a dirge, and he began to rock forwards and backwards in distress.

Brenda had seen this sort of behaviour amongst men who had returned from the war traumatised by the experience. 'Shell shock' as they called it.

But what happened next was altogether more alarming. He began to hiss, at first so softly that she barely noticed it, but quickly increasing in volume and tempo. He half rose from his seat, crouching like an animal in the corner of a room, looking wildly about him for a means of escape.

'Please, Reverend,' Brenda said, holding both hands

out, palms down, trying to pacify him. 'We will go now. We are very sorry to have disturbed you.'

He stretched out his left arm, lifting it up high above him, and he began to chant. 'You are a child of the devil and an enemy of everything that is right. You are full of all kinds of deceit and trickery. Will you never stop perverting the right ways of the Lord? Now the hand of the Lord is against you!'

The two women fled, out of the vestry, down the aisle and out of the church, and into the daylight where they hugged each other tight. 'Oh my God,' Agnes gasped. 'What a dreadful man. To call us the devil. To—'

'Not us, I hope. He was quoting something from the Old Testament.' Brenda was breathing heavily, alarmed, but she knew she had to focus. If the two policemen were not here and were not in the cottage, then where were they?

As she held her protective arms around Agnes, she looked up and noticed the birds. Rooks or crows – she didn't know which – were thronging the bare trees beyond the churchyard. They were silent, black and ominous, and then quite suddenly three or four of them took flight with a flurry of wings and strident cawing, and after that a host of them followed, filling the air with their noise. They began to swirl around the sky, and then individuals broke off, making sudden darts down towards the ground. Brenda squealed and let Agnes go.

She began to run as best she could down past the gravestones, slipping and sliding on a track that other feet had taken. She could hear Agnes racing behind her, calling her, but she didn't respond because she could see something now, lying in the snow-covered grass in front of a grave, a thin layer of snow over it. A mound, a pile of clothes, a body.

She slowed her pace and when she reached it, she stood still, stunned. She had found him. Kite surely? Not Sparrow because she knew what he looked like and in any case the dead man wasn't wearing uniform. She began to wobble on her feet.

Agnes pushed past her and knelt down, feeling the man's head, grabbing his wrist, leaning low to listen for any breathing.

'The cottage. Run and tell Mrs Ransom. We need help and fast. He's alive, but he's very cold.'

'No point wasting time with her. I'll go to the manor. We'll need some means of transport.' Brenda took off her coat. 'Put this over him. Besides I can move faster without it on.' And she set off with a determined stride.

ALL (OR MOST OF IT) IS REVEALED

DETECTIVE SERGEANT KITE was lying on a sofa which the men had moved closer to the fireplace. Piled with logs, it was blazing away, throwing heat out into the chill room. Agnes and Maud had removed his outer clothes and replaced them with warm, dry ones which Elizabeth had produced. Rose had brought in a bowl of thick soup and homemade bread, and Kite was being fed like a baby.

Brenda watched all this from a distance. Her help was not required, but she was aware of the grandfather clock ticking away in the corner of the room. Sooner or later her husband would turn up and then who knew what would happen? This was the perfect excuse he would need: to remove Kite from the case, to get him away from the house, maybe even to get him dismissed from the force on the grounds of ill health and whatever charges of incompetence her husband chose to bring. In short, this was the opportunity for the killer to go free.

The men were all in the other sitting room, and they were gathered around Constable Sparrow. After all the alarms of finding Kite collapsed in the churchyard, the reappearance of Sparrow had been no less dramatic. They had just placed the semi-conscious Kite in one of the traps – Maud had conceded that the circumstances necessitated accepting that one of her horses should be put to use despite the treacherous conditions – and had started up the slope when an ear-splitting scream had emitted from behind them. It was Mrs Ransom and she was trying to hold up a bedraggled, blood-stained figure.

When Sparrow too was transported back to the manor, the story of what had happened came out in dribs and drabs. How they had encountered a deranged Reverend Ransom who had fled into the church; how they had seen or thought they had seen – 'he was there one moment and gone the next' – a figure in the wood. How Sparrow had plunged after him, leaving a faint Kite in the churchyard – 'he ain't well, I can tell you. Said he was feeling queasy. Wouldn't eat any breakfast. But he was determined to show me something at the church.' How he had narrowly avoided putting his foot in a mantrap – 'who puts them in their woods?' And how he'd heard a noise behind him – 'a breaking of a branch, snap, just like that, and then "Alleluia, bang!" my head exploded like a whizz bang!'

Brenda, like the others there, had listened with fascination. It tied up with some of their own experience – the deranged vicar bit at least, the collapsed Kite – but there was something which bothered her. What was it Mrs Ransom had said about Sparrow? 'Quite a character.' And she had said it with a strange expression on her face and a glint in her eye. What exactly had she meant by that? And what about the footprints, the unseen visitor, and the hostility of the woman towards them? She had been determined not to let them in. She looked again at Kite, still asleep she thought, and yet his eyes suddenly flickered open and shut. Was he conscious of anything that was going on? If someone in the house was the killer, might he be the next victim?

'What about lunch?' someone had said. When Brenda tried to recall the details later, she couldn't remember who it was. All she knew was that it gave her the chance she needed and she quickly offered to sit with Kite while the others, including Constable Sparrow, sat down to eat a lunch of baked potatoes, stewed meat and vegetables.

After his food and trauma, Kite could barely keep his eyes open, but Brenda tapped his arm. 'You need to listen, Sergeant. If you don't, I am very much afraid of what might happen.'

He opened his eyes reluctantly and looked at her.

'My husband, Chief Constable Bostock, is on the way here with a Mr Tomkin. He wants to take you off the case.'

'Why?' His voice was that of a man at the end of his resources. 'I believe I know who the killer is.'

'That's why. He wants to protect the family.'

He considered this for maybe half a minute. Brenda thought he was about to fall asleep again, but he then gripped her arm with his free hand. 'Wake me when they have eaten. I just need a short rest. I am so tired.' He closed his eyes.

'Listen,' she said, 'I need to tell you about Mrs Ransom and the vicar and the footprints.' She pinched his arm, desperate to keep him awake. His eyes half opened for a second or two, then closed again. She pinched his arm again, leant down closer to him and began to talk, and she didn't stop until she had got to the end of her tale. But by then, he was deeply asleep, his breathing deep and steady.

Brenda straightened herself in her chair, and tried to think.

An hour later and they all reassembled in the large lounge. There was a flurry of activity until Kite's sofa had been moved back to its original position, other chairs adjusted, and an upright chair from the dining room brought in and placed in central position. Kite made his way to this chair, but rather than sitting on it, he stood behind it, his back to the welcome warmth of the fire, and holding tight to the chair.

He surveyed the room, anxious that everyone should be present. His eyes stopped on Sparrow and the rudimentary bandage around his head. 'Are you alright, Constable? I understand you took quite a blow to the head.'

Sparrow laughed. 'It'll take more than that to put me out of action. Besides Jane, Mrs Ransom, bandaged me up.'

'I can see blood on the bandage. I would like Miss Agnes to take a proper look at it. She volunteered as a nurse in the war.'

'No need, sir. More important matters to deal with now. I survived the Boche's bullets and bombs. A clonk on the head is nothing.'

Kite shrugged and resumed his sweep of the room. Then he cleared his throat and began. 'I believe I have identified the person or persons who killed Sir Wilfred Walker and Miss Mary Graves.'

'Isn't that obvious now.' It was Captain Alec, trying to take charge. 'Frank Tomkin did a runner, so it must have been him.'

'Please, Captain, I would prefer you not to interrupt unless you have some new information relevant to the investigation.' He paused and straightened himself up.

'Frank Tomkin has not gone on the run. Nor indeed did he steal Constable Sparrow's motorbike to make his escape. On the contrary, he drove it to Lincoln at my request to summon reinforcements from Chief Constable Bostock.'

There were gasps from all round the room. But it was Sparrow who spoke out. 'Why didn't you tell me, sir. Why didn't you tell all of us, sir?'

'Quite simply because I didn't know who to trust. I had my theories even then, but no certainty. You see, what I have discovered during my few days here is that Crowthorpe Manor holds many secrets.'

Lady Beatrice stood up suddenly, emitting a grunt as she did so. 'I would like to say something,' she announced.

'Mother, your stick.' Alec bent down and picked it up from the side of her chair. She advanced two paces and then stood still, staring at Kite. Her face was ferocious, anything but the face of a fragile old woman, but before she spoke she coughed, not once but several times, before wiping her mouth with a dark patterned handkerchief. Kite noted all this and felt encouraged.

She banged her stick on the floor as if to ensure that everyone was listening.

'I killed my husband, Sergeant, and I also killed Mary.'

There was a collective gasp from around the room.

'Mother!' Alec and Maud both said, almost in unison.

Kite looked at them, and then at the others. What were they thinking? What had so surprised them? That Lady Beatrice was the killer or that she was claiming to be the killer? Did they really believe it was her?

He started slowly. 'I can understand why a woman might murder her husband, but I do wonder why you would have killed someone like Mary? Unless she was having an affair with your husband.'

Lady Beatrice laughed. 'Poor little Mary. So devoted to my beast of a husband. She would have done anything for him. Except that he wasn't interested in her like that! All he wanted her for was as a bookkeeper. The problem was that Mary knew too much – about the parlous state of the company's finances and the deal my husband had negotiated with T G Tickler.'

She paused. Kite glanced around, looking for signs of who knew or didn't know about this deal. Yet no-one looked startled, no-one gasped with shock. Did that mean they were aware of it?

'So let me get this right,' he said quietly. 'Your husband agreed to sell the company to Tickler's, but didn't tell anyone.'

'He met T G Tickler in Lincoln a few weeks ago. Frank drove him there. At the time he pretended it was some new business opportunity. But of course he told me the truth only a few days ago, when he needed my approval – and my signature – for the takeover deal.'

'So are you saying that your husband had also told Mary, and when you discovered what had happened, you blamed her for not alerting you, and so you killed first Sir Wilfred and then her.'

'How very clever you are, Sergeant. Poor Mary! I feel sorry for her. Not for my husband, but for her.' She paused, and briefly swept the room with her eyes, before focusing again on Kite. 'You have to believe me when I say that she barely knew anything about it. She was so doped up on her sleeping pills. I just slipped her scarf around her neck and pulled. It was… it was easier than I expected. She seemed so surprised, unable to believe it. She clawed at my sleeves briefly, but then – quite suddenly – she gave up and died. Then I went back to my room and lay down.'

Kite was not convinced. She made it sound so easy, lacking in violence, almost a mercy killing, and yet the killer had rammed a Tickler's jam tin into her mouth. That had been an act of brutal savagery.

Alec moved forward and grabbed his mother by the arm. 'My mother is ill, delusional. It's completely ridiculous. She could never have strangled someone.' He propelled her back to her chair.

'You may be right about that, Captain. But what is undeniable is that your mother could not have killed your father on her own. Unless you are all lying – and I have considered that as a possibility – the idea that Lady Beatrice could have overpowered him, tied him up, doused him in petrol, produced a bomb which she had made with an empty Tickler's jam tin some time previously, and then scurried back upstairs to her bedroom before the bomb exploded is extremely fanciful. Which leads me to suppose that either she had help or that she is lying. And the reason she is lying is that she is protecting someone else.'

'For once, I agree with my brother.' Maud moved across the carpet and placed herself next to her mother's chair. 'She is not of sound mind and no judge is going to see it otherwise.'

'She is physically ill. I have noticed the coughing and the specks of blood on her handkerchief. I fear that she may not be long for this world. But my impression is that her mind is as sharp as ever.'

As if to prove his point, Lady Beatrice coughed heavily again. And when the coughing had subsided, there followed a silence, awkward and uncomfortable. Kite felt reassured. After the bluster of brother and sister, it seemed as though no-one else wanted to volunteer an opinion. Was that a sign that he was closing in on the truth? And that several of them knew or suspected what that truth was.

He cleared his throat. It was dry. 'I wonder,' he said, 'if I might have a glass of water?'

'Of course.' The voice was Elizabeth Walker's. Alone of all the people in the room she moved forward to give him a glass. Kite glanced at Rose, who remained rooted to her spot by the door. She looked notably pale.

'Thank you,' he said after he had drained the glass and then handed it back to her. 'Might I suggest, Mrs

Walker, that in your condition you might wish to retire and go and rest in your bedroom. I see no need to keep you here. I am fully aware that you could not possibly have been involved in your father-in-law's death, and I would be glad to spare you of any unpleasantness which I might have to discuss.

Elizabeth looked around, startled as a fawn. The room was even more silent than before and everyone's eyes were on her. Again it was Maud who spoke up. 'I think that's a very good idea.' By contrast Alec seemed bewildered by what was unfolding, rather like a rabbit blinded by a poacher's light.

'Perhaps Miss Agnes can accompany you,' Kite continued. 'She does have some nursing experience. But as for everyone else, I fear I will have to delay you here for some time yet.'

A nervous silence followed as Elizabeth and Agnes disappeared. Alec broke in. 'Can my mother not retire to her bedroom too? She has said everything that she could possibly want to say.'

Kite shook his head. 'I would rather she remained here. Indeed I believe she would be interested to know who it was who not only wanted, like her, to see Sir Wilfred dead, but had the capacity and determination to actually kill him.'

'What are you talking about?' he snapped. Anger never seemed to be far away with the captain. Was this an indelible part of his character or the consequence of his wartime experiences? A bit of both, Kite suspected. 'My mother has nothing to do with it, and I have to say I find your insinuations utterly intolerable. I shall inform the chief constable of this and I have no doubt that when I have done so, your career will come to a very sudden end.'

Kite rubbed his eyes. He was tired almost to the point of death, but he was determined to bring it all to a conclusion. As for his career, that seemed like an irrelevance. He was pretty certain that he knew who had committed the two murders, but he needed to make that crystal clear to everyone. The night before, as he had lain in bed, he had decided that they were all in on it and none of them would let him bring any of them to justice, indeed that he would be the next murder victim. But now he was clearer in his own mind who the killer was, but there had to have been an accomplice. More importantly, the appearance of Brenda and Agnes surely made his own situation much safer.

'I understand that the chief constable is on his way here as we speak, so you will be able to tell him whatever you like, but in the interests of everyone here – except of course the killer or killers of Sir Wilfred and Mary – the very sensitive matters which I now intend to raise are, I believe, better discussed here with you all before the chief constable arrives.'

He looked round the room, trying to assess the mood of everyone. He found that everyone was either looking at him or slipping glances at one another.

'What do you mean by sensitive matters?' Lady Beatrice said. She spoke softly, but her eyes were fixed on him.

'I will come to them shortly.'

He sighed deeply, then continued.

'It was the brutality of Sir Wilfred's murder that

most impacted me. Setting fire to someone who was very likely still alive and in addition blowing them up with a bomb made out of a Tickler's jam tin was an extremely callous act. But it must also have been a carefully pre-planned one. Making a bomb requires knowledge, materials and time. Once we had discovered the remains of the bomb in the debris of the car, I was convinced in my thinking that the murder was almost certainly not the act of a local vagrant who unexpectedly came across Sir Wilfred while trying to commit theft. As for who had the skill to make a bomb, there is no shortage of suspects: Captain Alec Walker and Frank Tomkin both served on the front line in the war. And, of course, both Mr David Graves and Rose Bates worked at the Burton munitions factory.'

He paused, curious to see if he got any reaction. After several seconds, it was David Graves who jumped in, full of bluster. 'Why on earth would I want to kill Sir Wilfred? He was my boss. He looked after me very well.'

Kite smiled grimly. 'Since you ask a direct question, then my direct answer would be that your position here as an inhabitant of Crowthorpe Manor and as a manager within the jam company was almost at an end. Your attempts to marry Maud have been firmly rebuffed, and Maud has over the past couple of years proved herself more than capable of taking your place in the company and indeed ultimately succeeding Sir Wilfred himself. Losing your home and your job and your hopes of making yourself indispensable to the Walker family – it seems to me that that must have been a very unpleasant pill to swallow. All this would have provided you with more than enough motivation to commit murder. The only doubt in my mind was whether you had the steely determination to actually do it.'

Kite paused. He felt a fleeting pang of pity for Graves, who looked like he wished the floor would open up beneath him, but he pushed on without a backward glance.

'By contrast, one person who I felt could readily have committed murder is Miss Rose Bates.' He looked across at her, but she looked back at him without a hint of trepidation in her face. 'As a "canary girl",' she could certainly have made a bomb had she wished to, and she most certainly had motivation. I've seen the grave of her brother Paul in the churchyard. You will all remember him. A young man with, as I understand it, considerable learning and behavioural problems. As you know, he had lived safely up here above the stables, helping out and doing odd jobs until, with Rose away at the munitions factory, he found himself being forced by Sir Wilfred to go and work at the jam factory, and live in the village away from his place of safety—'

'I blame myself for that,' Lady Beatrice said quickly. 'I should have intervened with my husband, but I—'

'I should have too,' Maud said, placing her hand protectively on her mother's shoulder. 'I should have realised what was going on, but I was distracted and—'

'I'm sorry.' Kite held up a hand. 'What do you mean by "what was going on"?'

Maud froze. Her face went pale and she looked at her mother for support.

'Maud? What did you mean?' Kite said again.

She held her hands to her neck. 'I meant that people there made fun of him. About the way he spoke, the way he behaved, the things he couldn't do. When he lived here, above the stables, we knew how to look after him. We knew what he could do. For example, he loved cleaning out the horses. And grooming them. But when he was there in the village, on his own, he felt abandoned.' Maud fell silent, apparently unable to continue.

'Abandoned? What are you saying, Maud?' Kite said.

'What she's saying is that Paul's death wasn't an accident. He didn't fall into the vat. He jumped into it.' Rose spat the words out with a bitterness which stunned the whole room. She glared around her. 'You all abandoned him. Because he was simple minded, because he was an embarrassment, you all ignored him. And because I wasn't there, I couldn't intervene and save him.'

Alec stood up and began to move across the room towards Rose, but before he could get any further Sparrow had intercepted him.

'Best to sit down, sir.'

Alec stopped, but didn't retreat. 'You bitch!' The words hissed from his mouth. 'Are you saying that you murdered my father because your half-witted brother killed himself?'

'I didn't kill him, though when I knew he was dead, and how he had died, I could have danced with joy.

The fact is, unlike the rest of you, I have an alibi. I couldn't have killed him, and Detective Sergeant Kite knows why.'

All eyes swivelled towards Kite. The tension in the room was as thick as a Thames fog, and as he looked around, taking in their stares, he realised something extraordinary: they really weren't all in it together. Most of them did not know who had done it. They may have had their suspicions, they may have all been glad that Sir Wilfred was dead, but they didn't actually know.

Kite cleared his throat. 'Rose has informed me that Frank Tomkin was in her bed at the time of Sir Wilfred's murder.'

There was more silence, and then a guffaw, from Graves. 'But Tomkin has done a runner, hasn't he!? You claim to have sent him to the chief constable, but in that case where is the help? So Tomkin being in bed with the slut isn't an alibi at all. The fact is, he must have done it himself. Fact is he was besotted with Mrs Elizabeth.' These last words slipped out, and Kite pounced on them like a predator on its prey.

'Besotted with Mrs Elizabeth? Why do you say that, Mr Graves?'

Graves looked down, averting his eyes from any of them.

'And let us suppose that it is true, what relevance has that to Sir Wilfred's death? Perhaps you can enlighten me – indeed enlighten all of us.'

'Nothing. I mean… I mean I've no idea who killed him, so how… how could I know anything about it.' He was now in full stumble mode. 'It's just that I don't like Tomkin. Never have. He is above himself.'

'I think you have said enough, David,' Lady Beatrice said crisply. 'Frank has served this family very faithfully. I will not hear you bad mouth him anymore.'

'Indeed he has,' Kite said. 'He served Sir Wilfred very well as chauffeur and as a man he could trust. He also saved the captain's life in no man's land, carrying him to safety. And, of course, when the captain was recuperating at Greystone Park, he drove Mrs Elizabeth there to see him and then three days later brought her safely home.' Kite paused. He could sense the tension in the room and resisted the temptation to look at Alec. He knew that if he had seen the anguish on the captain's face, he might not have been able to go on. But go on he had to.

'When the phone was still operating, I rang Greystone Park and spoke to a Miss Kempton. I regret to say that as a consequence of that conversation, I came to the sad conclusion that Mrs Elizabeth could not possibly have conceived her child at Greystone because the captain was so delusional that he didn't recognise her. Indeed he was so distressed that Miss Kempton had to ask Mrs Elizabeth to return home rather than cause him any more distress.'

Kite had been focusing on a painting of Sir Wilfred above the fireplace as he said all this, but now he scanned the room, waiting for someone to say something or scream or just deny it, but the silence was immense.

In the end it was Graves, who had been knocked back twice already, who intervened again.

'So it was Tomkin who… who…' He seemed unable to say what exactly Tomkin had done. 'The blaggard! He took advantage of Mrs Elizabeth, and when Sir Wilfred found out he killed him? And then poor Mary too. Death is too good for him. My God!' And he screamed a scream which echoed round the room before he sank onto his knees on the floor.

'Tomkin is not the baby's father,' Kite said as loudly as he could. 'I am as sure as I can be of that.'

'What do you mean? How can you know?'

Kite rubbed his forehead. It was hot. He was feeling dreadful, and he wondered with alarm if he might faint. And if he did, what might happen after that.

'We need to get to Lincoln, sir.' Constable Sparrow burst into life while all around the rest of them were stunned. 'Tell the chief constable. Get everyone looking for Tomkin before he disappears altogether.'

'Sit down!' It was the hitherto silent Brenda Bostock who barked this out, and such was her sense of command that they all did exactly that. Even Graves deferred to her. The only person still standing was Kite, but he was swaying on his feet, and she marched across, grabbed him by the arm and led him back to the sofa where he collapsed in a heap.

'Maud,' she ordered, 'Detective Kite is unwell, so would you please summon Agnes down here.' She waited until Maud had left the room, then turned her attention to Sparrow.

'And perhaps I should clarify, Constable, that there will be no need to send out search parties to find Mr Tomkin because I saw him last night and I know for a fact that he and the chief constable are on their way here even now.'

'What are you talking about, woman?' Sparrow seemed confused and alarmed.

'Tomkin isn't the killer,' she said firmly.

'You're in charge now are you, Mrs Bostock?' He laughed. 'Gawd help us all if you are.'

'What's going on?' It was Agnes, arriving at the doorway and then striding across the carpet to where Kite lay sprawled on the sofa. She took his wrist, checking his pulse, and felt his forehead. His eyes were open, but if they were focused it was on some spot on the ceiling.

'More water,' she ordered. 'And something to eat! A piece of pie or something. He shouldn't be here. He should be in bed, and someone should be keeping a close eye on him.'

Someone handed her a glass and she helped him sip it. Then a piece of bread with a slice of meat on it. Agnes watched him chew it slowly. When she was satisfied she looked around the room. 'I need some volunteers to get him to a bed. And we need to get a doctor out to look at him.'

'There's Dr Lightfoot in Crowthorpe village. But we can't ring him because the phone is still broken.' This was Maud, who had reappeared a short while after Agnes, apparently happy to leave Elizabeth unattended. 'And we have no car of course. I suppose we could harness up the trap again, though in these conditions I worry about my horse slipping and breaking an ankle…'

'Brenda and I got here on a motorbike,' Agnes said. 'But I suppose we are made of stronger stuff than the men here.'

'I'll go.' Sparrow was on his feet. 'I can ride your bike if there's fuel in it. I grew up in the village. I'll be able to find the doctor and bring him here in the sidecar. That will be quickest.' And with the alacrity of a man used to sudden action, he was hurrying for the door.

'Thank God for that.' Agnes looked at the others. 'Now some help please, if you will.'

Maud and her brother stepped forward, jolted into helping. Rose had already disappeared towards the kitchen. Graves had left the room too, shouting that he'd get the stretcher. Brenda waited and watched, alarm bells ringing. Something was wrong. She moved closer to where Kite was surrounded by Agnes, Maud and Alec. She trusted Agnes – of course she did – but there was a voice in the back of her head nagging away at her: *remember, one of these people is a brutal killer, and only Kite knows who.*

She bent down low, close to Kite. 'Sergeant,' she said. 'Sergeant?'

'Outside! Get me outside!' His breathing was strained, like an old man on his deathbed, but he gripped her arm with his hand so tightly than she winced. 'Stop Sparrow.'

'He needs to speak to Sparrow,' Brenda said, giving orders again. 'Get him to the front door. I'll tell the constable to wait.' She scurried out of the room, back along the corridor and out of the front door, which was wide open. Sparrow himself was turning the motorbike around.

'Constable,' she called, but he didn't seem to hear

her. Or maybe he was a man who hated to be told what to do by a woman. There were plenty of those in the world. 'Constable,' she repeated, as she drew closer, and this time he turned. 'Detective Sergeant Kite would like a word with you.'

'It can wait. There's no time for delay!' He kicked at the pedal, trying to bring life to the engine, but it failed to spark. He tried again.

'Why did you do it, Constable?' Kite was at the doorway, supported between Maud and Alec. He had recovered his voice. He stood there, and his eyes were alive with emotion. 'Why did you do it? Who promised you what?'

Sparrow kicked at the pedal again, but again the motorbike refused to start.

Agnes let rip a peal of laughter. 'Stupid man! Do you think I would leave the bike so that any passer-by could drive off with it?' She held up two ignition leads in her hand. 'It won't work without these.'

Sparrow stopped, his face full of rage. 'Give them here. I'm going to get the doctor.'

'You're not going anywhere,' Kite insisted as he and his helpers moved down the steps. 'I know it was you. You killed both of them. What I don't know is which one of them bribed you to do it. I thought at first that it was love, love for Rose, but I don't believe that you are capable of it. Sex, yes. But love, never. Poor Mary saw you, didn't she. But she couldn't believe what she saw, and she thought it must be a ghost. And that was why you killed her. Before she could say anything more. You were in the room when she told me, and your presence stopped her saying anything more. So when you got the opportunity you killed her most cruelly.'

'You're talking rubbish. Fantasy.' He was moving forward as he said this, closer not so much to Kite as to Brenda, who he grabbed and twisted in front of his body. 'I have a knife,' he snarled, brandishing it in his free hand. 'If Agnes doesn't get that motorbike started for me right now, then I'll gut this interfering busybody. Now get on with it.'

No-one moved. Kite began to sway, but firm hands tightened around him. 'Agnes,' he whispered, 'do as he says. But be very careful.'

She moved forwards, giving Sparrow and Brenda a wide berth. Sparrow wouldn't get far, she told herself. It was much more important to save her friend. God protect her. She focused on her task. Get the motorbike going and hope the bastard didn't use that knife. Within a minute or so, the engine burst into life. Sparrow dragged Brenda with him, back to the bike. Then shoved her hard away from him so that she sprawled on the floor. He mounted the bike, revved the engine and…

Amidst all the noise and confusion, there was a sharp crack of noise. Alec, who was suddenly transported back to the nightmare of the trenches, hurled himself to the ground, covering his head with his hands. Kite staggered, almost falling now that one of his supporters had relinquished their post. But Maud hung on and the vice-like grip of Rose, who had just emerged from the house behind them, locked itself round his other arm. But Kite was looking for Sparrow. He was the danger. But he was no longer going anywhere. The bike had skidded to a stop some yards away and keeled over. Sparrow was splayed across it, face down, hands outstretched. Kite turned and saw David Graves standing behind them in the doorway, a rifle in his hands. He moved forward through them, advancing cautiously. When he reached Sparrow, he knelt down and checked him for any sign of life, but there was none. He gave the body a sudden kick, nodded, and then walked towards Kite. He laid the rifle down in front of him. 'You can hang me for all I care. That bastard should never have done what he did to my sister. Never!'

Kite looked at him and then at Sparrow. Agnes and Brenda were hugging each other. Maud was crouched over her brother. Rose was still holding him up. 'I think we'd best get you sat down, Sergeant. We really don't want you dying on us.'

'One moment,' he whispered, then raised his voice. 'Constable Sparrow was trying to escape justice. He confessed murder in front of you all. He was fleeing on a bike he had commandeered after threatening to stab the chief constable's wife to death. In the circumstances, I think Mr Graves is more likely to receive a commendation than any punishment.'

Kite looked up, eyes focusing on the distance. He could hear the sound of an engine, loud and coarse. Brenda had seen it too. She watched as it drew closer. It was a lorry. She held on to Agnes' arm tighter. She knew who it must be. She turned round. 'I think you will find, Sergeant, that the chief constable is arriving just in time to congratulate you on solving the case.'

MUCH LATER

'DID I DO wrong?' Kite said suddenly.

He was sitting on a bench facing Lincoln Cathedral. He came here most days, walking determinedly up the hill, slowly improving his bodily strength. Most days he sat here alone, regathering himself before the slog home, but today Brenda Bostock was sitting next to him. It wasn't an assignation, merely the result of pure chance – him puffing his way through the Pottergate Arch at the top of Lindum Road and her coming the other way.

'Sergeant Kite!' she had exclaimed.

'Mrs Bostock!' he had replied.

And so here they were, sitting in the sunshine – the first hint that spring was around the corner – each of them needing to talk but not knowing how to start.

'Did I do wrong?' he repeated. Now that he had summoned up the question that dogged him day and night, Kite needed an answer. 'Please.'

'What's done is done,' she said firmly. 'There's nothing to be gained by looking back.'

'It's hard not to.'

Silence. A robin alighted several feet away from them and stared at them with cocked head. Brenda pointed at him. 'He doesn't look back,' she said.

Kite studied the bird. Did the robin even look forward? He turned and considered Brenda. 'You'll be going to Kent, then? I bumped into Constable Light and he was telling me about it.'

'My husband is going, you're quite right, but not

me. He can't turn down a job like he's been offered there. And I'm certainly not going to stop him.'

'But why are you not accompanying him?'

'Who wants a troublesome wife in tow? He'll go there, tell everyone how his wife will be joining him in due course, and wait until the questions die down, and then one day he'll let it be known to his cronies that I caught Spanish influenza and never recovered. He will receive commiserations, and soon after that the questions will stop.'

'But what will you do for money?'

'I have a job at a little school nearby.'

'And lodgings?'

'I have moved into a little house with Agnes. I am rather pleased to say that her husband's brother has moved out – he got a girl pregnant – and so there's lots of room. In fact…'

She didn't finish her sentence, or maybe it was a case of Kite no longer listening. He was staring vacantly across the grass. The robin had disappeared, and cloud had obscured the sun.

'I still wonder if I did the wrong thing.' Kite was a dog with a bone, forever chewing it though there was nothing left to chew. 'I mean, they got away with it.'

'Sparrow didn't.'

'No, but the others—'

'What others?'

'Lady Beatrice. If she hadn't egged on Rose, if—'

'Lady Beatrice is dead. Died a couple of weeks ago of whatever illness it was she had. My husband told me that with some pleasure. As far as he is concerned, it tidies up a loose end. Lady Beatrice held firm to her insistence that she planned it all and now she is dead. No-one is going to argue with that now. "Case closed" as he said.'

'But there's Rose too. I liked her, and I admit I let that colour my judgement. But when you look at it in the cold light of day, she was the one who planned and controlled things, who dragged Sparrow into it…'

'Are you sure she was behind it?' Brenda said.

Kite looked at her in surprise. 'She had the strongest motive. The death of her brother.'

'Surely Elizabeth had the strongest motive if she was raped by Sir Wilfred. But the mode of death rules her out. Of course Frank Tomkin knew the truth about Elizabeth's visit to Greystoke. And what was it that David Graves said about him being besotted with Elizabeth? He seems to me to be a man driven by loyalty. Not just to Alec who he rescued from death, but perhaps above all to Elizabeth, whose reputation he was determined to protect however he could.'

'I can understand he had the motivation to protect Elizabeth's and Alec's reputations, but if he wanted Sir Wilfred to be murdered, would he not have done it himself?'

'You could say the same about Rose. Or do you think a woman such as Rose is incapable of murder?'

'Of course not. But she wanted to try and avoid being hung for the murder.'

'So she persuaded Sparrow to do it? But how?'

'What are the facts? Sparrow tried to flee on the motorbike. He threatened to kill you when he was thwarted. So he was the killer. There is no doubt about that. The question then is why did he do it.'

'You mean Sparrow fancied her, or Rose fancied him?'

'That is possible. They both grew up in the village, and are of similar age. My observation of them was that they might have become involved with each other. I noticed a certain amount of teasing, even flirting, during those few days. I took no notice, although I found it unprofessional in a policeman. But I now believe it was more complicated that. I became aware of two other things. First, Sparrow liked to gamble. When we played billiards, he suggested we play for money, and when I won he made excuses about paying me back in Lincoln. He also showed a lot of interest in the pictures of race horses in the manor, and was also very knowledgeable about them, which of them had won races, and also especially which of them had lost.'

'You think he lost money on the horses?'

'Gamblers usually end up losing money and getting into debt.'

'So somebody bribed him? But surely not Rose. Would she have had enough money to convince him to commit murder?'

'It is possible. More likely she may have stolen it?'

'Stolen it!' Brenda clearly had not heard about this. But that was hardly a surprise. 'But from where?'

'Mary Graves told me that two hundred pounds went missing from the safe.'

'And you think Rose stole it?'

'Rose knew the house better than anyone. And was trusted. Like all servants, when she was in the room serving tea and cakes, or cleaning, I expect Sir

Wilfred barely noticed her. Sooner or later she may have seen him or maybe Maud or Alec handling the safe key, getting it out or putting it back wherever it was hidden.'

'It makes you think,' Brenda admitted. They fell silent. Kite shivered, feeling the cold of a sudden gust of wind.

'There is one more thing. Rose told me that on the night of Sir Wilfred's murder, at the time of the explosion, Frank and she were both in her bed. Rose didn't admit that at first, only much later.'

'But she could easily have been lying.'

'Of course she could. But what was interesting was Sparrow's reaction when I told him about it. He insisted Rose must be lying. At that point, Frank was on the way to Lincoln, so we could not question him about it. But Sparrow was clearly surprised and even shocked by this revelation, because he realised that whatever promises she had made – she had presumably paid him in advance, and had maybe even offered him some sexual favours – she had made sure she herself had an alibi. She had also, in Sparrow's eyes, been lying to him. It was Frank Tomkin with whom she had thrown her lot in.'

Brenda smiled. 'You really think that is how it was?'

'It is my best guess.'

'It's very convincing, and fits in with what I learnt from Maud. She came to one of our women's meetings yesterday. Anyway, she told me that both Rose and Frank have left the manor. "Gone to seek better things," she said. "With a generous financial gift, in thanks for all their loyal service to the family."

Or words to that effect. No looking back there.'

Kite shook his head vigorously. 'That's not right.'

'Isn't it? Why not? Rose's brother died essentially because Sir Wilfred drove him out of the only home he had, out of the only place he was cared for and had a proper role, to a place where he was so unhappy that he killed himself. Can you imagine how desperate he must have been to throw himself into a vat of jam? Sir Wilfred was a bastard. As you worked out, he raped his daughter-in-law. They all knew or suspected it. It was the elephant in the room that no-one talked about. But once he was dead, they all closed ranks. Whatever they knew or suspected, they felt that justice had been served and a monster killed. So the question you have to ask yourself, Sergeant Kite, is this. Is it better that Rose and Frank make a life together or that they are both hung from a gibbet?'

Kite didn't answer immediately. He tried to speak, but the awfulness of the realisation was much to voice. He had got it wrong. He hadn't seen it. 'Frank and Rose,' was all he could say. 'I trusted Tomkin too. I was convinced that all along he was as honest as the day is long. I sent him to Lincoln—'

'And he came back, didn't he? He could have done a runner.'

'But he was part of it.' Kite was desolate.

'Up to a point. I overheard some of what he said to my dreadful husband when he came to our house. Frank Tomkin wanted the investigation closed down. Just as my husband did. He couldn't believe that one of the family could have killed Sir Wilfred, and Tomkin, of course, was worried that you might discover the truth. Sparrow's panic and his attempt to escape, plus his death, achieved a very satisfactory conclusion all round.'

'Not satisfactory for me.'

'Oh, Sergeant Kite, Rose and Frank are not bad people. You have to weigh up the options and live with the consequences. The hangman's noose or the chance of happiness for the two of them. It's a very simple choice, Sergeant. And when you have made your choice, cast it behind you and no looking back.'

He put his head in his hands, dragged his fingers through his hair, and began to rock on the bench. She placed her hand on his shoulder and held it there until he slowed and finally stilled. He turned to her. He had the face of an old man. 'It's just that—'

'No looking back. I won't tell you that again because otherwise you will begin to think of me as a terrible nag. But there is happier news. Maud told me that Elizabeth has had a baby. They have called her Mary, which I think is rather nice. So the other thing you have to ask yourself as you flagellate yourself with self-pity is this: is it better for Mary to grow up happy and unaware of the circumstances surrounding her birth, or would you prefer that her life is blighted by the wild allegations about her paternity which would inevitably come out in any court case?'

She didn't wait for an answer. Instead she stood up, brushed down her coat and then asked him if he would kindly escort her home. 'Agnes will return in a little while. I am sure she will be very pleased to see that you are on the mend. Also, if you are not happy with your lodgings, we do have a very nice room which we would like to rent out to someone – that is to say, to someone we can trust.'

'It will be very nice to see Agnes again. And as it happens, I am looking for more amenable lodgings.'

She linked her arm through his, and they made their way slowly along the Bailgate. 'One more bit of gossip from Maud,' she said cheerfully.

'And what is that?'

'I think the constable has left something behind him on earth.'

'I don't understand.'

'Mrs Jane Ransom is large with child. The dates tie up rather neatly.'

'What are you saying?'

'I am saying that one can tell a lot from footprints in the snow.'

'I fear you are cleverer that I have given you credit for.'

'Agnes is too. After Mrs Ransom appeared dramatically supporting a bloodied Sparrow, Agnes took a quick look at his head wound. "Surprisingly little damage," she told me later. "A small cut, probably with a knife. It certainly doesn't tie up with his claim that had been struck over the head by a man in the woods".'

He laughed. 'In that case, all I can say is that Maud was right. The world might be a better place if women were in charge.'

THE END

ABOUT THE AUTHOR

Peter Tickler has lived the majority of his life in Oxford. He read classics at Keble College, then returned to the city a few years later to raise his family there. So when he decided to write a crime novel, it was almost inevitable that he would set it in Oxford – though 'town' rather than 'gown'.

His own unusual surname, and the part his great-grandfather played in the First World War as manufacturer of jam for the British troops on the front line, finally caused a change of direction in his writing. It took him back to Lincolnshire, where he grew up, and to the year 1919, a time of upheaval and re-evaluation for those who survived the fighting.

ALSO BY
PETER TICKLER

Blood in Oxford Series
Blood on the Cowley Road
Blood in Grandpont
Blood on the Marsh

Standalone
The Girl Who Stole the Apple

Doug Mullen – Private Detective
Dead in the Water
White Lies, Deadly Lies
Dead in Oxford
The Oxford Murders

Milton Keynes UK
Ingram Content Group UK Ltd.
UKHW010330050324
438811UK00001B/26